FIRST DOWN
and Forever
TO GO

Books By Leah Dobrinska

The Mapleton Novels
Love at On Deck Cafe
Good To Be Home
Together With You
Choosing Love

The Larkspur Library Mysteries
Death Checked Out
Mayhem In Circulation
A Killer Hold

The Fall In Love Series
Friends Don't
Enemies Don't
Exes Don't
Pros Don't

The Songwriter Sleuth Mysteries
Trebled Waters

The River Foxes Football Romances
First Down and Forever To Go

FIRST DOWN

and Forever

TO GO

Leah Dobrinska

Editing: Caitlin Miller, CM Editorial

Cover Design: Melody Jeffries, @whimandjoy

Author Photo: Beth Dunphy

Library of Congress Control Number: 2025927469

ISBN: 979-8-9885978-8-9 (paperback) | 979-8-9885978-9-6 (ebook)

For Nick.

Author Note

Dear Reader:

I am so excited to share TJ and Lucy's story with you! If you are the type of reader who likes to be made aware of heavier topics and potential triggers, please be advised that this book includes lost loved-ones (past), lost parents (past), and a passive discussion of suicide.

While I kept the overall tone of *First Down and Forever To Go* lighthearted and positive, I realize these topics and experiences are anything but that. Still, they are important for the characters' development. I have done my best to write these topics with great care.

I'm a firm believer in making informed choices about what we read, and it's my hope that this content warning allows you to do so. Be assured this is a closed-door romance novel, so a happy ending is guaranteed. Thanks for reading!

With love,
Leah

Chapter 1

Lucy

I f I wasn't convinced this was a terrible idea before, then the foot-long rip down the front of my sparkly, sequined couture evening gown would have sealed the deal. Or, I guess I should say, *unsealed* it.

I stare at myself in the floor-length mirror propped in the corner of my room at Daisy's Inn, where I've worked out a long-term rental in the quaint, small town of Cashmere Cove, and squish up my features at the sight of my reflection.

The gown, which I ordered from one of those fancy-dress rental places online and had shipped in time for tonight's ball, is a stunner. Correction—it *was* a stunner ... before I accidentally caught my heel on the sweetheart neckline when I was stepping into it and ripped it clear down the center. Now, the gown gapes open like a giant papercut. I have to hold the fabric to keep from flashing myself and my best friends, whom I video-called in a panic the moment I heard the telltale *rippp!*

My shoulders slump as I flick my gaze to where I have my cell phone propped up on the dresser next to the mirror. "I'm not going, you guys. This has to be some sort of sign."

"I don't believe in signs." Cassie, who also happens to be my literary agent, furrows her brow and leans closer to the camera, and now the porcelain skin of her forehead is the only thing I can see. "Can you sew it?"

I widen my eyes and quickly shake my head. "How many times have I told you I don't have any talents? You think I've been hiding a secret ability to sew?"

Cassie leans back so I can see her eyes again and shrugs. "Worth asking." She twists her lips to the side and scans my damaged dress.

"With all those sequins, it'd be impossible to stitch that." Classic Bex. She's the no-nonsense one in our little friend group.

My sweet friend, Philomena, Philly for short, winces. "I'm so sorry, Lu. Wish I could help."

I sigh. "Me too."

There's a metaphor here, with my current wardrobe malfunction. Something about how my life was ripped in two, exposing the real me, and there's no way I can ever be put back together. I'm like a condemned Humpty Dumpty, fallen from grace. Cancelled. Ruined.

I'm an author. My writer-brain has spun the story of my life a million different ways, with flowery words and built-out metaphors. I've delved into the backstory and prodded the pain points, and the ending is always the same. I messed up. I deserve all the misery I have coming my way.

I hate what happened at the People's Picks award show. I'd rather not dwell on it, but at the same time, I can't *not* dwell on it. Before I started getting ready for tonight's charity gala, I indulged in my weekly scroll, rereading the comments on one of the many, *many* articles that outline in painstaking detail what I've coined *The Incident.*

"Entitled much?"

"That's a lot of rage coming from someone so insignificant."

"Who does she think she is?!?"

"Wow, she was always the quiet one, but that's obviously because no one trusted her to speak … for good reason."

"Imagine having to live with her!"

"Not a good look, sweetie."

"She's the WORST!!"

"Wonder how it feels to be such a miserable person."

"She should take a flying leap."

"GIRL, BYE!"

"The world would be better off without people like her in it."

"Such a pretty face, but then she opens her mouth, and yikesss."

"The stick is so far up this girl's—"

Yeah. Brutal. Reading through the comments is my personal form of perpetual penance. I messed up, and I'm paying the price for it.

I blink my focus back to where Cassie, Bex, and Philly are staring at me through the phone screen, their faces a mixture of emotions—Cassie, determination; Bex, held-back laughter; Philly, apprehension. My heart squeezes. I wish they were here. I need an in-person pep talk from Cassie. I need Bex to laugh at me and tell me not to take myself so seriously. I need Philly to give me a hug. But since I'm holed up in a middle-of-nowhere town in the Wisconsin Cashmere County peninsula, none of that is happening.

"There's no way I'm coming back from this," I tell them. That's the truth in more ways than one.

"Not going is *not* an option. You need this, Lu. You know you do," Cassie says pointedly.

I bite my bottom lip. She's right. I know it. She knows it. I need to go to the ball to try to get some inspiration for my next book. I'm on a deadline, and things aren't looking good.

Cassie starts pacing in the living room of her New York City apartment. It's a tiny place, so she doesn't have much room, but she moves when she's anxious. "You need to go out and find a dress from someone."

I wrinkle my nose. "Absolutely not. I'm in hiding, Cass. The only reason I agreed to go to the gala tonight is that it's a masquerade ball. I'm not about to bring attention to my doorstep."

Cassie presses her lips together. She can't argue with me there. The whole point of moving here was to get out from under media scrutiny. I tried to stick it out in Los Angeles with my stepmom and stepsisters for the first couple months after *The Incident*, and while chatter around what I said and what I did died down a little, there was still this suffocating commentary anytime I was seen, detailing what an awful person I was. That, and my family was about to start filming the next season of our show, and we all figured it was better if I distanced myself. I didn't want to drag them down with me.

I haven't written a single word since the People's Picks. It's not because I got cancelled. I mean, I *did*, but mercifully, my author career was spared because I've always written under a penname. No one knows that Lucy Dupree, the girl who burned her whole life down on the People's Picks stage, is also Ava Reese, bestselling author of feel-good romance novels.

Writing has always been my outlet. Living in the fictional world of my daydreams was more fulfilling than living in the real world. Chalk it up to childhood trauma, I guess.

Even though my secret life has remained a secret through the fallout, all the negative buzz surrounding me as Lucy has been emotionally and creatively crippling to my alter-ego of Ava. I can barely even call myself an author at this point.

"What about your landlord?" Philly suggests.

"Daisy?" I knit my brows. "What about her?"

"She knows who you are, right?" When I nod, she continues. "So you won't be revealing yourself to anyone new. You've been there for a couple months now. She can obviously be trusted. Maybe she has something you could wear. Or she could find something for you?"

Cassie snaps her fingers. "This is the kind of thinking we need. Yes. Good. Lu, go find Daisy."

"And say what, exactly? That I'm a klutz who ruined my ball gown and I really need to go to this gala so I can try to get inspired to write a romance novel before my career implodes like the rest of my life?"

"Tone it down, drama queen," Bex says dryly.

I glare at her.

"That's exactly what you should say," Cassie says, ignoring the two of us. "Minus the part about being a romance novelist. Unless you're ready to let her in on that secret, too."

I shake my head vigorously.

"Didn't think so." Cassie makes a swishing motion with her hand, flicking her wrist like she's shooing me away. "Go on, now. You can do it. The ball starts in less than two hours. You don't want to be late."

"I don't want to go at all."

Cassie narrows her eyes at me, pointing a long, pianist's finger in my direction. "As your agent, I will not let you sabotage the career you've built over a ripped dress."

It's so much more than a ripped dress at this point.

I keep those thoughts to myself as Cassie's stern expression melts into something warmer, softer, before she goes on. "As your *friend*, I know you need this because you love writing, and I hate seeing you stuck. I want you to have some fun, get inspired by life again. I want you to write the best book of your career for the readers who are dying for the next Ava novel, but more so for yourself, because you're happiest when you're creating. I miss seeing you smile."

"Me too," Philly chimes in. "I miss you in general. I'm going to look at flights and come for a visit soon."

Tears wiggle their way to the corners of my eyes, threatening to fall if I make any sudden movements. I don't deserve my friends. I don't know why they've stuck with me through the last nine months, but they have, and I'll never be able to repay them for their support. Checking in to make sure I've eaten. Inviting me to our virtual writing sprints and not making me feel bad when I'm obviously *not* writing.

"I guess I miss you too," Bex says with a shrug, but her lips twitch, and it's enough to loosen the knot in the back of my throat.

"Okay." I blow out a long, slow breath. "I'll go find Daisy, and I'll try my best to get to the ball. I make no promises, though."

"Make us one," Cassie says, and I tip my head to the side. "If—no, *when*—you get to the ball"—she gives me a steely look—"do something you wouldn't usually do. Use the anonymity of the mask to let yourself be free. Just for tonight."

I twist my lips in disgust, demonstrating exactly what I think of this proposition.

"Just for tonight," Philly echoes, and she looks so earnest and hopeful that my shoulders roll forward.

"You've got this, Lu," Bex says, nodding as if it's decided.

Staring at their three hopeful faces, knowing how much they've done for me since *The Incident*, I can't bring myself to let them down.

I exhale. "Fine. I'll see what I can do."

Chapter 2
TJ

The Green Bay River Foxes are a force to be reckoned with on the gridiron. We're defending Super Bowl champions, and this year, we're playing like we've got something to prove. Our locker room is usually buzzing with pregame music and pep talks or post-game celebrations and speeches. There's always someone—often me—walking around in a towel.

Tonight, things look different. Sure, the locker room is still full of oversized dudes. Kennedy just sashayed by in a towel, bless his heart. There's music pumping through the built-in speakers and excitement crackling through the air. But the air itself smells of cologne rather than Biofreeze. We've traded in our uniforms, pads, and helmets for tuxedos, suspenders, and bow ties. My teammates and I are getting ready for the Green Bay River Foxes Holiday Gala, the first annual charity event of its kind.

"I feel like a penguin who had too much to eat." Lawrence Poe, our team's star tight end, tugs at his collar and frowns at his reflection in the mirror.

"Come on, man. Your attitude is stinking up the locker room," I tell him from where I'm sitting in my locker, lacing up my dress shoes. "This is going to be great."

"Says the guy who loves a party," Poe shoots back. "You thrive when you're the center of attention. A charity gala *and* being the featured player in a date auction are right up your alley. Some of us would rather fly more under the radar. Looking all flashy like this"—Poe points to his own chest—"isn't my idea of a good time."

"If I told you that you didn't look all that good, would it make you feel better?" I stand, flashing Poe a grin. He scowls at me, and I laugh.

These guys are like my brothers. We rib each other all the time. I have their backs; they have mine ... both on the field and in life. I'm not worried about ticking Poe off. I do love poking fun at his reserved, stoic self.

"Stand next to me. No one will pay you any attention because they'll be too busy swooning over me."

"Careful, Teej. Your ego is about to bust out of that tux," Anton, our quarterback and the team's leader, deadpans, but his eyes are framed with telltale crinkles of laughter.

Poe just stares at me like I'm being ridiculous. If I'm a golden retriever packed full of energy and enthusiasm, my tongue hang-ing out so I can lap up every experience with a hungry slurp, then he's a Great Dane: imposing in size with a calm, gentle demeanor ... and a killer side eye. Which he's giving me right now.

"I don't really dance. Not like this. Give me a sawdust-covered floor, some nineties country, and a line dance sequence, and I can hang with the best of them, but I'm with Poe ... I'll be out of my depth out there," Del, our team's center, says with a shrug.

"Don't worry, guys. I can show you some sweet moves." Anton does some sort of shoulder shimmy, hopping in my direction.

"Keep your sweet moves to yourself, please, and thank you." I shove him away, and Anton chuckles. "Still not sure what Rose sees in you."

Anton reconnected with his ex-girlfriend last year. They had to work through some things, but there was never any doubt that the two of them were endgame. They support each other and build each other up, and it's actually been pretty incredible to witness. I don't know that I've ever seen a pair more perfectly matched ... except for maybe my grandparents.

"That's because I save all my best moves for when I get her alone." Anton winks, but then he sobers. "I miss her. Is it pathetic that I miss her? I literally saw her two hours ago." He checks his wristwatch. "Think I have time to sneak out into the Atrium and find her before we're announced?"

"Dude. You are *whipped.*" I stand and put my hands on his shoulders, giving him a shake. "The definition of 'obsessed with my girlfriend' would have a picture of you next to it in the dictionary."

"There aren't phrases in the dictionary, TJ." Poe knocks his shoulder into mine, and we all shuffle toward the locker room exit where Ned Norbertson, our team's VP of Marketing and Fan engagement and our all-around communications manager, waits to bring us to the stage.

I roll my eyes. "That's beside the point."

"The point is"—Anton raises his voice over our bickering, used to being the one to reel us back in—"I'm not even mad about it. I'm happily obsessed with Rose. You guys should really find someone to love. Ten outta ten, would recommend."

I glance around to gauge the reactions of the other guys. Del looks wistful. Poe looks doubtful. Me? I'm grinning, but there's a slight ache at the base of my sternum—a wound that no one really knows about, hidden behind layers of skin and bone and buried deep in my chest cavity.

I had someone to love, once upon a time. Someone I thought I'd love forever. Then she was ... gone. You don't come back from a loss like that. At least I don't. I don't want to risk opening myself up to renewed pain. Not after years of healing. I'm a strong guy, but I'm not strong enough to endure getting my heart pulverized again.

I smile instead. "Pretty content with a new pretty woman every weekend, my man."

Anton shrugs, pinning me with one of his quarterback looks. The kind that tells the defense that he knows better than them and he's about to call a play that'll leave their heads spinning. "You're missing out, TJ."

"Maybe," I say noncommittally. Even if I am, I'm happy this way. I've got my friends and women who are happy to date me casually. I go out. I have fun. I come home. The end.

I've got my grandparents, and they're the one long-term relationship I intend to keep.

Speaking of them ...

I slip my phone out of my inside jacket pocket as Ned gives us our marching orders. Go onstage. Get announced for all the donors and big spenders we've invited. Yada yada yada. I tune him out and type out a message.

Heading into my event with the team tonight. I'll touch base with you guys later this weekend. Love you!

I pocket my phone without waiting for a response. It'll take my grandparents a solid twenty minutes to figure out who's going to text me back and then pointer-finger type out a response. When it finally does come in, there will be lots of capital letters and emojis and far too many exclamation points. The typos will be hilarious, and there will probably be four different texts because they hit send before they meant to. Gosh, I love them.

I follow the guys into the holding area behind the stage. Anton and Del are ahead of me and Poe. It's eerily similar to how we wait in the tunnel before running onto the field on gamedays, and a familiar zip of anticipation courses through me as the good-natured chatter of the guests reaches our ears.

I turn to Poe, brushing the lapels of my jacket. "How do I look, man?" I adjust my mask, pulling it down over my eyes. "Like a sexy running back Batman who's about to steal the show?"

Poe rolls his eyes. "What I wouldn't give for a modicum of your confidence."

"What's a mode-a-crumb?"

He shoves my shoulder, pushing me forward, and I'm grinning as we file out onto the stage. Raucous applause rings out, and I beam my million-dollar smile out over the crowd.

Scott Bass, our team's general manager, stands behind the podium, and the guys and I split off so we're standing on either side of him.

"I know I speak for the entire team when I say how grateful we are for your support not only tonight, but this season," Scott says.

We all clap, and those in attendance cheer.

"The city of Green Bay is a special place to play ball. No one else has the history we have, and as a River Foxes organization, we feel like it's the least we can do to give back to the town that gives us so much, right, gentlemen?"

My teammates and I all answer in the affirmative.

"To begin, I'm going to do some introductions. Up for auction tonight, we have some excellent options, including getting up close and personal with some of your favorite River Foxes."

A couple of people in the audience squeal. I try to find the source of the sound. I'm one of the guys up for auction. I'm hoping whoever bids on me is nice and normal. I can make conversation with a houseplant—and I do, on occasion—but it'll be more fun if I actually like the person who plunks down some cold, hard cash to have dinner with me.

Scott drones on about how the bidding will work on the silent auction and what's up for grabs there, but my attention is drawn to the top of the staircase that leads down to where we're all standing in the Atrium.

The sight before my eyes is arresting, and the air is zapped from my lungs.

A woman dressed in an antique ball gown stands on the landing. Her dress is a creamy white with a high neckline and long sleeves. The whole thing glitters in the dim lighting of the Atrium. Her dark brown hair is up in a curled pile with loose pieces softly framing either side of her face. A beaded band sits like a crown on her head. There's some sort of belt thing at her waist, and then a full skirt puffs out and around her like an upside-down wine glass. She looks like a vintage Cinderella, and I can't rip my gaze from the sight. I'm drinking her in. No, *guzzling* her in.

Her mask hides much of her face, but I'm enraptured as she scans the crowd below. I've seen my fair share of beautiful women over the years, but there's something about this one that makes my blood hum with a different kind of heat. A dangerous kind.

She's holding her shoulders back, and her spine is stick straight ... like she's nervous, almost hesitant. Like she might bolt in the other direction at any moment.

I hold my breath, eyes never leaving her, as she takes a step down the center of the staircase. A tremor of fear trickles through me because I realize that she could trip and stumble down the wide flight of stairs. Dresses and heels have got to be impossible to walk in, right? Especially when there's so much fabric and the floor is all shiny and slippery. Why isn't she holding onto the railing? Why is no one there to offer her a hand? Why do I want to offer her my hand?

I know why. I'm intrigued. She's stunning, and while she looks a little rigid, I'd bet money on my ability to get her to loosen up.

She makes it halfway down the stairs, and I blow out a relieved breath. She seems pretty steady on her feet. I don't know how women walk in heels, but she obviously has some skills in that department. Now I'm praying no one comes to join her.

"Dude!" Poe hisses from next to me.

"What?"

His eyes go wide beneath his mask. He waves his hand ahead, motioning toward Scott.

"Huh?" I flick my gaze toward the podium.

"TJ?" Scott beckons me forward. "Want to come on over here?"

I step forward, but not before I take one last look at the mystery Cinderella, hoping I can spot which direction she goes so I can track her down later.

With my gaze on her, I don't realize the up lights on the stage are right in my path, and I stumble as my foot connects with the nearest one, sending it skittering around. I manage to catch myself before I fall flat on my face. The crowd takes a collective breath, and my teammates start chortling.

"Easy, Teej! You trying to blind me?" Del has a hand over his face. The light spun around and is now spotlighting him.

"Just trying to make sure everyone knows what a good-looking center the River Foxes have," I say easily as I shove my hands in my pockets and stroll the rest of the way to Scott. The mic picked up my comment and the crowd ate it up. Del gives me a jaunty salute and steps forward, doing a pageant wave for the fans.

I lean toward the mic. "He's single, in case anyone's wondering."

Del's face turns bright red, and he gives me a murderous look. *You're welcome*, I mouth in his direction before turning my attention to Scott, who's shaking his head and smirking at me. The organization is used to my antics.

The crowd is cheering even more loudly for Del, and when the applause subsides, Scott puts his hand on my shoulder and squeezes, giving me a good-natured shake. "Here you have him, ladies and gents. The team charmer and—apparently— matchmaker?" He arches his eyebrows at me.

I lean toward the mic. "Wingman extraordinaire, that's me. Also"—I point at myself, having mercy on Del and putting the focus back on myself—"single and willing and able to mingle." I hit the fans with an overdone wink, and there's lots of squealing. I pan the crowd, but I've lost sight of Cinderella. I say a silent prayer that I can find her later. If I'm lucky, she'll be single and ready to mingle too.

Scott laughs, resuming his position behind the mic. "We're grateful TJ is a little more fleet of foot on the field than on this stage, am I right, folks?"

Chapter 3
Lucy

Someone needs to tell my fight-or-flight response to calm the heck down. I reach up and finger the edge of my mask. Daisy insisted I use her vintage, off-white lace one. "It matches the dress perfectly," she'd said. "It would be an honor to have a pretty thing like you wear it."

I can't believe I agreed. This is a wedding gown, for crying out loud. I'm not trying to draw attention to myself, but I can feel the stares.

No one knows who you are. I tell myself this over and over again, letting my fingers graze the delicate lace mask and feeling my heartbeat slow. This is fine.

I tune in to the activity of the room around me. The River Foxes spared no expense for this gala. There are large fabric swaths in ice blue and white draped tastefully around the room. Twinkle lights swoop in long lines, crisscrossing the high ceilings, giving the illusion that we're dining under a star-studded sky.

It makes sense that this event is done up so big. Tickets were outrageous. Cassie told me her agency was willing to pay, but I didn't take her up on the offer. Money isn't an issue for me. My dad's life insurance payout made sure I was set for life. Then, when my stepmom started monetizing her social media and day-in-the-life content, she made sure my stepsisters and I got a fair share of the profits. As much as I hated the spotlight, it raked in money. A *lot* of money.

Even if I'm not being featured on the family platforms anymore, I still have my writing income. Thanks to my sweet readers and

Cassie's hard work, I've had a lucrative career thus far, and I don't take it for granted.

I smile up at the waiter who clears my plate. The food was divine, but I only managed to eat a couple bites of my steak before I felt like I might pop a hole in Daisy's wedding gown. The waistline is tight with a capital T.

I spent the dinner hour chatting with a middle-aged couple from the Chicago area, Adelaide and Clark. Mostly I asked a few questions, and they were more than happy to launch into their entire life story. He came from old money, and she grew up on the wrong side of the tracks, but they fell for each other, and together they started what became a wildly successful event management firm. Their company also had a hand in planning this gala.

"Now, dear." Adelaide shifts in her chair to address me. I sit up straighter. "We've talked your ear off, but we haven't heard a thing about you. Tell us where you're from. What brings you out here alone tonight?"

Adelaide looks at me with kind eyes and a soft smile. Her face mask, the kind that's on a stick, is propped on the table. I reach up and touch mine again, needing the reminder that I'm invisible tonight. *I can lie. It's fine. Everything's fine.* Except my mind is blank. I literally make up worlds and fictional people for a living, and I cannot for the life of me come up with something adequate to tell this woman that will sound believable.

"She came to see me."

I turn in my seat at the sound of a smooth, deep voice behind me.

"TJ Wilson!" Adelaide squeals, and her husband pushes his chair back and stands to shake hands with the guy who tripped his way across the stage earlier. He's obviously a football player. Since I don't follow the sport or the River Foxes, I don't know much more than that, but from the way he played to the crowd and sent every woman here into a titter with his comment about being single, I could guess the kind of man he is. Right now, I don't really care that he's a player or a playboy. I'm grateful for the diversion.

He chats easily with Adelaide and Clark for a minute or two, and I get to my feet, even though they're killing me in these heels, so the four of us are standing together.

"We'll let you two kids get to it, then."

Get to what, exactly? I have no clue, but judging by the way Adelaide's wagging her eyebrows, she thinks there's some sort of history between TJ and me. Little does she know that while he may be a strong, sexy sports ball player of some kind, I'm a social media has-been who has never been kissed. Her suggestive eyebrows are misplaced.

Adelaide grabs her mask, holds it up to her face, and wiggles her fingers at me before tucking her hand into the crook of her husband's elbow and walking off.

I watch them go, aware of TJ's gaze on my face. My cheeks heat under his stare. I absently touch my temple, making sure my disguise is firmly in place. When I work up the courage to look at him, he's smiling at me, and I take a beat to size him up.

The guy is built. I don't know much of anything about football, but if I had to guess, I'd bet on him being someone who bulldozes people. Is that something that a sports player does? If not, they should. TJ would be good at it. The way his shoulders fill out his suit coat should be illegal. His tailor better be on speed dial because the stitching looks dangerously close to busting.

"What did you say your name was?" he asks, interrupting my mental cataloging.

I clear my throat. "I didn't."

His eyes twinkle behind his mask, and one eyebrow arches up over the top of it, like he's waiting for me to say more. I don't, and something fiery passes through his gaze, like he's recalibrating, but also like he respects my coyness. I've never considered myself particularly coy. Most people deem me standoffish.

"What should a person call you, then?" He leans in and points at himself. "Specifically, a person who swooped in during your time of need, at a moment when you obviously were desperate for saving from the sort of uncomfortable, prying questions well-meaning strangers tend to lob at beautiful women."

I suck in a sharp breath. It's been a long time since anyone offered me a compliment. TJ is smooth, I'll give him that. I open my mouth to respond, but he holds up a hand to stop me.

"You know what? I take it back."

My stomach gives an uncomfortable lurch. Did he decide I actually wasn't beautiful? Or am I such poor company that he's already going to excuse himself from the conversation before it's even begun? That's not so good for a girl's ego.

"Take what back?"

"You don't look like the kind of woman who needs saving."

I tip my head to the side. If he only knew the mess I've made of my life, he would take that back ... again.

"Mostly I was looking for an excuse to talk to you," he admits with an adorably boyish shrug.

There's something refreshing about TJ's openness. I don't know him at all, but I'm drawn to the uninhibited way he's carrying on this conversation. Even though he's wearing a mask, it feels like he's laying all his cards on the table. No games. No pretenses. A straight shooter. It makes me want to be that way in return ... at least, to an extent.

"Alright then, Mr. Football Player. You're talking. I'm talking. So can I tell you a secret?"

"Obviously, yes."

"I didn't come here looking for saving, but I did come here looking for something else."

He leans in. "I'm listening."

"I've got one night to have fun. To not think about who I am when I take this mask off. I need to pack a lot of experiences into the next"—I check the giant clock that hangs on one side of the Atrium—"two hours. I need to come away from tonight with inspiration that'll last me a lifetime. Think you can help me with that?"

"Oh. I am definitely your man."

"I'll be the judge of that," I fire back.

TJ's eyes twinkle beneath his mask. "I like a challenge."

"Good. I just have one simple rule."

"Name it."

"No personal questions allowed."

I'm pretty proud of myself for coming up with that one on the spot. It feels like a good safeguard to have in place. TJ crosses his arms over his chest. I wait for the fabric to rip, because he's really testing the limits with those muscles.

"You in, or not?" I say it so boldly I can hardly believe myself. I do *not* talk to men like this. I do not talk to *anyone* like this. I'm not direct. Except I guess tonight, I am.

"Oh, I am *absolutely* in." He reaches forward and collects my right hand, bringing my knuckles to his lips, holding my gaze as he lingers over the kiss for an extra second before shooting me a grin and tugging me toward the staircase I descended earlier. "Let's go."

Chapter 4
Lucy

TJ weaves us in and out of tables like he dodges things for a living. Maybe he does. I really should have brushed up on football before attending this gala.

A couple of guys whistle in our direction.

"Taking my advice, Teej?" asks a man who looks familiar to me. I stumble as recognition dawns. That's Anton *freaking* Bates. He's got his arm tucked snuggly around the waist of a knockout brunette in a skin-tight, strapless black dress. I'm immediately jealous of her toned shoulders and the killer red lipstick she's pulling off. Her mask is black with feathers at her temples, so I can't make out much more of her face, but I'm sure it's Anton's girlfriend, Rose. The two of them made a public splash last year when she took a bullet for him. Now her eyes crinkle with a smile as she glances between TJ and me.

"What advice?" she asks, looking up at Anton.

"Nothing," TJ interjects and then shakes his head at Anton. "And no."

"You sure about that?"

TJ glances back at me, and the look he gives me is piercing, like he's got X-ray vision, and he can see right through me. I wish I knew if he liked what he saw.

It doesn't matter. Not really. I'm not trying to impress TJ. I'm just trying to get inspired to write a romance novel.

TJ's eyes soften, and he winks at me again before returning Anton's gaze. "Not that sort of thing, Bates."

If I'm not mistaken, Anton's shoulders drop a little, like he's disappointed, but before I can be certain, he stands up straighter again. "Keep an open mind!" He turns his full attention to his date, pressing his nose to her forehead and dropping a delicate kiss on her brow. "Come on, Sammy Rose. Let's dance."

TJ leads me onward, but I look over my shoulder to where Anton pulls Rose to him at the edge of the dance floor. The song that's currently playing is fast, with a techno beat, but he wraps his arms around her waist, draws her to his chest, and gazes down at her, like they're the only two people in this crowded room. I wonder what sort of love song is playing in their heads. Or maybe it's their hearts. Whatever it is, his and hers must sound the same. They are totally in sync, totally enraptured with each other.

That's the type of connection I strive to write about in books.

I wobble on my heels and TJ tightens his grip on my hand. "You okay?"

"Yeah, sorry. I was watching your friend and his date. They're cute."

"They're madly in love." He makes an exasperated expression, and I chuckle softly as he tucks my hand into the crook of his elbow and leads me up the main staircase.

"Where are you taking me?"

TJ turns left, and we walk down the hallway that I passed upon my entrance. "I thought you said no questions?"

I roll my eyes. "No *personal* questions."

"Oh, well, in that case, I suppose it's safe to answer. I didn't want to break any of your rules."

"How noble of you."

He laughs, and it's a deep, throaty sound that sends a jolt of pleasure through my stomach. "I'll be your noblest knight tonight, madam."

"Eww. I'm not a madam."

"Then what?" He has his head angled toward me. "What would you like me to call you?"

I look up at him and arch my brows. He doesn't stop staring, a smile tickling the corners of his mouth like I'm amusing him. I find that hard to believe. I'm not a good time. That's what my stepsisters are always around for. They're the loud and outgoing ones. My stepmom, too. Those three can talk to anyone, charm anyone. They're outrageous, but they're also good-natured and funny. People like being around them. Meanwhile, I'm awkward, I never know what to say or how to start a conversation, and then I get in my head because I'm afraid everyone is bored when they're talking to me.

But TJ is here now. He's giving me his full attention. I can do this. I can be bold and have fun for one night, like I promised Cassie. It's good to flex a new muscle every now and again, right?

"You can call me Cinderella," I say before I lose my nerve. It sounds ridiculous the moment it's out of my mouth, but TJ's gaze hounds me, and he nods slowly.

"You look like Cinderella, not gonna lie. It was the first thought I had when I saw you."

He noticed me? Embarrassment and pleasure war for the upper hand in my gut. His intense gaze makes my pulse points fizzle. "Was that before or after you nearly blinded your teammate?"

He smirks, shaking his head but keeping his attention trained on me. "Del'll live. His scarred corneas are worth it if it means I caught your eye like you caught mine."

I feel a blush spreading from my forehead down to the soles of my sore feet. "Don't flatter yourself. You were up on stage, tripping over yourself … kinda tough to miss."

"Still chalking it up as a win."

"Whatever helps you sleep at night," I say airily and hide a smile when he snort-laughs. "Now," I continue, "you were about to tell me where you're taking me?"

"Well." He stops outside an unmarked door. "It's only fitting that Cinderella gets the best view of the ball." He pushes open the door to reveal another flight of stairs. "How are you with heights?"

"Not afraid of them, if that's what you're asking." I look up at the steep flight and then down at my shoes and my pinched toes.

TJ tracks my gaze. "But your feet are killing you, aren't they?"

Perceptive. That's a trait I definitely want my main male character to have in my next book.

"Like you wouldn't believe," I admit. "But I really want to see the view, so I can power through."

He sniffs. "Not on my watch. You won't be able to enjoy it if you get there and your feet are blistered. Here." He turns around and gestures to his shoulders. "I'll piggyback you."

I burst into laughter. "You will not."

"Why? It's a perfect solution."

"There's no way I can climb on your back in my dress."

He frowns, humming to himself. "You're right about that. It's very bottom-heavy."

"Just what every woman wants to hear."

His eyes bug beneath his mask. "You know I didn't mean ... I meant ... Your bottom is great, no matter how it looks. Not that I'm looking. Not that I can really *see* it at all, given the dress, which is what you were saying in the first place, and—" He presses his lips together. "I'm going to shut up now."

I can't help laughing. I add nervous rambling to my list of character traits.

"You sure you don't want to say anything else about my figure while you're at it?" I pop a hip.

TJ swallows. I hold out my hands, palms up, and do a slight turn. His eyes scan my masked face in micromovements, like he wants to see every inch, before he dips his gaze to trace the curve of my waist. He glances down at my toes and then casually brings his eyes back to meet mine.

The joke is definitely on me here, and this stairwell just became hotter than a stone-fire grill. I'm melting under his observation.

"I'll keep my comments to myself for now." There's a rasp in his throat that wasn't there before.

I need a thousand fans to combat the heat in my cheeks.

"I have a solution to our problem." He steps toward me. "Can I touch you here?" He motions to my back. "And here?" He points to my knees ... or at least, where my knees are beneath my dress.

I catch on to his plan pretty quickly. "You're going to carry me bridal style?"

"Is that what it's called?"

"Yes."

"Is that alright with you? The view's pretty great."

"I guess, but I don't—"

He scoops me up in one fluid motion, and suddenly I'm up close and personal with the muscles I've taken note of from afar. A pretty great view, indeed.

"—want to hurt you," I finish on a breath.

"*Pfft.*" He brushes off my concern with an exhale, and I feel the warmth of it on my cheek. His breath smells like peppermint, and there's a pleasant aroma of pine that surrounds him. My senses are in overdrive, and I don't hate it. I try to catalog everything. My skin seems to vibrate where he's touching me, and my stomach could be classified as a carbonated beverage right now. But beyond these physical sensations, I feel cared for and ladylike. I'm all for a strong female protagonist, but there's no rule that says you can't be strong and have a strong desire to be held. At least, not in my book. My *books.*

"You good?" TJ asks, and I feel the vibration of his chest.

"Yep," I squeak. I clear my throat and give myself a little pep talk as TJ starts climbing the stairs.

Pull yourself together, Lu. This is for research purposes. Put yourself in character. What would your FMC do? More importantly, what would fun, unrestrained Lu do?

"You have a very thick neck," I blurt.

That? *That* is what fun, unrestrained Lu would do? Comment on a man's thick neck? I'm mentally face-palming myself and wishing I could evaporate into my cloud of embarrassment.

TJ lets out a warm laugh. "Look at us—you with a heavy bottom and me with a thick neck."

"Shut up. You can't deny it." I decide to go with this, in all the awkwardness. I can't deny that it's fun, teasing and talking ... being close to him. "Your neck is like the column on one of those old Roman buildings."

He hums. "Which buildings are you referring to, Cinderella?"

"I have no clue what their names are. History and geography are not my strength. Honestly, math and science aren't either. Don't pick me for your trivia team."

"Same. We can be clueless about all things cultural, mathematical, and spatial together. I leave that sort of stuff to Poe."

"Who's Poe?"

"My teammate, Lawrence Poe." TJ tips his head back so he can look at me. Our faces are very close together. I can see the scruff of his five o'clock shadow. I have a weird and completely inappropriate desire to run my lips over it—to feel the coarseness of it under my tongue. Who am I and what is going on in my brain right now?

I shake my head slightly. "I guess I should admit that football is another thing I'm clueless about."

He gasps dramatically.

I hold back a smile. "This is probably a good time to ask you what exactly you do on the team."

"What do I do?" he asks, incredulous. He darts a glance down at me as he continues to climb up and up and up.

"Are you, like, a bench warmer? A manager? Are you any good?"

He blows out a breath and looks up to the ceiling. "Am I any good?" he mutters to the heavens. "You are crushing my ego right now, you know that, Cinderella?"

"Sorry!" I say again. "I know literally nothing about the River Foxes. Never watched a game in my life."

"Never?" He narrows his gaze at me. "Why are you smiling so big?"

I try to stop smiling, but I can't. "Because you're trying really hard to be casual when I've apparently insulted your football prowess. Let me guess, you're some sort of star?"

I feel his chest puff up against my back. "You could say that."

"So modest, too." I click my tongue.

"It's hard to be modest when you're as good as I am, Cinderella." The cool confidence in his tone makes my nerve endings feel like they've hopped on the backs of a stampede of buffalo. "That," he goes on, "and I have to be arrogant. I couldn't do my job if I didn't believe I could do my job."

My throat goes dry. There's that directness I noticed earlier. It's hot to hear him talk about his work with confidence in his capabilities.

"Noted," I say, swallowing a shiver at the intensity in his gaze and because I'm suddenly all too aware of the callouses on his hands. They're worker hands, and yet he's holding me like I'm made of glass and it's his one job in life not to let me shatter.

"If you watch a game, look for number twenty-five. That's me. I'm the running back, so I'll be in the middle of everything."

I've never had any desire to watch a football game until this very moment, but I'm supposed to be playing coy, so I shrug as much as I can, given my current position. "Might have to check one out."

"Might have to score a touchdown for you this weekend," he counters. "You'll know when I do."

I'm guessing a touchdown is a good thing, and the way my pulse spikes and my breath comes in short bursts tells me there's something to this sort of method-acting flirting.

"How so?" I ask, my voice a whisper. My heart whirls to life like a helicopter lifting off.

"Trust me." He dips his chin so our gazes lock in—complementary pieces in a puzzle. "You'll know."

He breaks eye contact even as there's a little voice in my head that's squealing like the little piggy running all the way home. I can't even believe this is my life right now. How did I end up here?

Oh yeah, a bossy literary agent, a killer case of writer's block, and a very expensive ticket. Not to mention a vintage wedding gown, courtesy of my sweet fairy godmother landlady.

"We made it." TJ stops on the last step. He's barely even breathing heavily after hauling me up here. How is that possible? "You ready?" he asks.

"Born ready," I tell him, because that feels like the sort of thing a self-assured, easy, breezy, beautiful Lucy would say.

Truthfully, I don't know what I was born for, and I don't mean that in a morbid way, just in a *my parents died and I've made a complete mess of my life, so what am I really doing?* sort of way.

TJ doesn't know these sorts of esoteric thoughts are rolling around underneath the jeweled crown I'm wearing, and it's very much for the best. I need to keep it that way. I need to channel fun Lucy for an hour or so more.

Then I can go back to Daisy's Inn and pore over every minute and detail of what's turning out to be an unforgettable night. I square my shoulders. If this is the one opportunity I'm giving myself, I'd better make the most of it.

Chapter 5
TJ

I ease my mystery woman down so she's standing on her own two feet. I immediately miss the warmth radiating from her body. I don't give her a chance to step too far away from me—not that there's anywhere to go. We're on a small landing in front of a nondescript door. I grab for her hand and, at the same time, use my other hand to twist the door handle, leading her toward the catwalk that crosses the rafters in the ceiling of the Atrium.

I step out first and look back to gauge whether she was honest when she told me heights don't bother her. Even though her face is covered with a mask and thick, artsy makeup spreading out from either side of it, I can still see her eyes—and while they're wide with surprise, they aren't darting around in a panic.

Calm in the face of a surprise. My kind of girl.

Wait. No. She's not my anything. She's my one-night good time.

That sounds ungentlemanly. My grandmother would bite my head off if she could read my mind right now.

But the point stands. This thing with Cinderella, or whatever her real name is, is for tonight. I don't need to get attached. I need to show her some fun.

She pauses and slips her heels off, leaving them safely on the landing before stepping out behind me onto the vented catwalk.

Calm and smart.

Instead of dwelling on how this woman is quickly becoming the most captivating person I've met in some time, I focus on leading her to the middle of the walkway suspended high above the Atrium. There are railings on either side, but it's a narrow passage, so I go slowly, giving her a chance to follow me at her own pace. I keep her fingers gripped in mine to steady her.

"Want to sit for a minute?" I gesture down to the walkway. "It's not the most comfortable spot, but you can't beat the view."

She laughs softly. "It's perfect. Yeah, let's sit."

We maneuver so we're seated side by side, our feet dangling from the catwalk.

"Wow," she says on an exhale.

I nod. We're looking down from above the strands of twinkling lights. It's like the party below is shrouded in a spider web of shining lights and we're on the other side of it, protected somehow. Part of it, but separate. It's like the best sort of out-of-body experience.

"This is incredible," my mystery woman whispers. She turns to look at me, and I meet her gaze. She smiles, and it's dazzling. "Thank you for bringing me up here."

"You said you needed to be inspired. This is where I come for…" I trail off. For what, exactly?

"Inspiration?" she fills in with a small smile.

I return the smile. "I guess, but also not exactly. More like perspective. Solitude. A reminder that I'm a small piece in the mosaic of this great big world."

This is the third time I've come up this way. The first was when I got signed to the River Foxes as a rookie. I was feeling pretty untouchable until I got turned around in the maze of hallways and was lost for twenty minutes until I found a maintenance worker who pointed me in the right direction. Before he let me leave, he told me he wanted to show me this spot. He didn't say why, but I'm pretty sure he knew I needed to be knocked down a peg or two, and coming up here is a good reminder that I'm not as much of a big shot as I sometimes like to think I am.

The second time was on the third anniversary of Tess's death. I couldn't get to the cemetery where she was buried like I had planned, and I needed to clear my head and be alone with my memories. This felt like the safest place to do that.

I blink a few times, realizing that Cinderella is staring at me as I've been lost in my own thoughts.

I tug at my collar. "Sorry. That got deep fast."

"No, it's good. It's a good reminder." Her gaze holds a lot of questions, but she doesn't voice any of them, clearly deciding to play by her own rules—rules I would do well to remember.

"Let's get back to the fun," I offer. "Since you're obviously not afraid of heights, tell me something that does scare you."

"That's your idea of fun?" she says, a teasing lilt to her voice. "Voicing my fears?"

She has a point. What can I say? Something about this woman is getting to me and making me want to know things … like what makes her laugh and what makes her scared and who's hurt her and who's healed her and everything in between.

"It could be fun." I shrug and then smirk. "Also, I'll tell you mine if you tell me yours."

"Hmm." She taps her chin, looking up.

I take the opportunity to admire the blush crawling up her neck, inordinately proud that I put it there. Even though I can't see her full face, I'd bet money on this woman having a sort of timeless beauty. Her skin looks milky soft, and I have a strong urge to brush my finger against her jawline. The thought makes a spark catch at the base of my chest.

"I'll allow it," she says, startling me out of my own head. "But you first," she adds quickly.

I blink and have to take a beat to rewind our conversation so I remember what we were talking about. The sight of Cinderella smiling over at me has every thought that's not *her, here, now* fleeing from my brain.

"I'm fearless," I quip, but she crinkles up her nose.

"Try again."

I chuckle. "Fine. I'm afraid of zebras."

She's quiet for a second, and I keep my eyes glued to her as she presses her lips together—wow, we haven't even talked about her lips yet—and raises her eyebrows high enough that they peek out over the top of her mask.

"You're serious?" she says.

"Very serious."

"Care to elaborate?"

"I don't know. It's like they don't know who they are. Part donkey. Part horse. All around weird. Their black-and-white stripes make me dizzy. Yuck." I shudder. "Don't even like thinking about them, honestly."

She bursts into laughter, and it's my new favorite sound. "What have zebras ever done to you? Have you ever even seen one in real life?"

"At the zoo!"

"Ah, yes. The zoo is a terrifying place. I'm sure you're just making it a regular thing to visit the zoo and be terrorized by zebras on what, a daily, weekly basis?"

I scowl at her, but it's pretend. Her teasing makes me feel like a helium-filled balloon—like I'm full and alive and nothing can bring me down.

"Alright," I say. "If my phobia is so funny to you, then you go."

She sits back and primly folds her hands in her lap. "If you must know, I'm afraid of car washes."

"Car washes?"

"Yes, the automatic kind that you have to drive into."

"What's so scary about that?"

She throws her hands up. "I don't know. Probably nothing! I've never gone through one by myself, okay? I'm afraid I'll mess it up, so I'm in this vicious cycle of being too nervous to try, and now I'm perpetually scared of it."

"Huh." I lean back as far as the catwalk will let me. Our shoulders are touching, my tux jacket brushing against the lace covering her arm. I keep an eye on her as she shifts next to me. She doesn't look uncomfortable, but maybe a little embarrassed.

"Thanks for telling me," I say, nudging her shoulder with mine. "If you ever want to give it a try, I'd ride shotgun while you face your fear."

She turns her head in my direction, eyes narrowed as if trying to determine if I'm being serious.

I hold up my hands. "I know this is a one-night-only thing we've got going, but the offer stands. You know where to find me."

Her lips twitch. "On the field, in the middle of it all … right?"

I nod. "You got it."

"This *is* a one-night-only thing," she says after a beat of silence.

Is it me, or does she not sound super happy about that? I mentally slap myself a couple times, trying to knock the wishful thinking from my brain.

"But," she adds carefully.

The wishful thinking roars back, doubled in size.

But then the music cuts out from the party below, and Scott's voice reaches us. "Ladies and gentlemen, it's that time! We're going to get started on the live auction. If I could have my players up here."

Just like that, the clock strikes midnight. My time with Cinderella is up.

Chapter 6
Lucy

"I 'm guessing that's you, Mr. Football?" I keep my tone light even as my heart sinks.

"Yeah, I gotta run." He stands and holds out his hand. I take it and let him hoist me up.

"Go ahead. I can find my way back down." My feet throw a hissy fit, pulsing with pain at the thought of taking all those stairs back down to the main level.

"Absolutely not. I'm not leaving you up here alone." TJ's tone leaves no room for argument. "But we do have to hurry. Come on."

We retrace our steps to the landing. I bend down and start putting my shoes on, but his large hand settles on my lower back, and I add that to my mental list of things to include in a book, because *hello*, the weight of his hand makes my stomach feel like it's free-falling.

"No time for those death traps."

I look over my shoulder, arching a brow. "You want me to go barefoot?"

He shakes his head. "Just hold them. I'll hold you again."

"I'm only going to slow you down," I protest. "Go ahead without me."

He looks torn, but then he steels his resolve. "I've got a better idea, as long as you're okay with me carrying you a little less ladylike?"

"Uh, I guess."

"Good." In one smooth motion, he hoists me up and over his shoulder. He's got his arm clamped around my knees and my head is staring at his perfectly formed butt. It's like the peach emoji in real life.

"Thank you." TJ's low voice is smug.

My face flames. "I said that out loud, didn't I?" I mutter.

"Sure did. Glad to know all my time in the weight room is paying off."

He jogs down the steps, and I can't help it. I start to laugh. If you would have told me at the beginning of tonight that I'd be carried fireman-style down a back staircase at the River Foxes Stadium by a handsome football player, I would have said there was a better chance of my nonexistent carriage turning into a pumpkin.

I can't stop giggling.

"You okay back there? Is my derriere causing you to swoon?"

I laugh even harder. "Derriere? Who even says that?"

I sound blithe and happy. Like I don't have anything else in the world to be doing right now other than teasing this hot football player about the word he used to identify his butt. I barely recognize my own voice. I sound shimmery and fun. I don't hate it.

"You're right. Anton is rubbing off on me. He talks all proper and formal sometimes. But also, you seem like a classy sort of lady, so I figured the words I'd usually use would make you blush."

"That's just the blood currently rushing to my head."

He laughs outright at that. He jogs down the deserted hallway and skids to a stop, carefully setting me on the ground. His chest rises and falls with exertion, but he keeps his hands on my waist, staring into my eyes. "You good?"

I feel for my mask, making sure it stayed in place while upside down. When I'm assured my identity is still undercover, I lean forward to brush off the sparkles that have transferred from my dress to the lapel of his tux, letting my hands linger. "Yeah, I am. Thanks for the lift." My playful voice is gone, replaced with a breathy whisper.

"Anytime." He winks.

I smile, but I have to work for it, because this is it. There won't be another time between TJ and me. No more back-and-forth banter. No more of his kindness and attention directed at me.

As fun as this was, it was all pretend ... just for this one night. It's better this way, because TJ and I would not be compatible in real life. I don't live in the moment like this, and I get the sense that he does ... all the time. He's outgoing and charismatic, and I stay holed up in my room, writing romance novels in secret. I've fallen from grace, and he's some type of beloved football star. The type of public figure I went ahead and lambasted on national television.

We're not meant to be.

But that doesn't mean that I don't feel a twinge of regret that I'm not even giving myself the chance to see him again. I waffle, wondering if it would be so bad to take the mask off, or to at least give him my first name and phone number. I could tell him to write me at Daisy's Inn.

Are pen pals still a thing? I haven't had one since second grade, but he seems like the type of guy who would be down for something goofy like that.

"Is TJ Wilson on the premises?" The question booms through the speakers, jostling me out of my pathetic train of thought. This isn't elementary school, and I'm not here to be TJ's friend.

"That's me." TJ is smiling, but he's also hesitating, searching my face for ... what, exactly? I don't know. "I guess this is where I leave you." He says it like a question, putting the ball firmly in my court.

My heart does a series of starts and stops. It's so tempting to do something stupid right now, like pull his ridiculously handsome face down to mine and kiss him, but my brain kicks into high gear, reminding me why it would be a horrible idea to push things further than I already have. So instead, I playfully shove him away. "Go ahead. You're late."

"Fashionably late," he corrects with a grin. My knees wobble under my dress. How can a man have so much charm? So much swagger? He takes a step backward, still facing me. "I hope you got your inspiration."

"I did." I hold his gaze, drinking in the ombre wave of his blue eyes and committing the kaleidoscope to memory. I never want to forget how it feels to be the sole object of TJ Wilson's attention. It's a heady sensation. It makes me feel powerful and alive in a way I don't think I've ever experienced before. "Thank you for tonight."

He steps back toward me. "I feel like we should, like I should ..." he breaks off, shaking his head.

"What?"

"Should I hug you right now?" His eyes are wide and searching my gaze from beneath his mask. My heart pounds. "Should I kiss you?" he asks, his voice lower still.

My body sways like I'm under some sort of spell. "If we were getting personal tonight, then maybe I would tell you that I've never been kissed before." I lick my lips, and his gaze darts down before ricocheting back up to meet my eyes.

"Never?" His voice scrapes like a wave against the sand.

I shake my head, forcing down the feelings of humiliation that this simple truth about myself conjures and telling myself to own it.

TJ leans in, and my stomach bottoms out. This is it. This is a moment I've dreamt up and imagined more times than I can count. Lately, I thought it might never happen for me. I might spend my days penning fictional love stories but never experience so much as a simple kiss for myself—for real.

He pauses and reaches forward, holding one of the tendrils of my hair between his fingers before tucking it behind my ear. My eyelids flutter closed.

I feel his warm breath against my cheek, where he places a lingering but chaste kiss.

I let out a gasp when he whispers in my ear, "If we were getting personal tonight, I'd tell you that I want to kiss you." I feel more than see him swallow, like he's fighting for control, and my blood starts to hum. My body is a live wire. "I want that very much," he rumbles against my earlobe. "But you deserve for your first kiss to be with a man who knows you. A man who'll savor the moment and take his time and treat you to the tender sort of embrace you deserve. Don't settle for anything less."

"Ah! There he is, ladies and gentlemen," the guy talking into the mic shouts.

I frantically step away from him, out of view, as TJ looks down into the Atrium from the top of the staircase. The crowd cheers, and he holds up both hands in salute, but then he casts one last look at me.

His words ring in my ears. *A man who knows you. A man who'll savor. Don't settle.* They're wrapping themselves around a fractured part of my heart I didn't realize was broken, and suddenly I want TJ Wilson to know me.

But this isn't about what I want. It can't be, so I muster up my brightest smile, even though my stomach is plummeting, and wave him onward. "Go!"

He hesitates for one more beat before he nods. "Goodnight, Cinderella."

And then he's gone.

Chapter 7
Lucy

I wait until the auction is well underway before I slip down the stairs. I don't want to draw attention to the fact that I was the reason TJ Wilson was late. I don't need anyone staring at me, trying to figure out my story.

I retrieve my purse from coat check and glance at my phone. I'd say I gave it a good effort. I can leave now and honestly tell Cassie I stayed out well past my bedtime.

Three players have been auctioned off on dates in the time it took me to put my heels back on, make it down here, and collect my things. Now it's TJ's turn.

The River Foxes have raised a boatload of money so far, and judging by the way TJ struts across the stage and the people in attendance squeal, they've saved the best for last.

When bidding for TJ gets underway, there is a lot of interest. My hands clench my purse, and I linger at the base of the stairs, looking on. The bids are rocketing upward, and the auctioneer can barely keep up. His head is on a swivel as he spots the numbers folks are raising from every corner of the room.

The price for a night out with TJ jumps to five thousand dollars, and several of the previous bidders drop out. It's clear this is going to come down to a war between an older guy with salt-and-pepper hair and a middle-aged woman in a pea-cock-blue dress with a matching mask that's lined with flouncy feathers. They're both sitting near the back of the Atrium, so I can easily observe them.

"Fifty-five hundred." Ms. Peacock stands and presses her hands into the table, staring down Mr. Salt and Pepper.

"Fifty-six hundred," he responds, massaging the back of his neck. He shifts in his seat, and I have a feeling his staying power is running out.

I can practically see the steam coming out of Ms. Peacock's ears. She obviously didn't expect anyone to last this long. The other players went for a couple thousand dollars apiece. "Six thousand!" she shrieks.

"Wow, six thousand dollars!" the auctioneer's voice rings out. "That's a great number. What do you say? Can we go any higher? I have it on good authority that TJ is a good time."

"I do, too," I mutter. He's also considerate and hilarious, and I can still feel the imprint of his lips on my cheek.

Don't settle.

His voice echoes in my ear. I feel like someone has taken eggbeaters to my abdomen and is running them at speed five, splattering batter all over the place. My fingers find the corner of my paddle number, and I absently play with the thick, shiny cardstock.

Ms. Peacock looks around the Atrium with her nose tipped up, all but daring someone to out-bid her. I pray Mr. Salt and Pepper has it in him, but he gives a slight shake of his head. A slow grin spreads over Ms. Peacock's face. It's predatory and triumphant. She turns to the woman sitting next to her at her table and says, loud enough for me to hear, "I can't wait to get my hands all over that fine specimen of a man."

Something unfamiliar and green seizes hold of my spine, yanking me upright.

"Six thousand, going once," the auctioneer calls out. "Going twice ..."

My hand is in the air with my paddle number raised before I can think twice. I don't know what I'm doing, but I do know there's no way I'm letting Ms. Peacock get anywhere close to TJ's *derriere*. Or any other part of him, for that matter.

"Seven thousand!" I shout.

Ms. Peacock spins around and glares at me, the feathers on her mask fluttering around like an angry bird. Everyone else looks in my direction, too, and that's when my brain catches up with my jealous heart and realizes that this was a no good, very bad, wholly terrible idea.

"Seven thousand dollars from the lady in the white dress," the auctioneer says. It's the same guy who announced the team earlier, and he's shaking his head in awe. He thumps TJ on the back.

TJ stares directly at me. A chill scampers up my back as a torrent of heat builds in my cheekbones. This man—this night—is throwing off my systems, making me feel and function like never before. *What* am I doing? I can't see him again. He can't know who I am. This can't go anywhere. Also, seven thousand dollars is a heck of a lot of money to spend on a date with a guy who I'm pretty sure would have given me his number for free if I'd asked for it. I was the one who set the terms of our arrangement.

TJ's eyes stay locked on me, and my heart takes off in a gallop when the corners of his lips hitch upward as the auctioneer calls out, "Seven thousand, going once, going twice ..."

"Yooouuu hoo! Ten thousand!" A little old lady with a helmet of white hair waves her paddle above her head from the front of the room.

The crowd turns collectively away from me toward her, and TJ flicks his gaze in her direction. Ms. Peacock audibly screeches with displeasure. I suck in a deep, relieved breath and slink away. Saved by the frosty-haired grandma. I toss up a silent prayer of thanks that she prevented me from doing something really stupid.

I retrieve my coat, quickly thank the attendant, and exit the Atrium through one of the side doors. I walk as fast as my heels will allow, letting the sounds of the player auction and the sensations of my night spent with TJ Wilson fade into the background. I don't stop or turn around until I'm outside. I lean against the stadium wall, placing one palm on my forehead and one on my heart. I don't know what came over me in there. My face is hot to the touch, so maybe I'm feverish.

I definitely know something's wrong with me when I linger for five whole minutes before walking to my car, hoping that maybe TJ will run out here in search of me. Then we could drive off together and talk all night, and in the glow of the orange-and-pink sunrise over the bay of Green Bay, where we'd be parked in his truck, he would kiss me. He'd take his time, and he'd treat me how I deserve. I'd feel the kiss in every nerve ending of my body, and we'd fall madly in love, and ...

It's almost scary how vividly I can craft the scene. I shake my head.

This isn't a movie, Lucy. This isn't a romance novel. You're not actually Cinderella.

Yet as I drive back to Cashmere Cove, my brain whirs as I replay every moment of tonight, and my body still sings with the echo of being in TJ's arms.

I'd be lying if I said he didn't feel a little like Prince Charming.

Chapter 8
TJ

"**S**old to paddle number 444! Congratulations, young lady!" Scott beams in the direction of the older woman who just forked over ten thousand dollars for a night with me.

I give the white-haired granny an overdone bow from the stage, playing the part of happy-go-lucky charmer, but my mind is on my Cinderella, who just fled the Atrium.

She bid on me. Seven thousand dollars, to be exact. *After* she said all she wanted was tonight. That has to mean something, right?

I follow my teammates off the dais, and Anton approaches with Rose. He slaps me on the back. "We're never going to hear the end of this, are we?"

"What?"

He laughs. "Your date going for over five grand more than anyone else's. Come on, man. You know you're going to be insufferable about this."

"Oh, yeah." I force a chuckle. "You know me."

I stand on my tiptoes, trying to spot Cinderella. She went toward the coat check, but if she comes back into the Atrium, maybe I can talk to her again before she leaves. I cannot wrap my mind around the fact that a woman like her—someone funny and adorable and stunning and smart—has never been kissed. I don't know if I made the right call in not kissing her. She seemed like she wanted me to. Was that the kind of inspiration she was hoping for? I didn't want to rush it. I didn't want something so significant to take place when I couldn't even see her face, when I didn't even know her name.

"Dude, are you even listening?"

My gaze snaps back to where Anton has been joined by Del and Poe.

"What? Sorry." I sink down to my heels again, keeping my eyes fixed on the back of the ballroom.

"Who was she?" Rose pipes up.

I glance at her out of my peripheral vision. "Who?"

She gestures over her shoulder. "The woman who bid on you. You were with her before the auction started, weren't you?"

Leave it to Rose. Freakishly observant Rose. She was Anton's secret bodyguard before they got together ... or maybe it was while they were getting together? The details are sketchy. I'm not surprised she picked up on my weird behavior. Since she and Anton reconnected, she's around the guys a lot, which means she's gotten familiar with us. She knows our tells. Right now, she's looking at me like she can see right through me, to the deepest part of my heart. The part that I don't let anyone see because it's a mess in there.

"Who? The woman in the white dress?" Ned Norbertson joins our circle. He's holding his cell phone. I'm guessing he was filming clips of the auction for our social media pages. "I was wondering that too. I saw you leave with her earlier."

Five pairs of eyes pin me in place, waiting for an answer. I rake a hand through my hair. "I don't know who she is. She didn't tell me her name."

"You like her, though, don't you?" Rose presses.

"What? I don't ... I—" If Rose saw me with Cinderella at the top of the steps, then she definitely saw me lean in. There's no use trying to bluff my way out of this. "Yeah. I do. She was"—I search for the right word—"intriguing. Funny and bold and—" I cut myself off. "You know what? It doesn't matter."

"Bull!" Del raises his voice, and we all flinch. He's a gentle giant. Oversized, but he wouldn't hurt a fly … except on the football field, where, as our center, he's like a brick wall who takes pleasure in pancaking anyone who tries to get past him to tackle Anton. "You're basically frantic," he continues, pointing at me before hooking his thumb over the door. "Go after her already!"

"I can't believe you didn't ask her name," Poe grumbles. "Dude, that's like Getting To Know You 101."

"I asked," I tell him. "She wouldn't answer. I called her Cinderella all night."

"Oh my word, this is straight out of a book," Rose says under her breath. And then, more loudly, she adds, "You should definitely go after her. Girls like to be chased."

"I'll keep that in mind," Anton says, nuzzling his nose into her neck. She swats at him, but her lips twitch and her cheeks blaze.

Something churns in my gut. I'm torn between a yearning to go after Cinderella and an awareness that the smart thing to do is let her go.

"What are you waiting for?" Ned asks.

I glance around the circle. Everyone is grinning and offering their encouragement. Del's eyes have welled with tears. Classic, Del. The man feels his feelings. I admire that about him.

"You're right." I pull in a grounding breath and act against my better judgement. Though right now, this choice feels inevitable. "I'm going."

I break away from the circle, and I'm halfway to the exit when my phone vibrates in my pocket. I have it set to sleep mode, so the only notifications that can get through are from numbers I've assigned as favorites. That means it's one of my grandparents. They never text this late.

My pulse hammers as I grab for my phone, and I swear my heart stops beating when I read the message from my grandpa.

Pa

Gram fell. I need your help.

Chapter 9

TJ

I get to the senior living neighborhood that Gram and Pa live in in less than fifteen minutes. I didn't run into any cops on my way, which is good, because I was driving well over the speed limit. I tried to call my grandpa, but he didn't pick up. I debated calling an ambulance, but I have no information other than the text message, and I could get to them faster than the EMTs anyway.

I slam on the brakes, skidding my truck into a parking stall outside their place. I leave the keys in the ignition and sprint toward the door, bursting inside while my heart threatens to burst out of my chest. "Gram? Pa? Where are you?"

There's a grunting sound and then, "Back here, Son!"

The unit is tiny, a simple living room on the front that joins an area where a small dining table seats four. Beyond that is the kitchen, and off to the back is a hallway leading to the bathroom and the only bedroom.

I sprint in that direction, bracing for the worst—my grandma unconscious or in terrible pain with a broken hip or a snapped femur. Something gruesome and awful.

I pause in the doorway to their bedroom as hysterical laughter reaches my ear. I blink a couple times at the sight before me.

My grandfather is on his knees, reaching over the edge of the far side of the bed. My grandma is nowhere to be seen, but then a leg flies up and tries to hook itself onto the mattress.

"You need to try, honey," Pa scolds with a huff.

More laughter from my grandma, who I now realize is wedged between the bed and the wall. "I am trying, but I'm stuck!"

My grandpa yanks, and my grandma hoots from her position on the floor.

"I don't want to pull your arm out of its socket." Pa looks over his shoulder, and I get my first look at his face. It's beet red, and he's wearing a wry smile. He turns back to my grandma. "TJ is here. He'll be able to help."

"Oh dear, this is embarrassing." My grandma bursts into giggles.

"You okay, Gram?" I ask, slowly walking to the foot of the bed and peering around the side. Sure enough, my grandma is on her back, her hips jammed between the boxspring and the wall. She's got one foot on the bed and the other pressed against the floor, trying to give herself some leverage.

"I'm as good as a person can be in this situation." She starts giggling again. "Look, Martin. I'm being rescued by Zorro himself."

I shake my head and take off the mask I realize I'm still wearing. I toss it onto the bed. My mind flits to Cinderella and the mask she wore all night. Now that I know my grandparents aren't having any kind of legitimate emergency, my heart thrums with regret. I have no clue who she is. Never will. But there's no use dwelling on that now. It's for the best anyway. That's what I tell myself as I fake a scowl at my grandma.

"Very funny, Gram. Do you want a hand up and out of there?"

"That would be good, dear. I've really gotten myself into a pickle."

"Do I even want to know how this happened?" I scoot between the bed and the wall and get my arms under my grandma's back so I can lift her upright.

"Nothing saucy was happening, if that's what you mean," Pa says. Does he sound disappointed? I'm going to try not to think about that.

"That's not to say nothing saucy never happens, though," Gram adds when I get her back up and onto the bed. She brushes her flannel pajamas.

I hold up my hands and take a step away from the bed. "I really don't need any details."

My grandma giggles again, and my grandpa looks proud. He shoots her a wink, and the same sensation of longing that burned like a white-hot brand being pressed into my stomach at the sight of Rose and Anton is back. I don't know what's gotten into me. When Tess died, I shut down the idea of having a love like that.

So why am I longing for a partner right now?

It's the Cinderella effect. It has to be. Which is stupid. I don't know anything about her. Not anything real, at least.

"We were trying out an exercise routine from one of those videos on YouTube." Gram talks animatedly with her hands, which draws my attention. "Did you know they make routines you can do right in your bed? Brilliant!" She frowns. "I didn't realize how close I was to the edge, and I rolled over and plopped right off."

"She started howling with laughter," Pa says, continuing the story. "I couldn't get enough leverage to get her back upright."

"I told him not to bother you," Gram hurries to add, shooting Pa a scowl. "We probably took you away from your fun before you were ready."

"What was I supposed to do, Lottie? Leave you to sleep on the floor all night?" Pa scowls back. "I never would have heard the end of how you'd wrecked your back."

"The real question here," I interrupt, "is why you were doing a workout routine at midnight on a Saturday?"

My grandma shrugs. "Insomnia is a weird thing, Teej, and when the inspiration strikes to move my body, I'm going to take it. Keeps me young. Why not work out in the middle of the night, that's what I always say."

I massage my forehead. I have a faint indent from where the mask pressed into my skin. I wonder if Cinderella does too. I wonder what her face looks like. Does she have laugh lines around her eyes? Does the skin above her nose wrinkle when she's thinking?

Focus, TJ.

"You can always call me," I tell them. "I'm happy to help, but next time, a little more information would be appreciated, Pa. I thought something was majorly wrong. You scared me." My voice cracks, and my grandparents immediately sober.

"I'm so sorry, dear." Gram stands and crosses the room, pulling me into one of her pillowy hugs. She's shorter than me by almost a foot, but her hugs are my favorite, and she always holds on extra-long. I relax into her, relishing the way she still strokes my back with her fingertips, even though I'm twenty-six years old. We have a shared history of getting really bad news—life-changing, soul-altering news—over the phone. Them, when my parents died. Me, with Tess.

"I didn't mean to make you worry," Pa adds, clasping a hand on my shoulder. "You know I'm not good with texting. Takes forever for me to get these clumsy thumbs to do what I want them to."

I smile at him when Gram releases me. "I know, Pa. It's all good. I'm glad you're okay."

They follow me back out into their living space, which they have decorated like a beachside oasis. Their décor would be more fitting in sunny Florida as opposed to the grey-and-brown tundra of Green Bay in November. But it feels like home. Gram has always loved turquoise and orange. This is how our house was decorated growing up. It's charming to me, and I feel instantly calm here ... especially now that I know they're safe and nothing is seriously wrong.

We make quick work of saying goodbyes, all of us stifling yawns. Gram and Pa promise to see me after our home game on Sunday.

I check my phone before pulling away from their house to find a handful of texts from the guys, asking where I went and wanting to know what was going on. I tell them that Cinderella got away because I went to my grandparents' house. They won't make fun of me for that. They all love Gram and Pa almost as much as I do.

I pause when I open a message from Ned, instantly feeling wide awake.

Ned

If you didn't track down your girl tonight, I have an idea of how we can find her. Let's talk.

Chapter 10
Lucy

It's Friday night, and naturally, I'm holed up in my room at Daisy's Inn. The remainder of a container of orange chicken and rice that I got delivered is balanced on the corner of my chair. My phone is propped up on the base of the lamp on the end table nearby, my computer open on my lap.

It's been exactly one week since the River Foxes Gala. One week since I met TJ Wilson.

"How's the word count looking?"

I pan to where Cassie's face stares back at me from my phone. I look at my computer and click out of the internet tabs I have open and over to my document. "Almost ten thousand."

"Look at you go! How do you feel about them?"

"Good." I allow myself a small smile. It does feel good to be writing again. To be flexing and working an atrophied muscle. It's been painful, but the good kind of pain. Something that used to be second nature now feels like I have to work a little harder at it, but I'm willing to put in the time. "I think they're pretty decent."

Cassie waves her hand in front of the screen. "They're fabulous because you're fabulous."

I smirk. She loves talking me up, but she knows my writing well enough to know that it's not always great. We do a lot of slicing and dicing between the two of us when I finish a first draft, tearing the manuscript apart so we can build it back up and put the story together in a stronger, more compelling way. "Thanks for saying that."

She closes her laptop and stands from her desk. I watch through the screen as her office background changes. She lives in New York City, so if it's almost seven o'clock here in Wisconsin, that means it's almost eight o'clock there ... and she's still at work. I know I'm not her only client, but sometimes it's easy to forget how much Cass juggles because we're friends, and she gives me so much of her attention, both for work and my personal life. If she's stressed by her job, she doesn't show it. I've never seen her looking anything but calm, cool, collected, and ready to kick butt.

"Aren't you glad you went last weekend?" she asks as she pushes her arm into the sleeve of her sleek, black winter jacket.

"I am," I say slowly. It's been a busy week for Cassie, and I haven't talked to Bex or Philly about my night with TJ either. I've wanted to call them. To go over every last detail of my time at the gala, analyzing it from all the different angles, but I've stopped short of picking up the phone at least a dozen times. I don't know if it's because I want them to tell me it was nothing or if it's because I want them to tell me they think there was an actual spark.

Cassie zeros in on my hesitation, her gaze narrowing. "There's a story there. I can see it."

"I, well ..." I sigh. "Yeah, there is."

"Give me thirty minutes to get home, put on sweatpants, and then we're going to call Bex and Philly. Don't go anywhere!"

Cassie ends the call.

"Where would I go?" I ask my empty room.

Because I have the very best of friends, they've spent the majority of their Friday night on a video call with me, dissecting everything that happened at the River Foxes Gala.

"You're really not going to tell him who you are, Lu?" Philly's eyes do their typical doe-eyed thing.

"What would be the point?" I say with a sigh. "I told him I needed one night of fun. That's what he delivered." *Along with a lifetime of memories.* Dramatic? Maybe. I don't get out much anymore, so it doesn't take much to have me overwhelmed with emotions and sensations, and a slideshow of that night will play on a loop in my brain for a long time to come. "He isn't looking for more than that, and neither am I."

"But you bid on another date with him." Bex pops a carrot into her mouth and crunches down hard. She screws up her face in disgust.

"Why are you eating vegetables at nine-thirty on a Friday night?" Cassie asks. "You're more of a popcorn and chocolate chip girl."

I nod, because that's exactly what I was thinking.

Bex waves us off. "Richie and I started a new diet together."

I frown, but I try to hide it with a yawn. Richie is Bex's fiancé, and there's something off about him. I can't put my finger on it, but I don't love how my feisty friend acts around the man who is supposed to be her biggest champion. It's like she shrinks herself down to fit the view he has of her.

Then again, who am I to talk or know anything about a relationship? I haven't ever had one.

Which brings me back to the point at hand.

"Your loss." Cassie pops a chocolate-covered blueberry in her mouth and hums with contentment.

Bex presses her lips together and tosses her carrot stick on her bed. "Anyway, Lu, explain yourself."

"It was a mistake." I shrug. "I got caught up in the heat of the moment."

More like the heat of jealousy. I have never felt so territorial. I had a visceral reaction to the thought of that peacock-colored-dress-wearing woman spending time with TJ. It's ridiculous. I acted on instinct. I know that now.

"Hindsight makes me see that I wasn't being rational. I wasn't thinking."

"Or maybe you should listen to your basic instinct and recognize that you like him and you want to spend more time with him," Cassie offers.

I flick my gaze over to my computer screen. A week ago, I would have agreed with her. Coming off the high of being in TJ's presence at the ball, I came home and did what any normal woman would do: I scoured the internet for anything and everything I could find about TJ Wilson.

I meant what I told him last week. I don't know football, and even though I've been living less than thirty minutes from Green Bay for the past several months, I haven't followed the River Foxes or their season.

Turns out they're at the top of the league. And TJ? Well, TJ is their star. He plays on offense, and he handles the ball a lot.

That tracks with how well he handled me.

The thought sends a blush screaming into my cheeks.

I caved and watched the game last weekend. I had no clue what was going on, but I had tunnel vision on number twenty-five when he was on the field. He ran into the endzone thing at one point, and then in celebration, he knelt and pretended to put a shoe on the foot of one of his teammates. It took me point two seconds to realize he was reenacting the glass slipper moment in *Cinderella*—for me.

I admit, it made me a little dizzy to be remembered by him. The fact that he kept his word and followed through was another indication that he's a genuinely good guy. None of that changes that he's not a good guy *for me.*

"Look at you. You're bright red." Philly presses her face closer to the screen. "You're thinking about him, aren't you?"

I roll my eyes and grab for my computer. I flip it around and show them the tabs I have pulled up. They've been up on my laptop all week. Am I torturing myself? Maybe initially. But the longer I looked at the pictures of TJ, and the more articles I read about him, the more certain I became that what happened on Friday night is all that's ever going to happen between us.

"I'm only thinking that my relationship with TJ started and ended last week. I mean, look at this, you guys." I start scrolling through pictures of TJ. There are shots of him in sinfully well-fitted tuxedos, out at different events, always with a different woman on his arm. Always laughing and being the life of the party. There are the photos of him in uniform at games, and then some of him wearing more casual athletic gear for what I assume are practices. In those, his white tank top looks painted on. His biceps don't look real. And no one—I repeat, no one—should have leg muscles like that. They're tree trunks. We've already established his impeccably peach-shaped *derriere*.

I've spent the week studying his face—solely because I need to describe the male main character in the book I'm drafting. That's my story, and I'm sticking to it. I may or may not have also spent an hour gazing at his chiseled upper body, my eyes drinking in the ink he has tattooed across his chest and his upper arms. They're intricate tattoos, and I want to know the meaning and significance of each and every one. I hovered over a link to an article that promised to give me *Everything You Need to Know About TJ Wilson's Tattoos*, but in the end, I didn't click on it. It feels too personal. Unfair that I know his identity and he doesn't know mine. I'd want to hear the stories behind his tattoos from the man himself, which is my crazy-train brain talking, because I'm never going to see TJ again, except on my TV screen.

I ignored the article and stopped ogling pictures of TJ's tattoos. Instead, I started dreaming up the backstory for my fictional lead character.

He's who I need to keep top of mind. The man I've made up in my head who is going to steal the hearts of my readers with his sweet heart and playful sense of humor.

"TJ was the perfect man to give me a dose of inspiration. He got me past my writer's block, and I'm grateful. But we're not meant to be," I tell my friends, turning the computer screen back in my direction. "Honestly, the thought of being in the public eye like him makes me break out in hives."

"Understandable, given your history," Bex allows.

"Exactly." I shut my laptop with a satisfying click. A person can only take so much of a hot football player staring back at her before she goes a little crazy. "He wouldn't want anything to do with me either." Especially not when he realizes I bashed his career right up there with the rest of the entertainment industry. "Anyway! Thanks for coming to my TED talk about TJ Wilson and my whirlwind night of fun with him. Now that you know all the sordid details, we can all move on."

"Can we, though?" Cassie's voice rises in question.

"Cass!" I groan. "Let it be."

She shakes her head, her gaze lit by the glow of her own computer screen, which is where I'd guess she's looking right now. "No, I don't mean to push you at him or whatever. If you say you're done with him, then that's good. But the River Foxes just posted something you might want to take a look at."

A strange sensation fills my lungs, triggering a sixth sense. I know once I re-open my computer and see whatever it is Cassie wants me to see that everything is going to shift in this safe little cocoon I've built for myself.

I navigate to my generic account, the one that's not associated with my real name or my pen name, and tap the River Foxes page, which, of course, I'm now following.

Sure enough, a new post went up ten minutes ago.

I read the graphic out loud, and my stomach pitches. "TJ Wilson is looking for his Cinderella."

"What?" Philly shrieks.

"Hold on. I'm looking it up now too." Bex sits cross-legged on her bed and pulls her computer into her lap, chucking a half-eaten carrot across her room.

I'm scanning the caption, even as my eyes are registering the thousands of likes and hundreds of comments that have been left since the post went up.

TJ Wilson, star running back for your Green Bay River Foxes, needs our help. He met a mysterious woman at the charity gala held at the stadium last Friday, but due to unforeseen circumstances, the pair had to part ways before exchanging contact information. We want to remedy that! TJ will be waiting in the Mezzanine at the conclusion of Sunday afternoon's game to rendezvous with his mystery woman.

The woman in question has dark brown hair, a stunning smile, a quick wit, and enchanting hazel eyes—his words, not ours, folks! We'll provide Prince Charming, but are you his Cinderella? To prove yourself, tell TJ one simple thing: What is he afraid of?

It's been a magical season so far for the River Foxes. Let's help one of our own make some magic happen off the field, as well, shall we? See you Sunday.

#bibbidibobbidiboo #fairygodmother #gusgus #jack #pagingcinderella #tjwilson

"Oh my gosh." I cover my face with my hands, leaning back in the four-poster bed.

"Seems like your boy might be a little hung up on you," Bex says, and when I open my eyes to glare at her, she's smirking.

"He's not my boy. He's not my ... anything!" I run my hands through my hair. "This is a disaster. What is he thinking?"

"He's thinking you have enchanting hazel eyes." Bex grins. "Guy's a football player and a poet."

"Bex! Stop!"

"Sorry." She doesn't look sorry at all. "I'm done."

"So you're not going to go?" Philly moves her face closer to her phone screen, her doe eyes imploring me to reconsider.

"Of course not!" I tell her. "This changes nothing. It only brings more unwanted attention to me."

"Relax," Cassie says in her usual no-nonsense tone. "It's not like anyone is going to hear that very basic description and think, *Oh, Cinderella must be the elusive Lucy Dupree.* There are a lot of women with brown hair and hazel eyes."

I flush as I think about TJ thinking about my eyes and my smile. I can't even count how many times I've replayed the moment when he touched a strand of my hair like he was holding a strand of gold ... right before I told him I'd never been kissed.

I'm an absolute fool for admitting that, especially now that I know TJ is my polar opposite in that department. Where I've never been kissed, he's very obviously been kissing a lot of women. Many of his kisses are documented for the entire world to see on social media and on sports and pop culture sites across the internet.

Which is fine. I don't expect anything from him, and it's another reason we very much would not work, even if I wanted us to.

"You're right." I take a deep breath. "I'm overreacting."

"You're really not going to go over there on Sunday?" Philly asks again. She's a hopeless romantic.

"I'm really not." I give her an apologetic frown. "The last thing I want to do is stir things up. TJ and I made a clean break. It's better for everyone if we put the whole thing to bed."

"To bed? Now we're talking," Bex says gleefully, but I narrow my gaze and she holds up her hands. "My bad, I can't help it!"

"Anyway." I cross my arms. "I'm sure if no one comes forward after the game on Sunday, this'll all fade away as the latest and greatest celebrity news takes center stage."

"You're probably right," Cassie says, stretching her arms over her head. "But," she adds, "I still think you should go see him."

I groan. "It's like talking to a brick wall with you people."

"Hear me out!" she argues. "You could go see him again, if for no other reason than to tell him not to push this any further."

"That would mean telling him who I am."

"I know." Cassie nods. "You'll have to figure out if that's worth it to you. Hearing you talk about your time with TJ last weekend makes me think he'd be someone you could trust with your identity, and maybe he wouldn't hold it against you."

She phrases her last statement like a question.

I sigh. "I don't know. I don't know him that well."

Cassie shrugs. "Just think about it."

All I've been doing for the past week is thinking about TJ Wilson.

"I make no promises. Now"—I level my friends with a look through the camera—"can we talk about someone else, please?"

Chapter 11
TJ

I'm sitting in a tufted chair, talking to the line of women who've shown up in response to Ned's social media post about how I'm hoping to find my Cinderella.

All in good fun, he'd said. *You don't want to always wonder who she is, do you?*

I told myself that's all it was—satisfying my curiosity where my mystery woman was concerned. But what's that proverb about curiosity and the cat?

"Taxidermy is my passion." The woman seated next to me leans in, holding a small, stuffed chipmunk in her hands.

I shift away as discreetly as possible, frantically trying to catch Ned's eye. He's at the back of the room. He and his team and several River Foxes' security guards are vetting people as they come through, making sure that no one too outrageous or dangerous ends up in my line. I don't know how the taxidermy lady snuck by. Ned's had run-ins with her before.

"Uhh ..." I stall for time. "Wow. We have, uh, very different passions."

"Tell me more about what makes you passionate." She angles her body closer to me. "I'd love to hear what gets you hot and bothered."

Well, right now I'm sweating, and I'm most definitely bothered by this conversation, but I hardly think that's what she means.

"What did you say your name was?" I ask.

"Marissa." She holds out her hand, knuckles up, as if waiting for me to kiss her fingers. I stare at them, not knowing how to get out of this situation without coming across as a jerk.

Most of the women who've come through the line have been nice—a little giggly for my taste—but mostly just here for a chance to meet me and say hi. Not one of them has known about my fear of zebras.

I'm trying not to be disappointed that the mystery woman didn't show. It was a long shot ... basically a shot in the dark. My Cinderella straight-up said she wasn't looking for anything beyond one night. Even if she changed her tune and bid on me, I wouldn't be surprised if time and distance made her remember herself and her mission.

I can't help but wonder if she saw my touchdown celebration. Both last week and today, I had Poe help me with a little Cinderella glass slipper reenactment. I owe him two steak dinners for going along with it, but it's worth it. I wanted to do something special for her, even if I never see her again.

The thought has my shoulders slumping slightly.

Marissa is staring at me, and she holds her chipmunk up next to her cheek and starts talking in a baby voice. "Tell me, my fair prince," she squeaks out. "What's your favorite animal? My lady here can get one custom-made as a token of her affection."

I laugh nervously and finally, *mercifully*, catch Ned's eye, bobbing my chin at Marissa in a *help me* way.

"That won't be necessary," I tell her. "Did you want to answer the question—what I'm scared of?"

"Of course." Marissa sits up straighter. "You're terrified of ending up alone. Lucky for you, if you end up with me, you'll not only have my love, admiration, and everlasting presence in your life, but also the presence of all my animal friends."

Ned skids to a stop next to her chair, saving me from having to formulate a response. The thought of being in the presence of

Marissa's animal friends has rendered me momentarily speech-less and, not gonna lie, a little creeped out.

"Okay. That'll do, Marissa. What are you doing here?" Ned asks.

"Shooting my shot, obviously."

Ned shakes his head and motions for her to get up. "We have lots of other women to get through, so since you are not TJ's Cinderella, I'm going to ask you to move it along."

Marissa doesn't put up a fight. I give her credit for that.

"Bye, TJ," she says in her chipmunk voice. "It's a shame we can't be lovers."

Ned makes wide, horrified eyes at me over the top of her head and mouths *I'm sorry* as he ushers her away.

I take the opportunity to check my phone while Ned's tied up. I've got a bunch of texts from friends, congratulating me on a good game, but I hardly notice them. My focus is completely taken up by an email from Sarah Stewart.

Dear TJ,

Great game today! We love watching you play. It's that time of year again, and I know you're busy with football and you haven't felt comfortable joining us in the past, but Roy and I wanted to extend an invite to you to attend Tess's benefit dinner. No pressure, but just know you're always welcome around our family. We'd love to see you. If you have someone special in your life, you're more than welcome to bring her. Maybe that's weird for me to say as Tess's mom, but I truly believe Tess would want you to live your life and find happiness. Come if you can! Hope to see you.

Love,

Sarah

I blink and let out a long, slow breath. My chest constricts at the thought of Tess and her sweet parents. They've been trying to get me to come to her benefit dinner for years, but I can't bring myself to. Guilt gnaws at my gut, and I take a sip of my electrolyte drink.

My fingers tremble as I tap out of the email, marking it as unread so I don't forget to reply later. As if I could forget. I haven't forgotten Tess. She's the reason I don't do relationships, even if her mom says she'd be cool with it. I know Tess would want me to be happy. But I don't know that I'd survive a loss like hers again. It's a sobering reminder as to why, even if I found my Cinderella, I would never let anything happen between us. No matter how much she intrigued me.

I run a hand over my face. What am I even doing here? This is a nonstarter.

Ned returns to my side after disposing of Marissa. "I am so sorry. I promise I won't let any more taxidermy enthusiasts through."

"How can you make that promise, Neddy?" I goad him, defaulting to humor to ease the tightness in my chest. "There could be an army of taxidermy queens just waiting to meet me."

"Don't even speak that into the universe, man." Ned rubs a hand along the back of his neck. "You ready for the next Cinderella candidate?"

"Ready or not." I tip my neck to the side, and it gives a satisfying crack. I need to buck up and fake some good humor. No matter how much my heart aches at the memory of what I once had and what I won't allow myself to have again, I can't let on to the persistent pain. I've got a line that's about twenty women long, expecting to see charming, fun, outgoing TJ Wilson, and that's something I always deliver.

Chapter 12
TJ

An hour later, it's just Ned and me and what remains of the security team.

"Well, that was something." Ned takes down the barricade rope he had in place to corral the line of eager women.

"It was alright," I say, stretching my arms.

"No Cinderella, though."

I shake my head. "Wasn't really expecting her to show." It's good she didn't, I remind myself, when a twinge of regret wiggles through the wall around my heart.

"Yeah, no." Ned nods. "It was a long shot. You were a good sport about it all." He holds up his phone and gives it a tiny shake. "The fans ate it up, so on behalf of the comms team, thank you."

"Anytime, man." I smile, forcing away the conflicting feelings in my chest. "You need anything more from me?"

"Nah, we got this. You head on home. It's been a long day."

"Alright. Later."

I get downstairs and am halfway to the exit when a person in a dark grey hoodie, baseball hat, and aviator sunglasses steps out from an alcove, holds up a slender hand, and flags me down.

"Can I help you?" I slow as I approach. I'm not super worried about stalkers or anything like that. I haven't had issues in the past, unlike Anton, who has dealt with his fair share of crazed fans, but my guard is up as I take in the way this woman shifts her weight, like she's nervous. Marissa better not have come back with more stuffed animals.

"It's me," she whispers, darting a look over her shoulder before facing me again.

"Pardon?" I glance around for hidden chipmunks.

"It's *me*." She accentuates the word. "You're afraid of zebras," she adds after a beat of hesitation.

My pulse thuds in my ears, all thoughts of taxidermy evaporating.

"You're here." My words wobble, like they can't decide if they want to reveal my happiness or my dread. Deep down, I know having another moment with this woman—another conversation—is only going to make me want more ... and more will only cause me pain in the end.

"I know." She looks around. "I can't really believe it myself."

"Why not?"

"Because"—she waves a hand in a circular motion in front of her face—"I don't want to be seen."

"By me, or ...?" I let my question hang in the air, forgetting my own uncertainty in the face of her obvious distress.

"By anyone. By everyone." She glances over her shoulder before grabbing my wrist and pulling me into the small alcove with her. She's got a strong grip for someone with such elegant hands. This isn't a big space, so when we face each other, there's maybe six inches between our bodies.

I angle my head to look down at her.

She tips her head up, her sunglasses mirroring my own reflection back at me. "The only reason I came is to ask you to please stop with the whole Cinderella hunt thing."

"I'm sorry." I wince, not really understanding the big deal but also not wanting her to be uncomfortable.

"No, it's not your fault. It's fine, I just ..." She shakes her head. "I needed to tell you not to draw any more attention to me because I'm sort of in hiding."

My eyes bug out. "Like witness protection?"

"What? No! Nothing that serious." She groans. "I should show you." She peeks out around the wall, down the hallway.

"I think we're alone," I tell her. I have no idea what's going on, but privacy seems paramount in her mind. "The security team's finishing up on the Mezzanine level."

She leans back and faces me, slowly taking her sunglasses off, and I stare down into the hazel eyes of none other than Lucy Dupree, disgraced starlet who left the spotlight after an outburst to end all outbursts on national TV.

"Whoa" is the first word that comes out of my mouth.

She flinches. "Yeah. Hi. It's me. It's okay if you hate me. I wouldn't blame you."

I hold up my hands. "I don't hate you. I don't *know* you."

"Well, I appreciate that, but I'm here to close the book on this thing." She offers me a tight smile. "I wanted you to know who you're dealing with so you'd stop with the hunt. That's what I came here to tell you." She pushes her sunglasses back onto her face and moves to leave.

Voices reach my ear at that very moment, and Lucy freezes. She spins in my direction, and though I can't see her eyes, I can picture the worried, frantic look in her green and gold flecks, and I want to erase it.

I reach behind me and blindly try the handle on the door in the alcove. It swings inward, and I step back, motioning for Lucy to join me. She doesn't hesitate, moving forward into the darkened conference room. I shut the door silently as someone walks past.

Lucy sucks in a breath, and we wait in silence until the footfall disappears. Since it's dark and quiet, all my senses kick in like a snare drum beat. There's a tropical scent emanating from Lucy's skin or her hair, something fruity mixed with a hint of coconut.

As my eyes adjust, I can make out the lines of her jaw. She's got a diamond face shape, with strong, defined cheekbones. I knew she was beautiful even when she was wearing the mask, but seeing her full face now ... even in the dark ... it's obvious she's a knock-out.

Of course she is. Everyone knows Lucy Dupree is beautiful.

"Do you think they're gone?" she whispers.

I clear my throat, pawing for the door. When my hand connects with the handle, I crack it open and peer into the hallway. "Coast is clear." I motion for her to go ahead of me.

She steps out of the room, but I catch her arm. She freezes and shoves her sunglasses up into her hair, giving me a clear view of her eyes. They're cloudy with apprehension. She arches her brows, and I'm rendered momentarily speechless by her freckles. *Your honor, I love them.* They were covered by her mask at the gala, but now my fingers itch to feel them. To connect the dots and trace the path from one to the next, like it's a personal roadmap.

It goes against every rule I've held for myself since Tess died. Rather, the one rule I've held for myself: Don't get attached. Before I know what I'm saying, I blurt out, "Let me buy you dinner."

Her eyes widen. "That's not necessary."

"I'd like to, though. You obviously went out of your way to come down here. It's the least I can do."

I tell myself this is okay. I've gone on plenty of first dates. Even a few second dates. That's all this is—a token of appreciation and a way to satisfy my curiosity about Lucy. And it's not even a date.

"I don't do public outings. Not anymore," she adds ruefully.

"You could come back to my place. I'll make you something."

Her eyes widen even further.

I backpedal. "I mean, only if you're comfortable with that. I've got chicken marinating, and there's plenty. I think I have a salad and maybe some grapes."

Grapes, TJ. Really? That's what you're offering Lucy Dupree?

Her eyebrows hitch up, and I'm certain she's going to politely decline, which I tell myself would likely spare me a world of potential hurt. But then she squares her shoulders and gives a firm nod. "Alright. Let's get out of here."

Chapter 13
Lucy

If anyone asks me how I ended up following TJ Wilson to his house, I'm going to say I blacked out and some overeager cowgirl crawled inside my brain and took the reins.

What am I thinking, going to a man's house when I barely know him? A man whom I absolutely have no intention of knowing.

Beats me. But here we are.

TJ pulls into the driveway of a modest little cottage. It's not even a five-minute drive from the stadium. The cool thing about the River Foxes, which I learned in all the research I conducted this past week, is that the stadium was literally built in the middle of a bunch of neighborhoods. Green Bay is small in comparison to other NFL cities. Most of the people living in these homes have owned them for years. They're diehard fans. They rent out their lawns for people to park in on game days. The house next door to TJ's has siding that's River Foxes-navy blue, with trim painted periwinkle, and an orange front door. The awning over the porch has the River Foxes logo painted onto the metal roofing.

I angle my car into the driveway behind TJ. I'm grateful for the darkness. I imagine a couple hours ago these streets were packed with gamegoers leaving the stadium after an exciting win. Now, the neighborhood feels mostly deserted.

TJ emerges from the garage and waves me toward a back entrance. I hurry forward and wait on his stoop while he unlocks the door. I dart a glance around the backyard, startling when I hear soft clucking sounds.

"Easy, ladies, it's me," TJ coos.

I flip my gaze to him. He's silhouetted in the porch light, his eyes focused on the back part of the yard. He must catch my confused expression, because he gives a slight shrug. "My chickens."

I open my mouth to respond, but no words come.

TJ pushes the door open and enters the house first, flipping on the lights. I take a careful step over the threshold. Maybe I should be nervous, being in a strange house with a man I don't know, on what feels like a desolate street, but I'm ... not.

Huh.

I felt completely taken care of by TJ last weekend, and that feeling hasn't gone away.

"I'm going to use the bathroom real quick." He tosses his keys in a small ceramic dish on the counter. "Make yourself at home."

TJ disappears, and I stand frozen in place, my gaze trained on that dish. It looks hand-painted, and it's so unexpected that I don't know what to do with myself. This entire house is that way.

I will be the first to admit I had formed an opinion of TJ Wilson based on the copious amount of internet stalking—I mean research—I've done on him in the past week. I figured he'd live in some fancy condo or mega mansion with high security and modern finishes and an at-home gym. We've all seen the man's muscles.

Instead, he lives here. In a small Cape Cod, in a neighborhood that's a stone's throw away from the stadium, with painted ceramic pottery and—I look around—a comfy, worn-in couch and a faded brown recliner. The TV hanging on the wall looks big and new, but otherwise, the room may as well have been plucked from the nineties. I look to my left, through the doorway that leads to the kitchen. The décor is similarly vintage with a wallpaper border on the soffits that's evergreen and cranberry. The cabinets are honey oak, and there's a painting on a wooden board behind the stove that reads *Live, Laugh, Love.*

It's so kitschy, it's cute. It's even cuter to think that TJ comes home to this humble little abode every night.

My eyes roam back over the living room, hungry for all the details. There's a canvas propped up on one of the shelves on the far side of the TV. It looks like a really bad painting of TJ himself. There's a basket of controllers for every gaming system imaginable tucked under the TV, and a sad-looking fake Christmas tree wedged on a table in the corner like an afterthought.

I slide my shoes off as TJ emerges from the bathroom and smiles at me. He looks like a giant in this tiny house, his head almost grazing the ceiling.

"I'm going to fire up the grill for the chicken, but can I get you anything to drink before I head back outside?"

"I'll have whatever you're having." I trail him into the kitchen. "You really don't need to do anything extra for me. You don't owe me anything."

He opens a drawer and retrieves a corkscrew before meeting my gaze. "So you've said."

He reaches for a bottle of wine sitting on the back of the counter. He deftly uncorks it and pours two glasses. He slides one over to me before removing the marinating chicken from his fridge, navigating the kitchen with ease.

This was not in my research. This domestic version of TJ … it's throwing me off.

"You're staring at me," TJ says, pausing with the chicken in hand, a small smile curling the corners of his lips. I've dreamt about those lips. About how close they got to mine when he leaned in on Friday night. I can honestly say I haven't thought too much about not being kissed. But that all changed this past week. Everything changed this past week, and TJ Wilson is to blame.

I shake my head once, clearing the vision that's formed of him cradling my cheeks and drawing my mouth to his.

"Sorry." My voice is weird and squeaky, so I clear my throat. "This is great. I just … I didn't know what to expect, and yeah. This is really nice." I wave my hand around the kitchen. "Can I help with anything?"

"There are a couple bags of salad in the crisper. Nothing fancy, but you can toss those together if you want. I'll be back in a second." He passes me on his way back out the door. He smells good. I noticed it at the stadium, too. Whatever he uses for shampoo and body wash is decidedly woodsy.

I make quick work of putting the salad together, finding a mixing bowl in the bottom cabinet and dumping everything inside. I stick it back in the fridge and wander into the living room again, crossing to the shelves to get a closer look at the painted portrait of TJ. He's got a couple other pictures in frames on the far side of the bookcase too. One is of a couple in their mid-twenties. The guy looks so much like TJ. His parents, I'm guessing. There's another photo of TJ with an older couple and one of a beautiful young woman. She's got jet black hair and bright blue eyes. She's not looking at the camera, but she's got her hands raised above her head and she's laughing. The background is blurry, but it looks like she's dancing somewhere. Maybe a bar? Her halter top shirt and cutoff shorts make me shiver, given the current temps outside, and I tug on the strings of my sweatshirt's hood, feeling like I'm intruding on TJ's personal space. I abruptly turn my back on the picture frames when I hear the door rattle.

"It's freezing out there." He sets down the now-empty glass container and rubs his hands together. I squint at him, and he catches my gaze. "What?"

"Didn't you just spend three hours playing football in short sleeves?"

"That's different. The adrenaline makes it so I don't feel the cold." He pauses and stares at me for a beat before his mouth splits into a grin. "You watched me play?"

I shift my weight. "I did."

You would think I told him I named my first born child 'TJ' with the way his eyes light up and his smile turns into a streak of sunshine.

"I'm honored."

"Millions of people watch you play every weekend," I remind him. I'm deflecting, hoping he can't see through me to know how I was glued to the TV, holding my breath every time he took the field. TJ wasn't lying when he said he was right in the middle of things. The man is either a human monster truck or a human motorcycle racer, depending on the situation. Sometimes, he flies headfirst into the other team's players, lowering his shoulder and plowing forward. Sometimes he swerves and cuts, zooming around the opposing team and leaving them in his dust. It's impressive on all counts.

"Yeah, but they're not you." He crosses to the sink and washes his hands before joining me in the living room, acting like his comment is no biggie. Meanwhile, my stomach is a yo-yo, dropping to the floor only to be yanked up again. He takes a seat on the far side of the couch and motions for me to sit. "I can't believe you're Lucy Dupree and you're here in Green Bay in my house."

I snort at his direct delivery. "Honestly, same." I perch on the opposite end of the couch. "I'm guessing you've heard of me ... seen the footage." A flush of shame crawls up my neck.

"Kind of hard to miss that."

I twiddle with a string hanging off the edge of the pocket of my sweatshirt. "Yeah."

I never know what to say next. I was bad enough in social situations before the People's Picks fiasco. I'd get around a group of people, and they'd all be laughing and lobbing questions and comments back and forth, and I'd stand by awkwardly, not knowing what to say or how to contribute. It's always felt like my brain was working in slow motion in comparison to everyone else's. I'm the boring one ... always have been. Add to it that now I've humiliated myself for the entire world to see.

"That's not really what I care about right now, though," TJ adds.

I blink. "It's not?"

"It's not that interesting." He shrugs. "I'd rather talk about something else—anything else."

My entire body exhales. It's weird, really. TJ's a star athlete. We're so very different. I shouldn't be relaxed. Then again, maybe it's that very reason that I am. There are no pretenses with him. I know this'll never amount to anything. He knows it too. So I can be myself.

"Alright then, I have to ask if you've seen the irony about a fox"—I point at the River Foxes hoodie he's wearing—"tending chickens. Tell me about this."

His eyes dance. They're even bluer than I remember. "What do you want to know?"

"Is it weird for you … or for them … to be grilling their brethren right in front of them?"

TJ laughs out loud. It's a rich, intoxicating sound, like a caramel waterfall over ice cream. "Wow, you really went there."

"It's a logical jump," I tell him, sitting up straighter.

He bobs his head. "I guess so, if your brain is all morbid like that."

"Rude." I stick up my nose, but I'm fighting against a smile.

He chuckles. "I got them last spring. I had them growing up, and I loved tending to the chickens. Taught me responsibility and all that stuff. The fresh eggs are nice too."

"Aren't they cold out there?" I peer toward the window where I can make out the frame of the chicken coop.

"Nah. I have the heartiest breeds. Wisconsin winters don't bother them. I built the coop myself and made sure they had some inside spaces to get out of the wind on the really frigid days."

"Chicken keeper," I say with a shake of my head. "That is not in your bio."

He arches his eyebrows. "I feel like I'm at a disadvantage here. You've had an entire week to get to know everything there is to know about me—"

"I do have other ways to spend my time," I interrupt him, even as my flushed cheeks are back, because he's not wrong.

"The point stands. I don't know anything about you, except what you told me at the gala." He tips his head to the side, waiting for me to argue, I'm sure. I don't really have a leg to stand on here. He's right. He knows it. I know it.

"You can ask me what you want to ask," I say.

"Are you going to answer me?"

"Depends on the question."

"Keeping up your track record as my mystery woman, I see."

I ignore the way my heart flutters at the thought of being *his* and shrug noncommittally.

"Alright then. How'd you end up living in Green Bay? Or around here, at least?"

"After everything that happened earlier this year," I begin, "I told my family it would be best for me to fly under the radar and not be front and center when our show started filming this fall. So I ended up here."

Dinner with the Duprees is currently filming its third season. My stepmom is so proud of the family empire she's built. I would hate to be the reason ratings drop. It's for the best that I left the spotlight for a while.

"Yeah, but why *here*?" TJ asks, taking a sip of wine but keeping his eyes on me over the rim of the glass.

He could have asked about my family. About the show. But I'm grateful he's not steering the conversation in that direction. It's nice not to dwell on my monumental screw-up.

"Honestly?" I tell him. "When Anton Bates's love story blew up last winter, I did some research on this part of the country. Cashmere Cove seemed like an idyllic little spot, and I figured it was as good a place as any to settle in for a while, so here I am."

TJ scoffs. "You're kidding me. This is going to go straight to Anton's head. Don't ever tell him he's your inspiration."

"Are you sure you're not just jealous you aren't my only source of inspiration?"

His gaze lasers in on me, eyes darkening to a more navy blue. "I can be all the inspiration you need, Lucy. Name the time and the place, and I'm your man."

I drop my gaze, because *good night*, the gravel in his voice is making my insides do Olympics-worthy flips. He has no idea he's already given me enough content for ten different romance novels. He's not going to know that, either, because that is something I'll be keeping to myself, thank you very much.

When I lift my eyes to meet his again, he's staring at me with intensity that sets the blood in my veins on fire.

"Next question," I murmur.

TJ opens his mouth, but then his phone chirps, and he reaches for it, silencing the alarm. "Gotta check on the chicken. Hold that thought."

I use the precious couple of minutes alone to give myself a pep talk.

No more flirting. No more mentions of inspiration. Come on, Lu. Act natural.

The problem is, I am not natural.

"Such a pretty face, but then she opens her mouth, and yikes."

The words from the comments section on one of the many People's Picks articles resound like a clashing gong in my mind. I swallow a couple of times, trying not to replay all the words that other people have said about me, and reminding myself that TJ knows who I am now. He's not holding it against me. At least, not right now.

I get a sense of peace at the realization, and by the time he comes back inside, I'm not quite so sick to my stomach. I still don't know exactly what to talk about, but at least I don't feel like I'm going to hyperventilate in his living room.

"Chicken'll be a couple more minutes," he says.

I nod. "This is a great house." I sweep my gaze around the living room.

"Thanks." TJ cracks a proud grin. "I love it. My commute is simple, and there's something about disappearing into the normalcy of a neighborhood that I really appreciate."

"How'd you end up in Green Bay?" I ask.

"Haven't you read up on all the details of my life?"

"I'd like to hear it from you."

He smiles at that. "I was drafted by the River Foxes straight out of college. They signed me for a three-year contract. When that was up, my agent negotiated a contract extension, so I'm here for a couple more years at least. I love this town, and I can't imagine playing anywhere else, but that's the nature of the job."

"I didn't realize that's how it worked." I tip my head to the side. It has to be tough to think about being shuffled to a different team after working hard and putting down roots in one place. "I wasn't lying when I told you that I don't know the first thing about football."

"What did you think of the games?"

"They were—" I search for the right word. "Entertaining."

He doesn't need to know that what I mean is *he* was entertaining. Because he was the only player I could focus on.

His smile is broad. "We aim to entertain."

"I could tell," I say, letting myself smile.

"I didn't figure you'd actually tune in."

I shrug. "Didn't have much else to do."

"Come on, a woman like you with no social life? I don't believe it."

"Yeah, well." I shrug again. "I burned every bridge I've ever had, and it's not like I'm flying home to see my family regularly. My friends who haven't disowned me live in different corners of the country; I talk to them often, but not in person. I'm kind of a lone wolf. Or whatever the female version of a lone wolf is. Jane Wolf? Wolfette?"

I snap my mouth shut. *What am I even saying?*

TJ laughs, and I steel myself. I'm used to people making fun of me, but when I meet his gaze, his expression is open and kind, and my shoulders relax.

"I've never thought about the name of a female wolf," he says, like he's actually considering what I was saying as a valid point and not something ridiculous my frazzled brain blabbed on about.

"I think maybe girl wolves are just called wolves." I splay my hands out in a *I have no clue what I'm talking about, so ignore me* gesture.

"Either way. I like Wolfette. You'll be a wolfette in my eyes from now on." He winks, and something snaps and sizzles behind my ribcage. "Let me go get our dinner."

TJ serves me a plate full of delicious-smelling chicken, a heaping portion of Caesar salad, and, as promised, a bunch of juicy green grapes. He stops to pray before we eat, which is unexpected, but sweet, and then he raises his wine glass. "To finding my Cinderella."

I dip my head, but clink my glass with his before adding a toast of my own. "To a River Foxes victory."

"Cheers." TJ holds my gaze, and if I were writing this scene into a story, I'd have included candles on the table so I could comment on the way his blue eyes sparkled in the flickering light of the dancing flames. Instead, we're seated at his tiny kitchen table beneath a chandelier from the nineties that casts the room in an orange glow. I don't mind it one bit. We sip our wine and dig in. I didn't realize how hungry I was until I had food in front of me.

"Can I get you anything else?" TJ asks when I polish off my last bite of chicken.

"No. I'm good. Thank you." I dab my mouth with my napkin. "I ate like a pig. Or a wolf ... ette, I guess."

He chuckles. "I'm glad. Proves that I know my way around my grill."

"I didn't eat much today. I was nervous about meeting you."

He swirls his wine around in his glass. "Why?"

I may as well be honest.

"Because you're you, and I'm me. I didn't know how you'd react."

He keeps his gaze on me. "I'm surprised, but in a good way."

Even without the candlelight, the air in the kitchen takes on a different type of charge. Like the electrons are winning out and all the molecules between us are crackling.

"I still don't want anything more from you," I hurry to clarify, because this feels dangerous, and I don't want to give him the wrong impression.

"I don't recall offering you anything more than dinner." He smirks.

I press my lips together. "Right. Of course."

Why am I assuming TJ Wilson would want anything to do with me romantically? Hello, Lu. Have you *seen* the women he dates? They're usually blonde and gregarious and gorgeous.

"That doesn't mean—"

The back door to TJ's house swings open with a bang.

Chapter 14

TJ

Lucy leaps from her seat and yelps as my grandparents come bustling into my kitchen with all the grace of a pack of baby hippos through a grocery store.

"Pa, Gram. What are you doing here?" I push my chair back and stand up to greet them, but it's like I'm nonexistent. They are focused on Lucy.

"Is this her? This is Cinderella? You've found her!" Gram claps her hands together and shuffles forward. "Oh, are you ever a looker!"

"Gram! Please." I shoot Lucy an apologetic look. Her eyes are wide as she flicks her gaze between my grandparents and me. "Sorry," I tell her with a wince.

She puts a hand over her heart, like she's trying to calm her pulse. "No, it's fine. I thought it was the paparazzi or something." She makes a face. "That's stupid, I guess."

"Not stupid. Understandable." I frown at the way she tears herself down. I wish she wouldn't do that. She said she was in hiding, so it makes sense that she'd be worried about unexpected visitors.

Lucy offers me a whiff of a smile, and I'll take it. I round on my grandparents. "You two ever heard of knocking? Or calling before you barge in?"

My grandpa arches his brows. "Sorry, son. We were anxious to come over and see if you had any luck with your little Cinderella hunt. From the looks of it, you did."

"I'm Loretta, dear." My grandma steps toward Lucy, her wrinkly hand outstretched. "Since my grandson has lost all his manners, I'll introduce myself. This is my husband, Martin." My grandpa doffs an invisible hat in Lucy's direction. "And who might you be?"

Lucy opens her mouth, eyes still the size of saucers, as she shakes my grandma's outstretched palm. "I, um, I'm Lucy Dupree."

"What a lovely name! A lovely name for a lovely lady." Gram clasps her hands together.

"You, uh"—Lucy looks up at me—"you don't know who I am?"

"Well, now I do!" Gram beams. "You're the lucky lady who caught my TJ's eye."

Oh boy. I need to do something about this before the dreamy evening I've been having with Lucy turns into a nightmare, courtesy of the two septuagenarians currently eyeing her like a pair of hyenas when faced with the prospect of fresh meat.

"Gram," I say with a hint of warning in my tone.

She wags a finger at me. "You stop it, TJ. You can't fault me for being excited to see you actually dating."

"I date all the time!" I remind her.

"Not really something I'd be broadcasting in present company," my grandpa says, giving Lucy a significant look.

I press a hand to my forehead. I've lost complete control. I drag my palm down my face and glance at Lucy to gauge how bad the damage is. I don't expect to see her fighting a smile. She twists her lips to the side and raises her eyebrows at me, as if saying, *What are you going to do about this?*

Heck if I know, Lucy. Heck if I know.

"Can we clear some things up real quick—?" I try again with Gram and Pa, but my grandma cuts me off.

"Are you two officially an item, then?" she asks, directing her question at Lucy. "I've raised my TJ well, dear, so you shouldn't have anything to worry about. I know he's dated around, but when he's serious about something, it gets his entire focus."

"Oh." Lucy's lips form a perfect circle until she presses them together and swallows a couple times. "That's ... nice. But we're not ... I mean, he's not my ..." She looks at me helplessly. I get it. There's something about my grandparents, my gram especially, that makes you feel like you don't want to let them down. I credit them for why I turned into a halfway decent human. I spent the majority of my life trying to make them proud.

"Lucy and I are not together like that, Gram," I say gently. "She's not my girlfriend."

Gram fists her hands on her hips and frowns. "Well, why not?"

I shoot Pa a look, begging him to help me, but he just shrugs. "She likes this one."

So do I.

The thought springs unbidden into my mind, and it startles me. I was telling the truth when I said I date a lot. It's all surface-level stuff. I haven't gone deep with anyone since college, and when Tess passed away, I closed off the depths of my heart so that I wouldn't ever feel that way again.

I'm not saying I feel for Lucy like I did for Tess, but I'd be lying if I didn't admit she's the first woman to give me pause and make me feel discombobulated since Tess.

It doesn't matter, though. I've made the decision not to attach my life to anyone else's. I'm happy with the way things are, and besides, Lucy doesn't want to date me, so there's that.

I sigh, trying to find the words to placate my grandparents. "She isn't ... She doesn't ... We're not ..."

"We're friends," Lucy interrupts me, drawing Gram and Pa's attention.

"Friends?" Gram repeats, like she's trying out the word for the first time.

Lucy nods hurriedly. "I was telling TJ that I don't have many people, especially not around here, and he was kind enough to make me dinner and ... we're friends." She glances at me as she says the final word, like she wants to make sure I'm on the same page. I nod.

Friends sounds good to me. I can do friends.

It takes only a second for a broad grin to spread across Gram's face. "Well!" She crosses the room to where Lucy is now standing up behind her chair and draws her into a hug. "Any friend of our TJ's is a friend of mine." She pulls away, keeping hold of Lucy's arms as she studies her. I'm ready to swoop in if I get the sense Lucy is uncomfortable, but she looks at ease, if a little shocked and amused.

My gram is always good for that. People swarm to her because she has a way of making them feel comfortable in their own skin. It's a gift. She often jokes that she must have a sign stamped on her forehead that reads, *Tell me all your problems.* I remind her that that particular sign is stamped on her heart, and people know they can count on her. They know she'll be there for them.

I get the sense Lucy doesn't have a ton of people who are there for her, so if my grandma wants to dote on her, I'm cool with that. I'll gladly share all the grandmotherly love, as long as Gram doesn't push her luck and try to force Lucy and me together. Now that she knows the truth about where our relationship stands, I'm hoping she'll respect it. I'm about sixty percent sure she will, but you never know with Gram. When she gets an idea in her head about what's best for people she loves, she has a one-track mind.

"What are you doing on Thursday, Lucy?" Gram asks.

Lucy glances up like she's flipping through a mental calendar. "I don't think anything. Why?"

"You simply must come to our chili cook-off and square dance. I insist."

"Oh, I wouldn't want to intrude."

"Nonsense." My grandma flicks her wrist dismissively. "As my friend, I'd like you there. I've got a whole bunch of people who'd love to meet you."

I feel my hackles rise, and I'm about to step in, but Lucy catches my eye and gives me a subtle shake of her head.

"That's so nice of you," she says to my grandma. "Do, uh, you know who I am?"

My grandma blinks. "Yes," she says slowly. "You told me who you are." She shoots a look at my grandpa, silently asking him, *Do these two think we're senile?*

"No, right. Of course. I just mean, I'm kind of famous, or, rather, notorious." Lucy winces. "I keep a low profile, so I don't like a lot of people knowing where I'm living or anything like that."

"Our friends and neighbors are our age," Gram says. "They don't care too much about famous people and their business."

Lucy's cheeks turn pink at this, and I want to put an arm around her shoulder and tell her that it's okay ... that *she's* okay.

"I don't think anyone would give you a hard time at all," Gram concludes.

Lucy looks up at me. "Are you going to be there?"

"We have a walk-through that day before we leave for our away game on Friday, but I hope to stop by. I'll be a little late." My heart flips to think that my presence would be a comfort to her. Something about Lucy Dupree has my protective nature kicking in. It's a weird feeling to have a desire to be there for someone else after living by myself for so long. I don't hate it. It's unexpected—like a dormant part of my chest is being tickled by a feather and starting to twitch back to life.

"I—" Lucy presses her lips together. "I'm honored to be invited. Truly. But I'm not sure it's for the best. Is it alright if I think about it? I can let you know."

"No need to even do that. Just show up if you can! TJ can text you directions. Does he have your number?" Gram flips her gaze to me.

"I'll get it, and I'll send you the address." I nod at Lucy and say a silent prayer of thanks that Gram somehow managed to give me an excuse to get Lucy's number and not make it weird. I could have asked for it, I guess. With any other woman, I wouldn't have thought twice about doing that, but something about Lucy is different.

Gram claps her hands together once and then pulls Lucy into a hug. "I really hope you can make it."

When Lucy leans away, she's smiling. "You're being too kind, Loretta. If I do make it out, can I bring anything?"

"If you've got a chili recipe you'd like to enter, by all means!"

Lucy's smile turns wistful. "I do." Her voice catches and she drops her gaze.

Instinctually I take a step forward, before reining in my desire to comfort a woman I hardly know.

My grandma catches Lucy's change in demeanor as well and somehow knows exactly what to do. She pats her hand. "Bring it along if you want. No pressure to, or to come at all. Just know it'll be a night of fun and flavor. Dress comfy to dance. They're bringing in an instructor for us." Gram shimmies her shoulders.

"Easy, dear. Don't throw out your back," Pa deadpans.

Gram clicks her tongue. "You watch that mouth, Martin, or there'll be no kisses for you."

Lucy's lips tick up, and I'm grateful to my grandparents for diffusing the moment. I'm not sure what it was about, but I'm glad Lucy is smiling now.

"Alright, then." Pa claps me on the shoulder. "We'll leave you two be. Come on, Loretta."

My grandma says goodbye to Lucy before she scuttles back across the room toward me, pulling me down into a hug. "Your pa is right. I *do* like her," she whispers into my ear. "I can tell you do too."

Without giving me a chance to confirm or deny it, she sweeps out the door.

Chapter 15
Lucy

*Y*ou *will not cry in the canned vegetable aisle. You will not.*

I stare down at the text message from my stepmom, Ruby.

Attaching the picture of the recipe card here for you, Lu. Is everything going okay? Need anything? Offer still stands if you want us to cancel or postpone this season so you can come home. Here for you. Kisses!

Not only is my stepmom's kindness causing tears to sting behind my eyes, but when I tap the image she sent and see my dad's handwriting and the splatters of chili on the recipe card, a lump forms thick and fast in the back of my throat. My vision blurs with unshed tears.

I swipe at my eyes and take a shuddering breath. I'm in the heart of the local grocery store in downtown Cashmere Cove. "Jingle Bells" is playing through the overhead speakers. Shoppers are milling about, so I've got my winter coat zipped all the way up and my hood pulled over my head. I'm trying to keep most of my face tucked down into my collar as I shop around, but now that I'm feeling emotional, my body temperature is soaring, and I'm going to overheat if I don't get some air circulation going.

I unzip my collar to let my neck breathe, blowing out a long exhale.

I'm fine. Everything's fine.

The chili cook-off at TJ Wilson's grandparents' senior living community is tonight. I wasn't sure I was going to go. I'm still not sure what made me ask Ruby to send Dad's recipe. I made a deal with myself that if she sent it in time for me to make a batch, I'd go. If she didn't get back to me, then it wasn't meant to be.

I should have known Ruby would be on the ball. The woman is freakishly organized, and she's worried about me, so when I reach out, she's always quick to respond.

Armed with Dad's recipe, I set off for the grocery store before I lost my nerve, but now, here I am, and I don't know if I can do this.

I stare at the ingredients in my cart. Celery, green pepper, onion. I've got my tomato soup and tomato juice, and I'm standing in front of a wall of canned beans, and it's ridiculous that this is going to be my undoing.

I find the kidney beans, and my stomach turns. I remember sitting on the counter in our house in California, Dad whipping up a batch of his mom's chili. I was probably about eight years old. It was a month or two before he met Ruby, so it was just him and me at home. I was complaining about the kidney beans he added to the mixture. I told him they tasted like dirt and that the texture made me want to throw up.

"*Why can't you leave them out?*" I'd whined aloud.

"Lu," he'd said, chuckling. "If I leave out the beans, it'll change the flavor of the entire soup. You don't have to like them—you can be disgusted by them—but that doesn't mean they don't have a purpose."

I'd complained some more, and my sweet dad had shaken his head, leaned over, and pressed a kiss to my temple. "You can always pick them out of your bowl if you must."

I miss him so much it hurts sometimes. Like right now. I'd eat kidney beans for the rest of my life if it meant I could spend one more afternoon with Dad in the kitchen.

About a month after that memory, he met Ruby. They fell hard and fast and were married six months later, and we became a big, blended family, with Ruby and Kait and Hilary, her two daughters from her first marriage. Less than a year after that, right before my tenth birthday, Dad left to get groceries and never came back.

"Are you okay?" a kind female voice stirs me from my memories.

I realize tears are streaming down my face when I blink and sense the wetness on my cheeks. I instinctively duck my head, averting my gaze. "I'm fine. I'm blubbering. Sorry. Don't mind me."

"No need to apologize. Sometimes you need a good cry."

I chance a look at the woman; her kind voice has some authority to it. I blink. It's Rose Kasper. Anton Bates's girlfriend, and an all-around queen, if even half of what the news articles about her say is true. She's around my age, maybe a couple years older, with wavy brown hair and a warm smile. Her eyes are searching, and they flare ever so slightly when she registers who I am.

"Lucy Dupree?" she says, her voice low.

I flinch. "Guilty."

"What are you doing here?" She sounds curious, but not out for blood. Something in her soothing, even tone has my defenses falling. I find myself wailing out the entire story for her in the bean aisle.

"I'm trying to buy ingredients to make chili so I don't let down TJ Wilson's grandparents at their cook-off tonight," I say with a sob. "I have no idea how to do this. Any of this. And I hate kidney beans."

"TJ?" she says, shock coloring her tone as she zones in on that little detail.

I nod, blinking away tears and staring at the put-together woman who is bearing witness to my breakdown.

"You're her, aren't you?" Rose crosses her arms. She smiles at me, and her eyes twinkle with delight. "You're the one he was with at the gala."

I open my mouth to deny it, but then I close it again. There's no use trying to backtrack now. I nod, my eyes welling with traitorous tears. "Please don't make a big deal out of this," I whisper.

She tips her head kindly. "Oh, honey. I'm on your side here."

My shoulders slump with relief. "Thank you."

She smiles. "Of course. I'm the one who told TJ to go after you at the end of the gala. We saw you leaving, and he obviously felt like there was some unfinished business between you two. Sometimes a man needs a nudge, so I shoved him in your direction."

"Wait." I frown. "TJ came after me?"

"He tried. Then he got a message from his grandpa saying his grandma was in trouble or something."

My heart thuds painfully as my adrenaline spikes. "She's okay, though, right? I saw her on Sunday at TJ's house."

Rose's eyebrows fly up. "You were at TJ's house? Interesting," she hums. "Very interesting." Before I can say anything, she goes on. "Anyway, yes, he was going to follow you out of the stadium. He wanted to talk to you some more, I think."

I shake my head, trying to sift through this new information. I figured the social media call to find his Cinderella was a publicity ploy, nothing more. I didn't realize he actually tried to prolong our evening. That maybe he actually wanted more time with me.

Not the real me.

The thought stalls my racing heart and brings me back to reality. TJ wanted more time with the bold, carefree woman behind the mask ... but she's not really who I am.

"Well, he got his time. I came to the Cinderella call, and he brought me to his house to have dinner. I told him I couldn't date him. We're not compatible that way," I explain.

Rose nods slowly. "But you met his grandparents ... and you're going to their"—her eyes dart to my cart and then to the shelves of canned vegetables—"chili cook-off party?"

I twist my lips to the side. "TJ was so nice, and so were his grandparents, and we all decided to be friends, and it sort of snowballed from there. I told them I'd think about going, and now here I am, buying ingredients to make my dad's chili, so I guess I'm really doing this, even though it's a horrible idea."

Why do I keep spilling my guts to Rose?

"I'm sorry. I'm blabbing. That happens when I get worked up." I shove some hair behind my ear.

Rose smiles. "You're good. For the record, I don't think going to TJ's grandparents' chili cook-off is a bad idea at all. They're great, and, for the record, TJ's one of the good ones."

I consider her, feeling a swell of relief to have my assessment of TJ as a decent human confirmed by someone who obviously knows him.

"My sisters and I all live in Cashmere Cove, if you want to get together," Rose continues.

My pulse kicks up again. "That's so kind." In another life, I'd jump at the chance to hang out with someone as cool as Rose. "I'm trying to keep my identity under wraps, though ..." I trail off with a shrug.

"Don't worry. Cashmere Cove protects its own. If you ever need anything, I have a background in personal security."

The story of how this woman took a bullet for Anton, single-handedly saving his life, flies through my mind, and I stare at her in awe.

"The offer to be a friend or a bodyguard is always on the table. Or if you're a reader, come see me at Mood Reader. That's my full-time gig now."

"The cute bookstore downtown?" I've wanted to stop in there a million times, but I've been afraid of drawing too much attention.

She nods. "The one and only. I'm a part owner."

"Dream job," I say on an exhale.

Her eyes light up. "You're a reader."

And a writer.

I swallow the words and nod. "I love to read. Romance, especially."

"Come see me sometime, then. I've got the new Philomena Grace book in, if you're a fan."

I smile at that. I can't help it when I think about Philly's success. Little does Rose know I have a signed and personalized copy from Philly herself in my nightstand at Daisy's Inn. She started as an indie author and got so successful that Cassie picked her up. Her newest book is her first traditionally published title, and it hit the big bestseller list. The success couldn't have come to a more deserving person.

"I'll swing by. I love Philomena Grace."

"I've been trying to get her to come for a book talk and signing, but so far I haven't heard back. Keep your fingers crossed for me."

"Will do." I make a mental note to talk to Philly and Cassie about scheduling a trip to Mood Reader. Would it be a selfish way for me to get some in-person time with my friends? Yes, yes, it would. I'm not above it. I'd love to help Rose out too.

A pinch of FOMO pricks at the base of my spine. If I wasn't writing behind my Ava Reese pen name, I could offer to come for an author chat myself. I reel in that thought. If I wasn't writing behind my Ava Reese pen name, my author career would have been cancelled right along with the rest of my life. I've never worried about missing out and not getting to claim my stories publicly before. It's been enough to write them for myself and know I'm bringing joy to my readers ... even if I'm gauging their reactions from a distance. It's for the best this way.

"I should run. I've got to get back to Mood Reader with snacks in time for book club. If you're ever interested in coming, all the details are on our website. We'll post next month's title there, too." Rose smiles and my heart tugs. In another life, I'd be there with bells on.

"Thanks for the invite."

"Door's always open," she says with an easy shrug, like she knows I'm not going to take her up on her offer, but she really hopes she's wrong. I get the sense she's not wrong about many things. "I hope you have a good time with TJ's grandparents." She leans in. "If you happen to give TJ a shot ... outside the friend zone"—she winks—"the other wives and girlfriends on the River Foxes are great. We'd welcome you with open arms."

I'm shaking my head before she's finished. "He needs a different type of woman than me."

"I'd say that's for him to decide." She flashes me an easy smile. "For you to decide for yourself, too. Not my place to butt in." She holds up her hands in surrender. "Nice to meet you, Lucy."

"You too," I say as she disappears around the corner.

I stare after her. What is going on with my life these days? I've gone from a hermit troll, sequestered away in my room at Daisy's Inn, to attending a ball, going to TJ's house, planning to go to a chili cook-off and square dance, and now I've got Rose Kasper inviting me to join the WAGs. Yeah, I looked it up. That's what they call the wives and girlfriends of professional athletes.

I get out my phone and text Philly and Cassie, letting them know that the owner of Mood Reader in Cashmere Cove is super cool and they should maybe, hopefully, consider a book event in town. After I send the message, I pocket my phone again and pause to assess my circumstances.

I'm dying to stack another layer of bricks onto the walls I've built around my life. To pull everything back in on myself and stay tucked safely away, where nothing can touch me. But as I stare at the line of kidney beans in front of me, I think about what my dad would say.

The mantra I haven't thought of in years pops into my head, and my vision blurs again.

"*You glow, Lu. Don't hide your light.*"

Dad used to recite it every morning before school. I was a shy kid, and he never pushed me to be anyone I wasn't. He always reminded me that I was good enough, just as I was, and that I had something to offer.

He wouldn't want me to hide away.

But he's not here. And putting myself out there is easier said than done.

Chapter 16
TJ

I step out of the locker room showers and saunter over to my cubby. What started out as me forgetting my towel one time has turned into a tradition. This far into the season—and since I've been doing this for two years now—I'm not about to change things. In the words of Michael Scott, football players may not be superstitious, but we are a little stitious.

"Dude, put a towel on," Poe grumbles, holding up a hand to cover his face.

I smirk. That's exactly how Poe always responds. It makes me feel like we're firing on all cylinders ahead of our game in Buffalo this weekend. We haven't been as dominant this season as we were during our Super Bowl run last season, but we're playing scrappy, and I like our chances. We're gelling like usual in the locker room, and if I have to walk around naked to keep things status quo, it's a sacrifice I'm willing to make.

"Everything is better when I let myself air dry," I quip.

"Better for *who*?" Poe mutters, and I chuckle.

I start putting myself back together in my post-practice gear. River Foxes sweatshirt. Gray sweatpants. I pull on my socks, humming a song I can't get out of my head. I realize it's "Bibbi-di-Bobbidi-Boo" when a throat clears behind me. I look over my shoulder to see Anton holding up his cell phone.

"Why is Rose telling me to ask you about Lucy Dupree?" he asks, his eyebrows arched.

I lose my balance and tip forward into the locker.

"Graceful," Del deadpans from next to Anton when I right myself and turn toward them.

"Care to explain?" Anton presses.

"How did she—" I press my lips together. "Curse Rose and her superspy abilities."

Anton snorts. "Don't curse my woman, Teej. But she does have some pretty amazing abilities." He wiggles his eyebrows.

"Nope. Don't want to hear anything about that." Poe plugs his ears, and Anton grins.

"What gives?" Anton waves his phone in front of me.

I sigh, plopping down into my locker as the three of them circle up. I should have known I wouldn't be able to keep my interactions with Lucy Dupree a secret from them for long. Honestly, it's impressive I made it from Sunday to Thursday without someone sniffing us out.

Not that there's anything to sniff. But these guys are the brothers I never had. We know things about each other. We share. Healthy male relationships and all that. Besides, I think it makes us better on the field since we're so invested in each other's well-being.

"Lucy Dupree is Cinderella," I tell them.

Three jaws drop in unison.

Anton recovers first. "Lucy Dupree? *The* Lucy Dupree?"

"The one and only."

Del lets out a low whistle. "How'd you track her down?"

"I didn't. She found me." I spend the next few minutes telling them about Sunday. "So we're friends now, I guess."

Poe frowns. "Is she as stuck-up and entitled as she was on that stage? What was that for again?"

"The People's Picks," Del supplies. "She really snapped."

Anton scrolls through his phone. "I've got the video right here." He spins it around, and the replay is rolling before I can say I'd rather not watch it.

I won't admit to the guys I've watched it every night this week. I told Lucy we didn't have to talk about it, but that doesn't mean I'm not curious. The woman I've gotten to know seems so different from the woman standing on the stage in the video, off to the side of her stepmom and stepsisters as they're accepting the award for Best Social Media Family.

I hold my breath because I know what comes next.

Another social media sibling duo charges the stage and grabs the trophy from Kait, one of the Dupree sisters. They get into a tug-of-war. They're screaming at each other. The crowd is losing its mind. Lucy's stepmom bursts into tears, and then I zone in on Lucy. Her hands go to fists at her sides, and she strides toward the microphone. She rips it off its stand and says, "Enough. Stop it, all of you! Right now! Would you look at yourselves? You are being childish and stupid. Don't any of you get it? None of this matters. None of *you* matter. This is vapid and irrelevant, and you all should just get over yourselves and shut up. Nobody cares who won this award. Or nobody *should* care. Social media is not real life. It's entertainment. We're all being paid way too much money to do absolutely nothing but be a distraction for the masses who are too stupid to do anything better with their time. Please, just stop all of this."

The entire room goes silent. No one moves. The fight on the stage stalls out as everyone turns to stare at Lucy, their expressions incredulous.

Lucy's bare shoulders heave with exertion. Her evening gown clings to her petite figure, navy blue sequined fabric glittering in the stage light. The camera zooms in on her, and she blinks a couple of times, like she's coming back to herself. Her cheeks blush a fierce red, and she sucks in a breath before squeaking out an apology into the microphone.

She drops the mic to the ground, and the feedback echoes with an unpleasant thump and screech as she sprints off the stage as fast as her high heels will allow her.

Anton presses pause on the video, and the guys stare at me.

"Well," Del says slowly. "Is she as screechy in real life?"

I frown. "She's not screechy at all. She's …" I search for the right word. "Unlike anyone I've known before. I mean, I don't know her that well. We only met at the gala and then had that one dinner together, but yeah. She's something … different."

Lucy's bashful, with an undercurrent of self-assurance. Like she wants to believe in herself, but checks the impulse. She's got a quick wit and she's a good listener. I noticed it in the rafters and again at the dinner table. I'm itching to ask her about the People's Picks, if she meant what she said, and if she regrets any or all of it. But I get the sense Lucy is as skittish as one of the chickens in my backyard. She doesn't know me well enough to trust me. I'm afraid that if I press her now, she'll run away. I'm biding my time, trying not to think about her, and I'm failing miserably.

I blink out of my reverie to see a smile spread across Anton's face.

I point at him. "I don't like that look. Whatever you're thinking, don't say it. She and I are *friends*. Friends with a capital F."

Anton holds up his hands. "It's nice to have friends. We're your friends, right, fellas?"

"'Course we are," Del says, and Poe nods.

"But we don't have you tongue-tied and involuntarily humming 'Bibbidi-Bobbidi-Boo' like Lucy Dupree does," he says.

"I'm not tongue-tied," I defend. "I'm doing nothing involuntarily. I'm my own man. I have a date when we get back from Buffalo."

"With Lucy?" Del's eyes brighten.

"No, with a woman I met a couple months back at that mixer in downtown Milwaukee."

They don't need to know that I cold-texted someone because I had gone down a Lucy Dupree rabbit hole, and I was in a dangerous spot of starting to care, starting to become too invested in this enigma of a woman. I needed to do something about it. I scrolled through my contacts, and "Amber, hot girl from the MKE mixer" seemed to be what the doctor ordered.

Anton frowns. "Another jersey chaser?"

I throw up my hands. "How many times do I have to tell you? I don't mind when a woman appreciates my profession."

"So you've said." Anton shakes his head with dismay, but then shrugs. "That's good, then. All good. You probably don't care that Rose told me she ran into Lucy shopping for chili ingredients. Sounds like she'll be at your grandparents' place tonight."

The hair on the back of my neck stands at attention. As much as I'm trying not to dwell on Lucy, I add every little thing I learn about her to my mental puzzle. I have the pieces of her I experienced at the gala. Fearless. Fun. Flirty. The not-so-insignificant piece of information that she's never been kissed, which, I can't lie, I've thought about on more than one occasion. Then I've added in what she told me when she came to the Cinderella call, about how none of that other stuff was the real her. How she's solitary and introverted. I mull over what this new bit of information might mean. Either Lucy has a soft spot for chili and square dancing, or she doesn't want to let my grandparents down. The thought of that makes my chest feel tight. Lucy cares.

Could she potentially be going because she wants to see me?

I shake my head ever so slightly. Doubtful. When I texted her the address earlier in the week, her only response was a thumbs-up emoji. She may as well have shut the door in my face. No quicker way to end a conversation than to drop one of those in the chat.

I started to think I came on too strong. I was my usual outgoing, flirty self. She seemed into that at the gala, but I'm a lot, and I'm not for everyone. So that thumbs-up felt like she was saying *thanks* and *leave me alone* at the same time.

So I did.

But now ...

"What are you waiting for?" Anton motions me toward the door. "Get over there."

I stick up my nose and start shoving my stuff into my bag. "I was going there already to see my grandparents, thank you very much."

"Uh-huh, and you had exactly zero percent urgency." Del strokes his beard. "Now, you can't wait to get out of here."

I force myself to move more slowly.

"Don't forget about us when you become obsessed with Lucy Dupree," Poe goads.

I roll my eyes. "Not going to happen."

Not because I don't think I could. Because I do. That's exactly why I won't. I'm not going to get myself entangled with a woman who becomes my true north, only to have the map of my life flipped on its head.

That's happened already, and I'll guard my heart from it happening again until the day I die.

Chapter 17
Lucy

I've been at Loretta and Martin's for less than an hour, and I feel like I know these people already. In a good way.

When I showed up in the gathering room in the main building of their senior living community, Loretta was so excited to see me that she wrapped me and my slow cooker in another one of her pillowy hugs.

"You came!" she cheered. "I'm so glad you did. Let me introduce you to everyone."

I didn't even have time to get panicky about who "everyone" was and what they might think of me or if they'd seen the footage of me calling them "stupid" ... at least by proxy. Three other ladies swarmed us, all similar in age to Loretta, and started talking all at once. No one seemed to recognize me, and if they did, they didn't call attention to my very public faux pax.

"We need some young blood around here," a woman named Carol said. "I try to stay up with the times. Tell me, Dolly, what exactly is *the rizz*?"

"Isn't that the fancy hotel in New York?" a woman named Titi spoke up.

"That's The *Ritz*," Carol corrected with a huff.

"The Ritz is my favorite kind of cracker," Susie added. "I get myself a plateful and add some pepperoni and some artisan cheese and *voilà*, girl dinner!"

It was all I had in me not to cover my mouth to bury a laugh. "Rizz is like charisma," I told them. "You ladies have it in spades."

Loretta's pale blue eyes twinkled, and they reminded me so much of TJ's that I had to stop myself from blurting out something stupid like, *You know who else has rizz in spades? Loretta's grandson, who I can't stop thinking about and who, it turns out, I'm basing an entire book character off, without his knowledge or consent.*

These thoughts tumbled around in my brain, but Loretta hooked her arm through mine. "You're going to fit right in here, I can tell. Come on, let's make the rounds."

The chaos has only ratcheted up from there. Good chaos. I've received several compliments on Dad's chili recipe, and while I knew it would be hard, it's actually been really nice to remember him—to talk about him when people ask where my recipe originates. I love Ruby and Kait and Hilary—I totally lucked out where our blended family is concerned—but my stepmom and stepsisters live big and loud lives, and it sometimes feels like they're going at a hundred miles per hour with the show and the social media and the brand deals, and Dad's memory seems to get buried. This has been a good reminder that it's okay to talk about him. That it won't kill me, and that it actually might make me feel better.

I pull out my phone and snap a picture of Loretta, who has her head tipped together with Titi, Susan, and Carol as the square dance instructor begins her spiel. I send a message to Cassie, Philly, and Bex.

Lucy

Can this be us someday, pretty please?

Their responses are immediate.

Philly

YES PLEASE!

Cassie

Dibs on being the one with the good cowboy boots.

I smile at the older ladies. Carol is the one rocking the bright red boots, and it seems very appropriate that Cassie would notice. Her attention to detail and eye for the latest trends is impeccable. It's what makes her a killer literary agent.

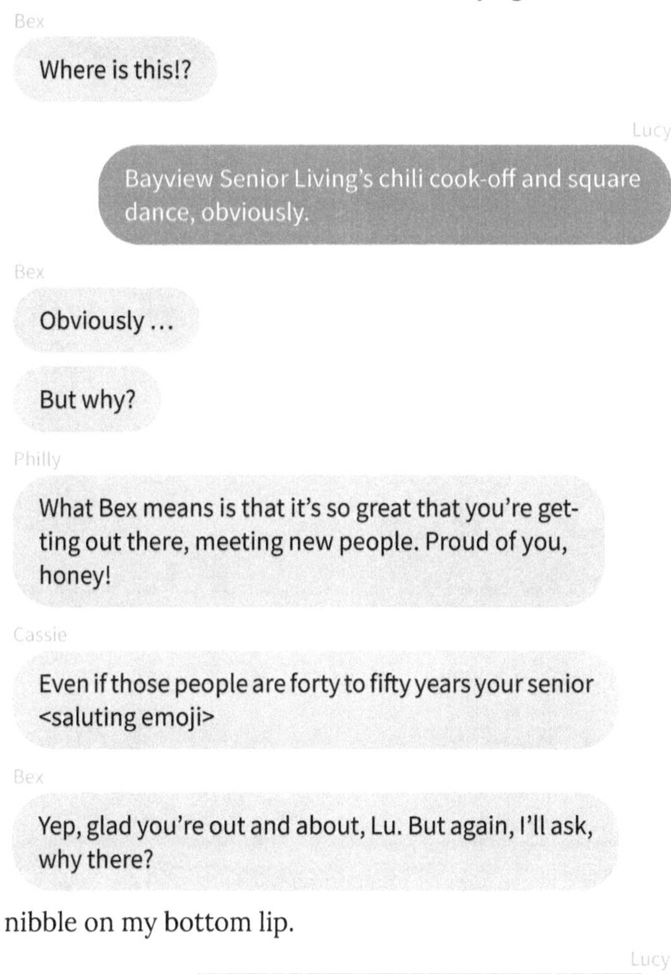

I nibble on my bottom lip.

Nobody responds for a solid minute. I start to wonder if they've jumped to a group chat offshoot, without me in it, so they can talk about me behind my back.

Lucy

Hello? Anyone home? Guys, it's no big deal.

Cassie

First of all, you're not a disgrace.

I can practically hear Cassie's firm tone, and it makes me smile.

Cassie

Second of all, are you alone there?

Bex

Cut to the chase, Cass. Is TJ there too?

Lucy

No.

Philly

Boooo! We want TJ! Give us more TJ.

I laugh despite myself.

Lucy

He had practice tonight, but he said he might come later.

Cassie

Look at you, knowing the comings and goings of one very attractive, very available professional football player <wide eye emoji>

A flush creeps up my neck.

Lucy

It's not like that. He's story inspo. Nothing more. Nothing less.

I tap out of the message string with my friends and over to my text conversation with TJ. If you can even call it a conversation. I read it back, as I've done no fewer than twenty times this week.

TJ

> Hi Lucy, this is TJ. Thanks for coming tonight.

Lucy

> Hey, thanks for having me.

TJ

> My grandparents' place is at Bayview Senior Living. 333 Bayview Lane, Green Bay.

Lucy

> <thumbs-up emoji>

I frown at my screen. That's it. That's the end of it. He didn't respond. Which is something I should absolutely not be over-thinking. But I absolutely, positively *am* overthinking.

Did he text me to tell me his grandparents' address and then, when said task was completed, he figured he'd done his duty and was done with me? Did he get distracted by another message from someone else who was way more entertaining and wittier and funnier?

It was his turn to respond, right? And he didn't.

End of text conversation. End of story.

"Hey, there." The sound of TJ's low voice behind me has me jumping in my seat. I fumble with my phone, and it drops to the ground.

I quickly bend over and snatch it up, checking the screen for a crack.

"Sorry to startle you," TJ says with an easy smile, but there's a glimmer of hesitation in his gaze, an uncertainty that hasn't been there when we've interacted before.

"You're fine. I'm always clumsy. Not your fault." I set my phone face down on the table. "You're here," I say, and heat licks at my cheeks. *Duh.*

TJ looks effortlessly handsome, and it's unfair, really. He's in gray sweatpants and a sweatshirt, but it's all working for him. He must've gotten a haircut since Sunday, because there's a design shaved into the close-cut hair behind his ear.

"It's a lightning bolt."

I blink and meet his eye. He rubs the patch of hair.

"It's new." I'm knocking it out of the park over here with my observational and conversational skills. No one would ever guess that words are literally my job.

"Thanks for noticing."

I blink back at him, because I'm incapable of coming up with anything to say in response.

"It's a tradition this time of year for me and the other backfield guys," he goes on. "We all get designs like this in December."

"Oh. That's cool." I don't know what a backfield guy is, but I'll figure that out later.

He arches his brows and raises his hand, rubbing it over the design again. His lips droop on either end, and he shifts his gaze away from me. "Do you hate it or what?"

I shake my head quickly. "No. Not at all. I think it's sexy."

Truthfully, I'd like to run my fingers over his hair, getting a feel for the lightning bolt carving myself.

For research purposes.

I make a mental note to have my MMC, Theo, have some sort of playoff tradition like this with his teammates. Maybe he'll buzz his head altogether. It could be an intimate moment between him and the FMC, Monica. She could tentatively ask if she could run her hands through his hair, or lack thereof, and then she could feel self-conscious about it and turn to walk away, but he'd grab her wrist and slowly bring it up to the top of his head, bending slightly so she could have better access to run her hand over his buzzcut.

I swallow, coming back to myself, even as my fingers itch to touch TJ's hair … I mean, to go write the scene.

"Sexy, huh? Good to know." He's smiling broadly.

Dismay and pleasure slosh around in my gut as I replay what I admitted to him. What is wrong with me? Sure, *sexy* was the first word that came to my mind, but why couldn't I find my filter when the moment called for it? Have I learned nothing after the People's Picks?

"Objectively sexy. I mean, friend to friend, I thought it was good for you to know it looks good. Objectively speaking."

I'm making this worse.

"Are we friends?" TJ asks, and he's back with the uncertainty in his gaze.

"Oh." I tug in a breath. "Uh, I thought so. I don't want to assume, but didn't we decide that at your house?"

He nods. "You said we were friends, but I didn't know if you meant it. You thumbs-upped me."

I furrow my brow. "Pardon?"

He fishes his phone out of the pocket of his sweatshirt.

Note to self: Write Theo wearing a sweatshirt in a future scene. Have him loan it to Monica. I'd love to get a feel for the fleece lining of TJ's sweatshirt right about now.

"See?" TJ holds up the phone, screen facing me. "You thumbs-upped, and that was it."

"I'm sorry? Was I not supposed to?"

"I thought you didn't want anything to do with me."

"That's what a thumbs-up means?" I pitch my brows. "I was letting you know I got your message. When you didn't respond, I figured *you* didn't want anything else to do with *me*."

"I'd like everything to do with you." My pulse spikes. He clears his throat. "As a friend," he amends.

I refrain from fanning my face, but barely. The man standing in front of me is a known flirt. He doesn't really mean anything by those words. But it *is* nice to know he wants to be my friend.

"I didn't want to press if I was making you uncomfortable," TJ goes on. "I'd already forced you to come to dinner at my place. Then my gram all but forced you here. We were being flirty and fun together. Or at least, I thought we were." He waves his hands around like he doesn't know what to do with them, and it's oddly endearing to see him off his game. "When you gave me a thumbs-up, I figured that was your polite way of ending the conversation."

"That wasn't my intention. Leave it to me to give standoffish vibes via text," I huff out a self-deprecating laugh. "I guess I've been hiding myself away for so long, I don't know how to interact with people in a normal way."

"It's not your fault. I could have responded differently instead of leaving you hanging. Honestly, the thumbs-up thing is proba-bly more of a me issue. I let my own insecurities get in the way."

Huh. My writer instinct twitches. *Self-aware and self-reflective.* Check and check. I need to give Theo a scene that exemplifies both. It'll endear readers to him, and it'll make Monica see him for who he is—a genuinely good guy.

"Sorry if you were expecting me to respond and I left you hanging," TJ concludes.

I wave him off, even though, judging from the relief coursing throughout my entire body, I needed to hear those words. It's really nice having someone tell me I'm not the problem. It's felt like I'm the problem a lot lately.

"You're fine," I say aloud. "Can we start over?" I hold out my hand. "Hi, I'm Lucy Dupree, and I'd very much like to be your friend. I have to admit, I'm not usually fun or flirty. What you saw of me at the gala wasn't really who I am."

TJ engulfs my hand in his. His skin is calloused and warm, and the squeeze he gives my fingers sends lightning shooting up the length of my arm. "I guess we'll see about that."

The words feel like a challenge and a promise entwined in a double helix formation. My heart feels like it has grown legs and is scampering about like an excited octopus. My writer brain knows that's a terrible analogy because octopuses swim in water, but I'm going with it anyway.

TJ's soul-searching gaze makes me feel like he wants to know everything there is to know about me. I only hope he's not disappointed with what he finds out. He sinks into the chair next to me. "So, what did I miss? Did Carol's chili make anyone cry this year?"

My eyes widen, trying to remember which chili sample belongs to her. "Not sure. Which one is Carol's? Is it that bad?"

"Not bad at all. Just wickedly spicy."

"Ah." I nod. "Must've been this one." I point to the empty bowl at the corner of my tray. "It was delicious. That's my second bowl."

TJ lets out a low whistle. "Impressive. Not many people finish Carol's chili, historically."

I shrug. "I like it hot."

"Noted." TJ winks, and if only the floor would swallow me whole, because seriously? I walked right into that one, like the talking-to-hot-men-newbie I am.

I bury my face in my hands. "The chili," I mumble. "I meant the chili."

He just laughs.

"I'm such a dweeb," I say between my fingers. I'm not flirty or fun. I'm a walking, talking, personified foot-in-mouth. "When I tell you I'm out of practice with people, you see what I mean now?" Why do I have to give oxygen to the first thought that pops into my brain?

"Quit it." He reaches over and pulls my hands away from my face. "I like looking at you."

Chapter 18
TJ

Lucy sucks in a breath, and I retract my hand, severing the skin-to-skin contact. She's not the only one who's out of practice when it comes to being friendly. Then again, I'm not so much out of practice as I am out of my depth with this woman.

She's wearing a white, flowy top over wide-legged jeans and emerald-green sneakers. Her hair is hanging down, and it's either got a natural wave to it or she's curled it. She looks effortless, casual, but still somehow put together, and I am in awe of the whole package.

I've spent lots of time with women—stunning, gorgeous, fun women—shamelessly flirting my way through first and second dates like it's my job. It's easy and nice. I don't have to think too hard.

This thing with Lucy … it's different.

In my defense, it's been a long time since I looked at a woman and was so arrested by her. By the softness of her voice and the sweetness of her laugh. By the curve of her neck. By the map of freckles charting a course across the bridge of her nose. And those are just her physical features. If it's possible, I'm even more taken with Lucy's presence. I may or may not have spent the first five minutes after I arrived lingering in the entryway, just watching her.

Not like a creeper, I promise.

Like a man enraptured.

She was talking to Gram's friends, Susie and Titi. The two older women were gesticulating wildly as they recounted whatever story they were telling. Lucy nodded along, giving them her full attention. She's attentive and treats people like they're deserving of her time. I admire that about her. I watched as Susie and Titi drew her into the conversation, and she chatted with them like they'd known each other for years. Lucy had them laughing and leaning in, like they couldn't get enough of her.

Honestly, same.

Now, she's got me tripping over my words and off my usual game.

Flirting is my default, and I *want* to flirt with Lucy. I want to make her blush and let her know that she affects me. But we're friends. Just friends.

My brain knows that. My mouth hasn't gotten the memo yet.

"Rule number one when conversing with friends," I say quickly, trying to salvage the moment. "It's best to look each other in the eye so you can read facial cues and so that things don't get lost in the translation of thumbs-up emojis."

Lucy presses her lips together and nods sagely. "Excellent advice. Anything else I should know?"

There's so much I want to tell you.

I stop myself from saying that aloud. It's terrifying to feel like I *want* her to know things about me. I haven't had a thought like that since Tess died.

"I guess I should tell you that I don't like it hot," I say. She arches her brows. "At least, when it comes to chili. Carol's recipe has made me cry three years in a row."

Lucy laughs, and it's like the first chirps of robins out my window after a long winter. I want to bottle it up so I can listen to it on repeat later.

"I love that you're close with your grandparents and their community here," Lucy says.

"It's a cool place." I nod, steering the conversation in that direction. "Gram and Pa raised me after my parents died."

I rarely talk about my parents. But something about Lucy's willingness to be here tonight, to fight through the awkwardness and put herself out there, causes a crack in my usually shiny, surface-level front.

She nods slowly, her hazel eyes warm and her expression earnest. "I read about your parents and their passing when I looked up your bio." Her face is pink, like she's still embarrassed that she's researched me. "I'm so sorry for your loss."

I dip my chin. "Thanks. I didn't really know them, but I've heard all the stories from Gram and Pa, and my parents were good people." I let out a breath. "I guess I miss all that might have been and the experiences I never got to have with them, you know?"

"I do know." She offers me a sad smile. "I'm not sure how much of my family you've followed over the years, but I lost my mom as a baby and my dad passed when I was ten."

How could I have forgotten that? I have a baseline knowledge of what goes on in the entertainment and pop culture world. I haven't watched a ton of her family's show, *Dinner with the Duprees*, mostly because its usual airtime is Sunday evening, and I'm either playing or watching football. But the Duprees have been a staple for two cycles of seasonal TV, much longer than that if you count the family's social media presence.

I have a vague memory of hearing Ruby, the family matriarch, sharing her origin story on some morning talk show. She's Lucy's stepmom, if I'm recalling correctly, and she got her start in the industry when she began posting online vlogs of raising three kids after her husband tragically died in a gas station robbery. He was a good Samaritan caught in the wrong place at the wrong time. My heart cracks open for the woman sitting in front of me.

"That's right. I'm so sorry." I reach across the table and instinctively cover her hand with mine again. I give it a gentle squeeze and then pull back.

I have so many questions. Did her stepmom treat her well? Does she get along with her stepsisters? It didn't look like it during the People's Picks, but you never know. I hate the thought of Lucy being a real-life Cinderella. Suddenly that feels too on the nose. My protective instincts flare.

"It's a club no one wants to be a part of, right? The dead parents club." She winces out a wan smile. "Only people in it can understand what it's like."

"Very true." Come to think of it, maybe it's the fact that we've both lost our parents that makes Lucy feel more like a kindred spirit to me. Maybe the magnetic draw I feel toward her and this strange desire to protect her at all costs has more to do with that shared life experience than anything else.

"Yoohoo! You two! What are you doing sitting like bumps on a log?" Gram sashays out of the square-dancing formation she's been in since I arrived and hurries over, stopping in front of our table. "TJ, glad you could make it. Best get out on the dance floor. We've only booked the instructor for another forty minutes."

"I'm not much of a dancer, Loretta." Lucy puts up her hands in the universal stop sign. "I'm enjoying watching, though."

"Nonsense. You simply must join in. You think we're all dancers? Have you really been watching? Carol's out here acting like she's a *Coyote Ugly* understudy, but the rest of us can barely put two steps together."

I grimace. "Gram, what do you know about *Coyote Ugly*?"

"Enough." Gram tips up her nose. "Now, come on. I won't take no for an answer."

"Gram, I've got a game this weekend. I'll stay over here and keep Lucy company."

"We're not doing anything that body of yours can't handle." Gram grabs for my hand and pulls me upright. "You can keep Lucy company on the dance floor."

"Alright. I'm coming, I'm coming." I turn to Lucy, who has her eyes roaming over, as Gram puts it, *that body of mine.*

"You are not at all obliged to join us," I tell her, drawing her attention to my face and relishing the pink hue of her cheeks.

"You're a guest." I say the last word with a pointed look at Gram, who has the presence of mind to incline her head, reluctantly agreeing with me. "Feel free to watch me attempt to dance from here."

Lucy twists her lips to the side, and her gaze darts toward the geriatric dance party happening beyond me, then back to my Gram, and then in another quick perusal of my body, which I do not hate, and then up to meet my eyes.

"I suppose I could give it a try," she says after a beat.

Gram cheers. "I knew you were a gamer, Lucy. That's my girl."

"You know," Lucy says to Gram as my grandmother leads us to the center of the dance floor, "my friends call me Lu."

"Lu it is!" Gram claps her hand and takes her position across the square, next to Pa, who winks at me. Carol and a man I don't recognize stand to my left. Titi and a guy who looks vaguely familiar are on Lucy's right.

I'm paired with Lucy, and as I glance down at her as she takes in the whole scene, I mumble "Lu" under my breath, trying out the sound of it on my lips. I like it. I like it a lot.

"Yes?"

I blink, and she stares at me expectantly.

"Nothing." I give my head a slight shake. "Your nickname. It suits you."

She smiles. "Thanks. What does TJ stand for, anyway?"

"Theodore James."

She gets a startled look in her eyes, but before I can ask her about it, the instructor gets our attention.

We spend the next several minutes trying to learn the steps to a simple square dance. All I've learned is the words to "Tie a Yellow Ribbon 'Round the Old Oak Tree" because I've heard it on a loop three times over.

Neither Lucy nor I are very smooth, but there's a lot of giggling and shared amusement as we watch Titi, who has taken the yellow ribbon that was woven through slits in the neckline of her cardigan sweater, and is waving it around like she's a member of a high school color guard team.

Lucy leans over to me during a dancing interlude, her chest heaving slightly from the exertion of the dance. "Is Titi involved with that man?"

I have to stifle a laugh when I see Titi using the yellow ribbon from her sweater to tickle the cheek of an older gentleman whose face is bright red. "Don't think so, but I'd say she wants to be."

Lucy presses her lips together, but a smile breaks free despite her efforts. "He's absolutely adorable. So awkward and sweet. I could write an entire story about him." Her eyes widen. "I mean, I ... don't they look like characters in a book? You could write a story about them, too! I bet yours would be even better than mine, because you know them. Or, you know the community here. Gram and Pa would give you great first-hand info, and..."

She continues to prattle on, and I catch myself grinning. This seems to be the tell for Lucy's nerves: Words pour out of her. It's got me wondering what's so nerve-wracking about admitting that she could write about Titi and that older man.

"Alright, my fine folks, let's give 'er another go." The dance instructor's voice rings out through her headset microphone, and Lucy snaps her attention to the stage. "Line up! Or should I say, square up."

The music starts, and I clasp hands with Carol on my left and Lucy on my right. I give her hand a squeeze as we start doing as the music instructs us and circling around the old oak tree. When we get back to our starting position, I let go of Carol's hands and swing with Lucy around in a circle. I lean closer to her and say into her ear, "Do you write a lot of stories, Lu?"

She sucks in a breath, but before she can respond, we're separating, and I'm dosi-do-ing with my corner girl, who happens to be Carol. Lucy is matched up with Titi's man of the hour. When we come back to our home position, Lucy has her lips pressed together, and her eyes are darting around my face. I take her hands, and heightened color dots her cheekbones. Maybe I shouldn't be enjoying this as much as I am … with my friend. I push my luck, leaning into Lucy's airspace again and speaking into her ear as we promenade around the circle. "I think you do."

"Do what?" She feigns innocence, but gives herself away when she breaks eye contact.

I squeeze her hand, and she glances back at me. "You tell me." I *tsk*. "Friends don't keep secrets from friends, Lu."

Lucy looks like she swallowed her least favorite food and is trying to keep from spitting it out. There's obviously something going on here. Something Lucy isn't telling me. If she tells me to buzz off and leave her alone, I will. Until then, I'm letting my curiosity run the show.

I arch my eyebrows at her whenever we make eye contact as we dance. We go in and out of the same formation several more times before the song concludes. Every time I'm tugged away from Lucy, my adrenaline spikes with anticipation to get her back in my sightline. When our fingers brush, my pulse takes off faster than I do when I've got a full head of steam on the football field. It's like there's a thread between us that's pulling tighter and tighter by the second, until it's kicking out sparks.

Do I pull her a little closer the last time we have to promenade around the circle, making it so our arms are pressed firmly against each other's? I can't be sure, but our proximity allows me to catch a whiff of her perfume, and the tropical scent is like a shot of espresso, stirring me up inside until I feel wide awake.

When the song is finally over, I join the other dancers in clapping. Gram hoots and Titi lets out an ear-piercing whistle of approval before turning to the guy next to her and wrapping her arms around his neck. He lets out a startled yelp, but recovers himself and pats her primly on the back. In my periphery, I catch sight of Lucy, gaze locked on the two of them, mouth curled in a delighted smile. It's a good look on her.

Carol turns to me and does a theatrical curtsy. "Thanks for the dance, TJ."

"Likewise, Carol." I bow back at her before excusing myself.

Gram and Pa are caught up in conversation with someone who grabbed them from a different group, and I take Lucy's hand and pull her away from the dance floor. "Let's get out of here for a sec."

I feel semi-guilty for sneaking off, but I'd like to talk to her and not have our conversation interrupted by the square dance sequence or my well-meaning but very invasive grandparents.

"Where are we going?" Lucy hurries to keep up with me.

"To get some fresh air. To talk about the secret you're keeping." I lead her out the door and into the lobby of the gathering space.

"You can't possibly guess my secret based on one interaction!"

"Ha! So you're admitting there's a secret," I say victoriously.

"I—" She stops talking at the sight of the worker who's staffing the desk. It's a younger woman, and she looks up from her cell phone when we appear. Lucy instinctively ducks her head and steps behind me.

I curse under my breath. I forgot the desk in this community building is manned twenty-four-seven to meet the residents' needs. I spin around and tuck my arm around Lucy's shoulder, pulling her into my side. She stuffs her face into my shirt, and I angle my body so she's cocooned.

"Can I help you, TJ?" The woman bats her eyelashes at me. I've never met her, but she must be a River Foxes fan.

"We're good for now. I've got everything I need." I wink at the woman behind the desk before I drop a kiss on Lucy's head, nuzzling my nose into her hair for good measure. I hold her firmly against my side, keeping us moving in the direction of the exit. I want her all to myself. There's nowhere in this retirement community that doesn't have eyes and ears. My best bet for some privacy is my truck.

The desk lady flicks her gaze from me to Lucy, her brow taking the shape of a V. I don't think there's any way she could figure out who I've got tucked into my chest, but to make sure she doesn't try, I continue with my fib.

"Some of the chili is messing with her stomach," I tell the woman, who, according to the name placard in front of her, is named Summer. "Couldn't handle the heat."

I jump when I feel fingers digging in below my rib cage. Lucy's found a sensitive spot, and I tug her closer to me, trying to cut off her access to tickling me.

"Anyway, I'm going to get her home." I grin at Summer.

"Of course." She flips her hair behind her shoulder. "Let me know if you ever need anything while you're visiting your grand-parents. I work the evening shift on weekdays, and I'm always up for some company." She wags her brows suggestively at me before dropping her voice. "I can definitely handle the heat."

I have to fight back a grimace. Having women throw them-selves at me because of my profession has never bothered me. I've always considered it a perk of the job. But maybe my team-mates are right. Tonight, with Lucy tucked under my arm, I can't get away from Summer fast enough.

I paste on a smile. Lucy tries to take a step away from me, but I don't want to let her go until we're out from under Summer's watchful gaze, so I keep her close.

"See you around," I tell Summer noncommittally as I push open the exterior door.

Chapter 19
Lucy

T J's truck is parked near the front entrance, and he holds the door open for me to climb inside. By the time he seats himself behind the wheel, I have fully recovered from my momentary lapse in judgment wherein I was about to blab to TJ who I was and what I write.

I'm claiming temporary insanity and thanking the dear Lord I came to my senses before I spilled my guts. I'm also thanking Summer for reminding me that TJ—social butterfly, outgoing, big personality, flirty-with-everyone-and-their-sister TJ—is not a guy I can confide in or trust with something as major as my pen name and secret author career. This is for the best.

"So, where were we?" TJ turns in his seat and wags his brows. "Oh yes, you admitted you had a secret."

The cab of the truck is dim and only lit by the overhead lights outside in the parking lot. Still, his blue eyes glint with mischief. On the dance floor, they had me ready to tell him anything. But not anymore.

I've gotten good at keeping my author career to myself. TJ is another in a long line of people whose charms and forces of persuasion I have to remain impassive to.

"Hardly," I tell him, brushing a stray thread from the hem of my shirt. "You're reading into what I said."

"So you don't have a secret?" TJ crosses his impressive arms. "Why'd you get all antsy when you were watching Titi and Arnold?"

"I was merely commenting on how a pair like that would make for an excellent story."

"Uh huh." His voice is laced with skepticism. "You said *you* could write a story about them."

"I'm sure I could," I say easily. "So could you. You've been around them more than I have. I've known Titi for one night, and I can already tell that she's got a personality that could carry an entire movie franchise. Arnold was so cute being bulldozed by her." I smile now, thinking about them. It gives me something to focus on that's not TJ's penetrating gaze.

I have an entire idea for Monica's grandparents based on the pair. I can work it into a subplot about her family history, and it'll add some levity to an otherwise difficult past she's been working to overcome.

TJ squints at me, his eyes crinkling ever so slightly, like he's trying to make out my sincerity. I sit up straighter. I don't owe him anything.

Even as I think it, that hint of guilt returns, pricking at the base of my neck. I *have* been using TJ as inspiration for the story. He's an unwitting accomplice. Does that mean I owe him the truth? Inside, on the dance floor, with his body pulling mine to his with confidence and ease, feeling his hand splayed on my back and against my palm, catching the scent of his shampoo and having his smile aimed at me, I would have said yeah, I'll tell him. He wore down my defenses with his fleetness of foot and sweetness of smile.

But Summer was a good reality check. I'm nothing special to TJ. Just another girl in a long line of girls whom he's crossed paths with. He can be my friend, and that's all well and good, but I don't owe him the truth. Even if he's given me a lot of material for the next phase of my current work in progress.

"How are you feeling about your game this weekend?" I ask, breaking the silent stare-down we're in and putting my thoughts in much more neutral territory. Thinking about my story and my main character, who is based on TJ, in the presence of the man himself is making me trippy. What's real? What's fake? I don't need another slip-up.

He blinks slowly and then eases back into his seat, as if deciding to let me off the hook. Crisis averted. "Good," he says. "We leave tomorrow. Quick flight, and then we'll have a day and a half to acclimate and relax before Sunday afternoon's game."

I've been trying to read up on football to learn at least the bare minimum to write a pro-football character, but I still feel woefully uneducated when it comes to TJ's livelihood. "Are you guys, um, being picked to win?"

He shoots me a sly grin. "If people are smart, they'll never pick against me … or the River Foxes."

He's laying his cockiness on thick, and usually I'd consider that an off-putting trait, but I can tell with TJ that he's doing it in good fun. He knows he's good. He knows his team is good. He owns that. It's got to be a burden to carry the pressure that comes with talent and a record like the River Foxes have. I would hate to be in the spotlight and under the microscope. He doesn't seem fazed by it. In fact, it almost seems to energize him.

I shake my head. "Pretty confident in yourself, huh?"

"You've seen me play," he responds, as if his game speaks for itself.

I shrug in response, facing the windshield and not giving him the satisfaction of agreeing with him that yes, he's impressive. Yes, even if I have no clue what he actually does, even a novice like me can tell he's a beast out there. Yes, it's all kinds of hot.

Wait. I shouldn't be thinking about TJ and how attractive I find him. We're *friends*.

"Will you watch this weekend?"

Something in his tone catches my attention. I expected continued cockiness, but instead, there's a vulnerability there, and when I side-eye him, I see it in the stiffness of his posture, the way he's leaning toward me, jutting his chin out like he really hopes I say yes. This is a different side to the overly confident, more-swagger-in-his-pinky-toe-than-I-have-in-my-entire-body man who was teasing me a minute ago.

This TJ feels more real—and my entire body melts.

"Of course I will. What are friends for?"

He relaxes in his seat and smiles back at me.

"Speaking of that. Do you need me to take care of anything for you while you're gone?" I ask.

He opens his mouth, but words don't come out. He blinks at me a couple times.

"Is that a weird question?" I reach up to pull my hair into a tail, twisting the end around and swirling it into a bun to give myself something to focus on. "I'm sure you have people, closer friends or whatever, who help you out when you go away," I prattle on. "I was thinking with your house and your chickens and whatever. If there's anything I can do—"

TJ presses a hand on my knee, and I stop speaking, staring at the point of contact between his palm and my jeans. I bring my gaze up to meet his, but his expression is unreadable. I shift in my seat, and his hand falls away. I tell myself not to be a total cliché and miss the contact immediately, but here we are.

Come back, I think before I can stop myself.

Dang it.

"That's really nice of you to offer, Lu." His voice is ten shades of gravely, and I have to stave off a shiver at his use of my nickname.

"Of course. Whatever you need, let me know."

"It *is* supposed to be pretty cold this weekend. Especially Sunday. If you could check on the chickens and make sure their water hasn't frozen, that would be great. I'd ask my grandparents, but I worry about them coming out in the cold, and I guess my neighbor could maybe check things out, but as a die-hard River Foxes fan, he usually tailgates at the stadium even for away games, and yeah."

TJ cuts himself off, and I don't think he realizes how much more at ease in my own skin he's making me feel. I wouldn't have pegged him as a rambler, but it's a comfort to know he doesn't always have the exact words ready to go either.

I smile. "I'm happy to help."

Chapter 20

TJ

I snap a picture of myself, pointing to the corner of my back-door welcome mat, and send it to Lucy. I make the quick drive to the stadium, where I'm getting on the team bus so we can head to the airport. We fly out to Buffalo for our game in a few hours.

By the time I park and check my phone, I've got a message waiting for me.

I smile as I walk through the player lot.

You're really not going to let that go, are you?

Not until you tell me the truth.

I spent an absurd amount of time on the internet last night trying to figure out if my hunch about Lucy is true. I have nothing to base my speculation on except for the way she looked at the retirement community when she was studying Titi and Arnold. It was like she was in another world and she'd already dreamt up entire backstories for them. That, and the guilty look that flashed in her eyes when I asked her about it. For a second, I really thought she was going to admit to being a secret author or something. But then she clammed up, and now I'm wondering if I imagined it all.

Still, it fits. If she came to the gala looking for inspiration, it could have been inspiration for a new book idea. I know I'm reaching, but I can't help it.

Unfortunately, my hours of scrolling turned up nothing to support my hypothesis. Lucy Dupree's online footprint pretty much starts and ends with her stepmother's brand. I read a lot of old posts from the days following Lucy's dad's death. They're heartbreaking, and my stomach clenches every time I think about Lucy, as a child, shouldering the loss of her only remaining parent. My protective impulses for her flared.

Most of Lucy's public posts are collabs between her and her stepsisters, originating from their accounts. She never shared much herself. There's nothing to indicate she has some sort of alter ego; no news articles speculating on her as a secret author. I might be barking up the wrong tree. But something tells me I'm not. I'm known for having good instincts on the field, and I feel like those same instincts are at play here.

I stow my phone when I get into a team meeting, but by the time we're loading up the bus, I check it again to find another message.

Lucy

> I don't know what you're talking about! But since you love your chickens so much, maybe you should write a book about them.

Interesting. I can't type back fast enough.

TJ

> Whoa, we've moved from a simple story to a full-on novel now, have we? Tell me more.

Lucy

> I'm speaking hypothetically.

TJ

> Hypothetically, but for real, right?

I run into Anton's back. He stopped in the aisle of the bus. "Easy, killer," he says and then furrows his brow. "Why are you smirking like that?"

I relax my face. "What? Like what?"

Del pops his head over my shoulder. "He's texting Lucy."

I tuck my phone into my sweatshirt pocket. "Dude. Is nothing sacred?"

"Did you have a nice time with her last night?" Anton asks, eyes twinkling.

I roll mine back at him. "Oh yeah, surrounded by two dozen old people. It was a rocking evening."

"He's deflecting," Poe says from behind Del. "He doesn't want us to know what's actually going on between the two of them."

I nudge Anton forward, trying to get out from under their scrutiny ... and if I'm being honest, back to texting with Lucy.

"I told you guys. There's nothing going on between us. We're friends. If you must know, she's checking on my chickens for me while we're gone."

Anton looks at Del and Poe over my shoulder, his eyebrows arched.

"Why are you making that face?" I ask him.

"No reason." He waves a hand. "You haven't once had a woman over to your place in all the years I've known you, and suddenly Lucy Dupree comes along and it's like Grand Central Station over there."

"It's really not that big of a deal." I shrug. "She's a friend like you're my friends. If you weren't getting on the same plane with me, I'd have one of you check on the chickens. Seeing as you're all tied up and she offered, I figured, why not."

"Okay, then." Anton nods, but I can tell he doesn't believe me.

Whatever. I don't need the guys to understand, and if they want to rib me for my friendship with Lucy, I can take it. As I take my seat on the bus, I recognize that the feelings stirring in my chest when I see a new message from her pop up are different than the reaction I have when one of the guys texts me. But I'm not going to overthink that right now. I'm going to sit back and enjoy chatting with her.

Lucy

You're ridiculous and relentless.

TJ

What I'm hearing you say is I'm ridiculously smart and relentlessly funny.

Lucy

Now you're projecting.

Don't you have anything better to do than text me right now? Not that I mind. But I figured ...<shrugging shoulders emoji>

I frown. There she goes again, putting herself down.

> **TJ**
> Nope. Boarding the bus to head to the airport. You're actually doing me a favor, keeping me out of my own head before the game.

> Lucy
> Do you get nervous?

I chew the inside of my cheek. I don't admit this because it runs in the face of the entire outside persona I project—the fearless, not-a-care-in-the-world guy who saunters around on the field like nothing can touch him.

> **TJ**
> I do. Don't tell anyone, or I'll lose my street cred.

> Lucy
> You? Street cred?

> **TJ**
> Very funny. I thought you were on my side!

> Lucy
> Just keeping you humble <angel emoji>

> Seriously, though, your secret's safe with me. You'll be great on Sunday. You always are ... at least, you have been the past two games, which is the extent of my football watching.

> **TJ**
> We need to get you caught up on all you've missed. I'll send you my highlight video <winking face emoji>

> Oh boy, I can hardly wait.

I snicker, and Del's face pops up over the seatback in front of me. I shoo him away. I can't tell if Lucy's being facetious. I don't actually think she'll want to spend her time watching my greatest hits, but it's a balm to my ego to think that maybe, just maybe, she's interested in seeing what I bring to the table. I leave it all on the field, and I'm proud of my play. I find the link and send it over, because why not?

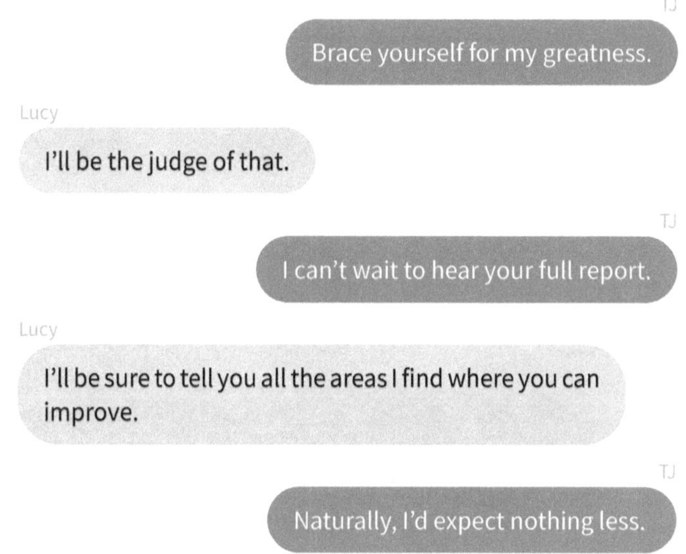

I'm smiling like a goofball, and I don't even care. Talking to Lucy is *fun*. I'm having fun.

I take a break from texting when we make it to the airport and file onto the private team plane headed for Buffalo, but as soon as I can, I'm checking my messages again, and I'm rewarded with:

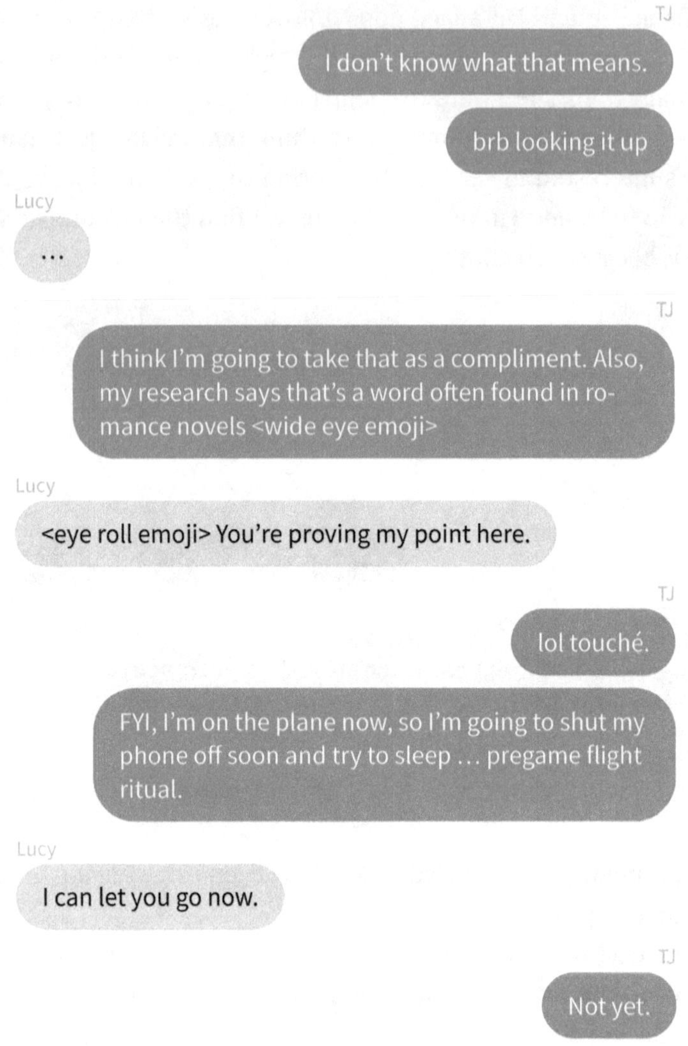

Shoot. Did that sound pathetic? Did I come on too strong? Too demanding?

I smile, grateful that Lucy seems to be enjoying texting with me as much as I am with her. I settle into my seat.

Other than critiquing my highlight reel, what are you up to today?

Lucy

Nothing very exciting. Hanging out at home.

I wonder if she does anything for work. She probably doesn't have to. Based on what I read, if she's entitled to any of the Dupree social media fortune, she's financially set. That, and if her dad had life insurance, she wouldn't have to work a day in her life. I don't peg Lucy as the type of person to sit around and twiddle her thumbs.

Hmmm. You say that, but what I'm hearing is you're about to write the next great American novel ...

Bubbles pop up on my screen, but then they disappear. I hold my breath, then chuckle when her message finally comes through.

Lucy

INCORRIGIBLE

The announcement comes over the intercom to put our devices into airplane mode, and that's my cue. I'll send off one last message to Lucy before settling in for a nap. Somehow, I think I'm about to have some very sweet dreams. The thought should freak me out, but I'm in too good a mood to care.

And yet you won't deny it. <smirking face emoji> So you're saying there's a chance ...

My fingers hover over the keys. I don't know how to end this conversation.

Warmly.

Sincerely.

Have a great day.

Wishing you well.

Talk soon.

All these random email sign-offs pop into my head, but none of them feel quite right.

"Dude, quit overthinking this," I scold myself.

Del appears in front of me. "What's that?"

"Nothing," I mutter, staring at the screen.

He points at my phone. "You're supposed to power that down, Teej."

"I know, alright. Give me one second."

I tap out the first thing that comes to my head.

TJ

> Taking off here. Say hi to the chickens for me. And enjoy rewatching my highlight video. I'll text soon to check in!

Was the exclamation point too much? It feels like it was too much, but there's no going back now.

Chapter 21
Lucy

"Act cool. Act natural. This isn't weird at all. Being at TJ's house … without him. To check on his chickens." I slam the door to my car and dart a furtive look over my shoulder like I'm some sort of undercover operative. I check my posture. I'm hunched like a turtle ready to bury its head in its shell.

"Pull it together, Lu." I stand up straighter, even as the wind howls all around me. "And stop talking to yourself," I add, realizing full well I'm being ridiculous. "I'm a writer. I always talk to myself." I roll my eyes at the conversation I'm carrying on with me, myself, and I. "Okay enough."

I suck in a breath and cast another glance toward TJ's quiet street. I left Cashmere Cove at two, before the River Foxes game started, but Daisy's Inn is a solid thirty-minute drive from Green Bay. Factor in the snowstorm that hit when I was about halfway, and my thirty-minute drive turned into an hour and fifteen-minute harrowing commute. The River Foxes game is now well underway in Buffalo, and everyone who lives in this neighborhood is glued to their TV or has made the trip east to catch the action in person. Or so I'm assuming. It's deadsville around here.

I tuck my chin deep into my coat and hurry to TJ's back door, clutching my bag to my side. Honestly, I could use a turtle's shell right about now. Wisconsin winters are brutal.

On his back stoop, I bend and run my mittened finger under the mat. The photo TJ sent me of himself crouched right here flies to the forefront of my mind. Nobody should look that good pointing at the corner of a doormat, and then there's TJ, effort-lessly cool.

I fumble with the lock and manage to shove the door inward. It's dark, and thanks to the winter storm, the afternoon sky is a murky gray, so there's not much daylight coming in through the windows. I flip on the overhead light in the back entrance and let my eyes adjust. My gaze snags on a notebook next to the ceramic key bowl.

Dear Lu,

Make yourself at home. There's food and drinks in the fridge. Don't feel like you have to get right back on the road to Cashmere Cove. What's mine is yours, so feel free to stay awhile. Thanks for helping out with the ladies. I owe you one. Go River Foxes!
TJ

Okay. How cute is a handwritten note? I grab the notebook and reread his message as I walk into the living room. The sad-looking table-top Christmas tree in the corner is still undecorated. I wonder if TJ's not really the Christmas-y type. It's strange, con-sidering the man doesn't seem to do anything at half-strength, and yet the Christmas tree is decidedly unfinished. I could ask him about it. It seems like something friends would know about each other.

I've been walking this fine line where TJ is concerned. Trying to figure out what's appropriate friend behavior. I'm significantly out of practice. His text messages on Friday felt flirty. I chalked it up to TJ's personality. I'm pretty sure the man flirts with anything that has a pulse. The way he square danced with me should not have turned me on, but it definitely did. Still, that's a me-problem. It's not his fault. I need to tread carefully, or I'm going to wind up hung up on TJ Wilson.

I set my bag on the couch and notice the remote. I power on his TV. I promised him I'd watch the game, and I'm a woman of my word. Friends watch other friends play sports. It takes me a few attempts to figure out what buttons do what, but eventually I get the River Foxes game playing. The score at the bottom of the screen reads Green Bay River Foxes, 28, Buffalo Cavalry, 3.

I do a little jig, happy to see the River Foxes taking care of business. I watch as the skinny guy from Buffalo stands back from a long line of other, less skinny guys. The skinny guy runs up to the line and kicks the ball. It sails in a high arc above the field and lands way at the other end.

Everyone from the River Foxes ignores it, so I figure it must be out of bounds. The camera pans to a group of River Foxes players jogging onto the field. I recognize Anton Bates, the player the camera currently has in focus. Behind him is TJ.

I will neither confirm nor deny my body's instant reaction at the sight of him. Suffice it to say, my eyes drink him in like a kid chugging down a juice box. All of him. All at once. I'll never admit this to him, but I watched his fifteen-minute highlight reel five times in full since he sent it to me. It's impressive watching him on the field. He's like a man on a mission, and I'm totally here for it.

Right now, he's wearing his helmet, so I can't see the lightning bolt in his hair. Pity. He's grinning and clapping his hands. Hands that were on my waist and spinning me around the square dance floor less than three full days ago.

I let my mind wander again to the way TJ's touch sent fire coursing through my veins. I shiver at the memory his lips, grazing the side of my cheek when he leaned toward my ear to whisper words for only me to hear.

It's sad that a square dance at a retirement community chili cook-off is the pinnacle of my real-life romantic endeavors. I'm not complaining. I store it all away as story fodder, and I sigh—in either relief or dismay, I'm not sure—when the screen fades from Anton and TJ to a commercial.

I hoist myself off the couch, remembering what I'm here to do, which is *not* to pine over TJ Wilson. That ship has sailed. Actually, there never was a ship. Ships are too romantic anyway, and a ship sailing away implies all sorts of things like kisses goodbye and longing and letters. Nope. TJ and me? We're more like a platonic city bus.

I pull my hood up and head out into the elements, grateful that, if nothing else, tending to the chickens will give me something to focus on. The chickens are in their run, which TJ has wrapped in some sort of thick plastic. They're seemingly unperturbed by the snow swirling around outside. They are perturbed by *me*. I slip on the boots TJ instructed me to wear and step inside, and one chicken flaps its wings and seems ready to charge at me before it settles back down.

"Easy!" I use my calmest voice. "I'm here to help you. I'm a friend."

I make eye contact with a majestic-looking brown-and-red-feathered hen. Her beady black gaze bores into my soul, and I swear if she had eyebrows, she'd be arching them at me right now. It's like she's saying, *I don't trust you as far as I can throw you.*

"Truly. I come in peace. Just checking on your water. I told TJ I would."

At the sound of his name, the chickens start clucking, a low, plaintive sound, like they miss their main man. Which is ridiculous. What does he do? Refer to himself in the third person in their presence? How do they know him?

Who knows? I'm in no position to argue.

"I get it," I say, making nice. "He's your favorite guy, huh? He takes good care of you."

The brown-and-red hen continues to stare at me, and I feel like it's getting personal now.

"Don't worry." I hold up my hands. "I'm not going to steal him away from you. Some other women might, but not me. I'm on your team. I'm TJ's friend."

More clucking.

"I'm talking to chickens. I've officially lost my mind."

A particularly loud cluck emanates from the brown-and-red-feathered hen, seeming to second the motion that I'm going crazy. It's enough to jolt me into action, so I make quick work of knocking the snow build-up from their feeder and checking their water, just like TJ explained how to do before saying goodbye on Thursday night.

Mission accomplished, I head inside.

I shuck the chicken boots on the stoop and scrub my hands for a solid two minutes in the kitchen sink. I'm not grossed out by chickens, but I also want nothing to do with chicken diseases. That seems like a fair stance. When I turn off the water, I hear the announcers on the TV talking about Anton Bates. I walk back into the living room and see him lined up behind a row of hunched-over River Fox players. The ball is on the ground in the center of the line. TJ stands behind Anton. I don't understand why they call it football when there's not much kicking involved. Except for what that skinny guy did before. The majority of the playing doesn't seem to involve feet. Football is not a fitting name for whatever is going on here.

"Wilson in the backfield and two receivers wide-set," the announcer says. "Bates takes the snap and drops back ..."

I have no clue what the broadcaster is talking about, but my gaze never leaves TJ. He sprints out from behind Anton and runs directly into a giant of a man from the Buffalo team who is charging at Anton from the other side of the line. The dude is twice TJ's size, and TJ is not small. I gasp as TJ gets plowed over, but my gaze flips to Anton in time to see him throw the ball. The camera follows the course of the ball, so I can't see if TJ got up. I barely register the cheers and the River Foxes player sprinting down the field until he's knocked down by a guy from Buffalo. My heart is in my throat as I wait for the chaos of the play to subside and the camera to pan out.

I don't take a breath until I spot number twenty-five jogging off the field, looking no worse for wear.

"Take it easy, TJ," I breathe aloud to the empty room. "You've got chickens who are counting on you. And a friend named Lucy who'd like to see you again in one piece."

I flop down onto the couch and watch as Anton tosses the ball to somebody else. The name Poe is on the back of this guy's jersey when he gives the ball back to the referee and huddles up with the rest of the team. They've gotten almost all the way to the far side of the field. I know from my research that they're trying to get the ball over the endzone line. TJ joins the circle, and I bite my lip. I also know from my research that this is either going to be a play to him, or Anton is going to try to dive over the line of big guys himself.

I watch the action unfold, and sure enough, Anton takes a step toward the huge scuffle of oversized men, but then at the last second, he lunges to the side and flips the ball backward to where TJ is trailing him. TJ snatches the ball out of midair, tucks it under his arm, and runs untouched into the endzone.

"Thank you, Jesus." I throw up the prayer of gratitude in all sincerity. Football is vicious. My research led me down a rabbit hole of gruesome injuries and ... yikes. Even some of the hits TJ took in his highlight reel had me wincing. Anytime a guy can get through a play unscathed, it's a miracle.

The guy with the jersey that reads Poe joins TJ in the endzone, and together, they do their Cinderella skit. I roll my eyes at the empty room, but I'm smiling like Christmas came early. I place my hands on my cheeks because they're burning up. The camera gets in TJ's face as Poe slaps his helmet, and they jog off the field together. TJ grins and winks. The tiny gesture is magnified on his giant TV screen, and I swear my heart flutters like a feather caught in the wind.

I shake my head. That wink wasn't for me. It was for the millions of fans watching the game.

The Cinderella Act was for you.

My brain is short-circuiting, coming up with unhelpful thoughts like that.

It's true.

I have a very convincing brain, I must say. TJ didn't have to do the Cinderella celebration. He found me. I told him I didn't want to date him. But he's still acting out our little inside joke. Something about that makes me feel warm and gooey inside. It's proof that the guy has staying power. Like he actually wants to be my friend.

I sit with that idea. I'm grateful for my girlfriends, definitely, but I don't have a lot of close guy friends in my life. My dad died when I was young, and when my stepmom made our family famous, I could no longer trust a guy's intentions. Ruby was very discerning with which crowds she let me and my stepsisters hang around, and I'm grateful for that. We were young and rich, and she didn't want us to get taken advantage of. As a result, I'm awkward around men. I know I am. The only reason I could act semi-normal with TJ at the gala was because I was hiding behind a mask.

But I've been normal—or as normal as I get—around him *without* my mask on. Here at his house and again at the retirement community. Even via text, if we ignore my errant thumbs-up emoji.

Inspired, I pull out my phone and tap out a message. He's been a friend to me, and I want to be a friend to him, too. Apparently now we're the type of people who text, because ever since TJ sent me that picture of the doormat, we've kept up a constant stream of conversation.

Lucy

> You scored! Good job, Prince Charming <winking face emoji>

I send the message, feeling proud of myself. Look at me go, having a functioning relationship with an adult male. But then I read my text back. And regret immediately kicks in.

Prince Charming, Lu. Really!?

I hadn't meant to sound flirty. I was only trying to let TJ know I noticed his touchdown celebration. I lean back into the couch and sit there for a second, debating whether or not to edit the message. But I don't want to be edited with TJ. Changing my words now would almost be worse than having sent them in the first place.

Lucy

> Your chickens are doing great, btw. I said hi for you, like you asked. FYI, I don't think they like me. But they're tucked in and all watered. Heading home soon!

I send off my message, satisfied that it sounds friendly and down to business. My work here is done. I get up from the couch and grab my bag. I get out the small gift I brought for TJ. It makes me smile, and I hope it makes him smile, too. I lean it on the tiny table behind his key bowl and cast one look back at his home before I head out into the snow.

Chapter 22
TJ

I'm at an upscale restaurant, sitting across the table from Amber, also known as "hot girl from the MKE mixer" in my phone. We're having a delicious lunch. She's as gorgeous as I remember, and she's trying really hard to engage me. She keeps leaning in and giggling at things I say, even when I'm commenting on something stupid like the impressive quality of the table napkins. Usually I'd be eating this attention up right along with my salmon and salad, but today all I can think about is Lucy.

My *friend* Lucy.

I keep telling myself that, but it's no use. I didn't want to get invested, but I'm afraid it's too late.

"I'm going to freshen up." Amber bats her eyelashes at me and slides out of her seat. Before she leaves the table, she leans over and places her long fingers on my bicep. "I'm free all afternoon."

I smile at her, hoping she can't tell it's forced. She leans forward and places a kiss on my cheek, which is an aggressive move for a first date. Props to her for her boldness. She hits me with a sultry smile before sauntering off. She must've picked her dress, which hits above mid-thigh, and her soaring high heels for my benefit.

I feel bad that I'm not holding up my end of this date, but the only feeling I have as she struts away is relief. I take my phone out of my pocket and pull up the picture I took of Lucy's gift.

It's a cross-stitched hoop. There's a chicken in the center, and beneath it, she's stitched the words *S-lay all day*.

I grin just looking at it.

Lucy can cross-stitch. Lucy made a chicken pun. Lucy left this at my house ... for me. It's all I can think about. *She's* all I can think about. I want to see her and talk to her, and none of that is lending itself to a very good date with Amber.

I don't know what's gotten into me, but for the first time since Tess died and I decided I never wanted to get so hung up on a woman again, I *want* to get hung up on a woman.

Or at least, spend more time with one woman in particular. I fear I'm already hung up on my friend.

A text notification drops down at the top of my screen from Anton.

Anton

> Look who I found <wide eye emoji> <winking face emoji> <fire emoji>

He's attached a picture, and when I open it, I'm greeted with the sight of Lucy curled up in a chair with a laptop resting on her knees. She's wearing a baseball hat, and her hair hangs like curtains around her face. The way my pulse kicks up is borderline concerning, but I'm typing back before I can think more about it.

TJ

> Where are you?

Anton

> Mood Reader with Rose. In Cashmere Cove. <book stack emoji> <kissing face emoji>

I hold up my hand, signaling to our waitress that I'm ready for the check. She nods in acknowledgment.

TJ

> Someone needs to talk to you about the appropriate usage of emojis.

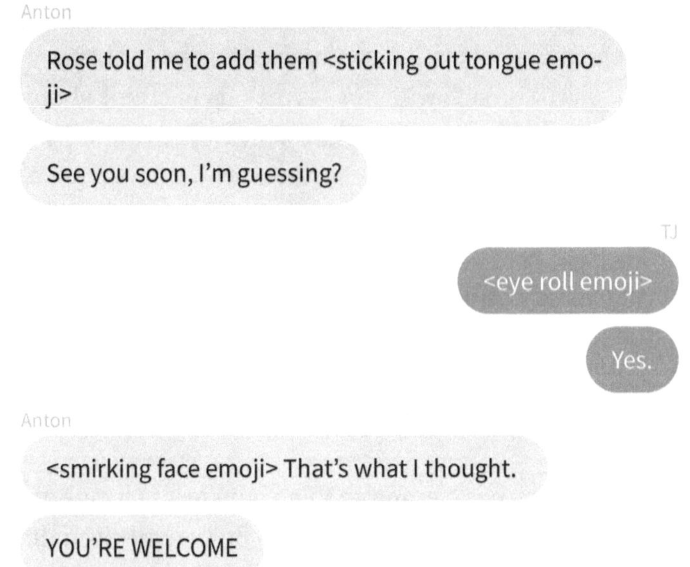

I roll my eyes for real, stashing my phone as the waitress hands me the check. I thank her and hand over my card.

"You ready to get outta here?" Amber purrs as she slips back into her seat.

More than she knows. I'm reenergized at the thought of seeing Lucy. I'm on the north side of the city, but I probably have about a thirty-minute drive to Mood Reader.

"Actually, something's come up," I tell Amber. "I've gotta run."

She pouts. "That's too bad. Rain check?"

"I'm not really interested in anything serious right now. With my busy schedule, I don't know if I'll have much free time in the future."

A sour expression crosses her face. I can tell she thought this lunch date was going to end much differently.

"Well, you know how to get a hold of me. I can be available, even for just a quick rendezvous." She wiggles her eyebrows, and I fight against a sour look of my own. Suddenly, hooking up with women feels shallow. Like it's not good enough ... for me or for them. It seems the guys' pep talks are finally getting to me.

That, or thinking about how Lucy has never been kissed—which is a subject I am very curious about but have very little idea how to broach with her—is making me think about how kissing anything that moves and looks my way isn't how I want to act.

There was a time when I thought Tess would be the last woman I ever kissed, and I was content with that. After she passed, I snapped. I knew I could never let myself get attached to another woman like I was attached to her. The pain of losing her was enough for a lifetime. So why not have some fun in the meantime, right? It felt like a foolproof plan. It was. Until now ... when it ... isn't.

I walk Amber to her car and then all but sprint to my truck.

I make the drive up to Cashmere Cove in twenty-five minutes.

The bell above the door at Mood Reader jingles when I walk inside. Instrumental Christmas music greets my ears, and my shoulders tense, but I feel myself relaxing when I spot Lucy through the shelves. She's in the corner, at the back of the store, curled up in the same chair from the picture. She doesn't look up when I enter.

Anton is leaning against the check-out desk in the center of the bookstore, angled toward Rose, who calls out a welcome. Anton waves to me, but I motion for them to be quiet. I don't miss the look they exchange, but I ignore it. I saunter through the cute book shop toward Lucy. There are several patrons perusing the shelves, but they seem to be more interested in their book selections than they are in me. I'm used to people making a big fuss when I walk into a room. It's kind of nice to blend in. To not feel like I have to put on a show.

Mood Reader is done up for Christmas. Twinkle lights are draped from the top of bookshelves. The display tables are all covered with red-and-green fabric, and lots of the books feature holiday titles. It smells like cinnamon and pine, and I have to admit I don't hate it. As I get closer to Lucy's chair, I spot earbuds in her ears.

I drop into the empty chair next to her and stare. It takes a solid sixty seconds, but eventually she blinks as if coming out of a daze and looks over at me. She sucks in a breath.

"TJ," she practically shouts. She pulls out her earbuds and tips the screen of her laptop down, angling it away from me. "What are you doing here?" she adds in a whisper.

I grin at her. "I came to thank you for the cross-stitched chicken."

Lucy's cheeks blush holly-berry red. "Oh, that." She looks down. "It was silly."

"Not to me. I love it. I didn't know you could cross-stitch."

"I can't do it very well," she downplays. "But yeah, I picked up the hobby a year or so ago. Something to do for my creativity that I don't feel like I have to be perfect at, and … yeah …"

She works her jaw before pressing her lips together, almost like she feels like she said too much. I wish she would keep talking.

She squares her shoulders and finds her train of thought again. "How were the chickens when you got home?"

"Right as rain. Thanks for checking on them."

"It was nothing. Happy to help."

I nod. We stare at each other. I can't get over how beautiful Lucy is up close. It shouldn't still hit me like this. I've seen her a couple times now, but wow, she's got this glow that steals my breath every time. Her freckles may as well be sugar crystals, and I've developed a sweet tooth.

I stretch my legs out in front of me, crossing them at the ankles. "So. Whatcha up to?" I motion to her computer. "Working on that novel?"

Her eyes bug out, and she darts a nervous glance around. "Shhh," she hisses.

I arch my eyebrows, and the guilty look is back in her eyes. I sit up slowly, shifting so I'm facing her and blocking her view of the rest of the store. "Wait. I'm right, aren't I? You're a legit writer."

Lucy looks almost pained. "Nobody knows. You can't tell *any-one*."

This three-minute conversation with Lucy is already three times more enjoyable than my entire lunch date with Amber.

"I'm an excellent secret keeper." I cross my heart.

Lucy slouches into her chair and buries her face in her hands. "I can't believe I told you." She peeks through her fingers. "We can't talk about this here. Come on."

She stands and surprises me when she grabs for my hand and hoists me up. I follow her like a dog on a leash as she weaves through the store.

She pauses by the check-out desk. "Thanks for having me, Rose. I'll be back."

"Where are you two off to?" Anton says, and the lilt in his voice isn't lost on me.

"TJ is having some digestion issues, and I have medicine at Daisy's," Lucy says without missing a beat.

"Aw, feel better soon, TJ," Rose responds.

Anton arches his eyebrows. I shake my head at him over the top of Lucy, but he grins.

"I'm not—" I cut myself off when Lucy glares over her shoulder and levels me with a look that says, *Don't say a word.* "I will," I amend.

Chapter 23
Lucy

T J follows me to Daisy's. We park, and he trails me inside. My shoulders immediately relax as the warmth from the hearth room thaws my chilled bones.

"It looks like St. Nick threw up in here," TJ mumbles from behind me.

I turn in time to catch him pulling a face like he's got a bad taste in his mouth. I arch a brow, and his smile turns mischievous. "You were about to tell me all about your—"

"Shh." I hush him, grabbing for his wrist and pulling him toward the grand staircase in the center of the entryway. "Come on."

I haul him up the stairs and to the end of the hallway. I fish my key out of my coat pocket, because yes, all the rooms at Daisy's Inn have old-fashioned locks with real, live turn keys. That will totally be making it into a book someday. I push the door to my room open and motion for him to walk in first.

He hesitates, flicking his gaze to me and then to the open door, before taking a tentative step inside.

"I don't have cooties." I push him the rest of the way through the door and shut it behind me.

"I didn't think that you did. I was only thinking that it might be weird for you to have me in your room. You weren't expecting to spend the afternoon with me."

He's not wrong. I wasn't expecting to tell him about my secret author life at all, but certainly not this afternoon.

"That's actually a good point. Why are you in Cashmere Cove?"

TJ opens his mouth, but I hold up a hand.

"I mean, why are you really here? Don't use the chickens, or the chicken cross-stitch, as an excuse."

He looks contrite before his features morph into a sheepish smile. "Anton texted that you were at Mood Reader, and I don't know, I guess seeing you sounded better than doing what I was doing, so here I am."

Mentally, I tell the excited puppy who's leaping around my stomach to sit and stay. I do not know how to handle this type of attention from a man like TJ, and I shouldn't like it as much as I do. I can't deny that it feels good to hear he wants to spend time with me. I've spent far too much time thinking about him the past few days, too. I can say it's in the name of research, but that's not entirely accurate. The more time I spend with TJ, the more I feel like my fictional version of him will never live up to the reality of the kind and considerate man before me.

TJ's lingering at the foot of the four-poster bed, looking unsure about where to go and like he wants to crawl out of his skin for admitting that he wanted to hang out with me.

"I'm glad you're here," I say. Honesty is the best policy, after all. "Even if you did wring my biggest secret out of me." I scowl at him, but I can't stop my lips from hitching up when he smiles.

"I have so many questions," he says.

I shake my head. "Here." I gesture to the chair in the corner of the room. "Let's sit."

TJ flops down in the comfy chair, and I slip my winter jacket off and sit cross-legged on the foot of my bed.

"Alright," I decide to get out in front of this. "Yes, I'm an author. I write under a pen name, and nobody knows this about me. I love creating stories, crafting worlds, and solving problems within the pages of a book. It's my dream job."

TJ's eyes go wide. "You have books published?"

"Yes."

"How many?"

I shift my weight. "Six ... so far."

"You've published *six* books, Lu? Are you kidding me?" His mouth hangs open. "That's incredible. *You're* incredible."

I'm also supremely self-conscious at the moment. I dip my chin. "It's not that big of a deal. You're a professional athlete, so ..." I wave my hand around like that speaks for itself.

"We're not talking about me right now." TJ makes a *pft* sound. "Let me be in awe of you for a second. This is the coolest. I can't believe I have a friend who's a published author. When did you start writing?"

I blow out of a breath. "It's a long story."

He leans back in his chair. "I've got the day off, so I'm all yours."

"I've been writing stories since I could write. Mostly I'd make up stories about little girls and their moms. It made me feel better about missing mine. My dad would tell me about how wonderful my mom was, and I'd use that as a starting point and write these lavish tales of a mother-daughter duo who saved the world." I can't help but smile. "I called my series The Glorious Girls."

Warmth emanates from TJ's expression. "That sounds pretty amazing."

I tip my chin. "It was good for me, I think. My therapist encouraged it, and I loved writing happy endings." I swallow. "When my dad passed away, I kept writing. I didn't have anyone to tell me stories then, and I mostly hated the real world, so I made up scenes that were happy as a way to escape."

TJ leans forward in his chair, resting his forearms on his knees. "It was how you coped."

"Pretty much." I pick at a pill on the comforter before dragging my gaze up to meet his. "It's the joy of my life to know that I can bring other people joy with my words." It feels raw and vulnerable to say that, especially because of how this year has gone. I've spent a lot of the past few months wondering if I'll ever be able to create something worthwhile again.

"Are your books popular? Do other people read them, I mean?" TJ's question stirs me from my dark thoughts.

I think about the call I got from Cassie telling me my third book hit the best-seller list, and I can't help but smile. "Yeah. People do, or at least they did."

Confusion mars his features. "What does that mean? They don't now?"

"I don't know if I'm going to be able to give my readers something new." I shrug. "I've barely written anything since what happened at the People's Picks."

He frowns. "Why's that?"

"Because I told everyone that being entertained was worthless, and here I am, making my living on books that literally entertain people. I feel like a fraud."

TJ leans back, studying me. "Do you want to talk about it?"

I chuckle, but it's mirthless. "What else is there to say?"

"I don't know. We haven't really discussed it, you and me."

"That's because I'm ashamed."

There's an unreadable expression on his face. "Can I tell you a secret?" he asks after a moment.

I flick my wrist, gesturing for him to go ahead. I'm bracing for him to tell me I'm a huge jerk and that he can't believe a person could be as condescending as I was up on that stage.

"I actually thought what you said was pretty great."

Wait. I replay his words and suck in a breath. "You're lying."

"Nope. Cross my heart ... again," he adds.

I shake my head. "I don't believe you."

"Why not?"

"Because I was entitled and belittling and the worst." I could quote that comment section all day and all night.

He tips his head back and forth like he's considering this. "But you were also overwhelmed and mortified at what was going on. I'm sure that impacted how things went down."

I suck in a breath. How can he read me so well? "How do you know that?"

"I may have watched the video a couple of times since meeting you." He looks sheepish.

My face flushes. "How many times is a couple?"

"A couple dozen."

"TJ! I'm mortified." I hide my face in a pillow.

"Don't be! I've studied the film, as any good football player would. I've broken it down and assessed your posture and your expression and your words, and you know what I keep coming back to? You *did* something, Lu. You said something. You acted. Not many people can say they would have stood up and faced something head-on. But you did. You were in a public pressure cooker situation, so maybe you came off patronizing, but I don't think what you said was all that off base."

I gape at him. I haven't talked out loud about this at all. I cried a lot to Cassie and Philly and Bex in the early days. I told them how sorry I was if I offended them, and they helped me sort through my life and figure out my next steps, but as far as getting into the nitty-gritty of what I said and what I meant? I haven't really gone there ... with anyone.

"The thing is," I say, summoning my courage and hoping for the right words to say what I mean without sticking my foot in my mouth. "I do stand by what I said. Most of what I said," I amend. "I definitely shouldn't have told my sisters and everyone that they didn't matter or called the masses stupid. That was wrong of me, and I fully own that. Everyone matters. But—I don't know—people get so caught up in social media or entertainment or sports." I wince. "Sorry."

"No, keep talking."

I take a deep breath. "Or books." I point at myself, to show him I understand that I'm a part of this narrative, too. A big part. "Whatever the fixation, in our society of materialism and comfort and consumerism, what we're fanatical over becomes our entire lives, but that's not how it's meant to be. That's not what we're put on this earth for."

I close my eyes and blink them open, trying to gauge his reaction. TJ stares at me, but he doesn't look offended or put off, just curious and attentive.

"I'm sure it sounds hypocritical now that you know I write books for a living," I go on, "but I don't want people to be obsessed with my stories to a point that they become the most important thing in their lives. I want to help people live their actual lives by encouraging them to love deeper or by giving them a moment of peace or escape when life gets hard, so then they can face whatever they're facing with renewed strength and spirit. When things get disordered and we put all our emphasis in the wrong places, then everything spirals out of control. *That's* what I was trying to say up there. That we'd all lost sight of what really mattered. People and doing good work and loving and serving those around us. Granted, I picked a terrible moment, and my delivery was all wrong. So now people think I'm the devil incarnate."

"Nobody thinks that," TJ says indignantly.

I snort. "Trust me. They do. I've read all the comments."

"Please tell me you haven't."

I meet his imploring gaze, tipping up my chin. "I read them weekly."

TJ looks physically pained. "Why would you do that?"

I shrug. "I deserve it. That's my comeuppance."

He shakes his head. "People in comment sections are unnecessarily cruel."

Tears sting the corners of my eyes as I remember one comment in particular. "Yeah," I say, my voice wobbling.

TJ's warm gaze never leaves my face as he tosses the pillow on the floor and leans forward in his chair. "Hey, talk to me, Lu. You've been carrying a lot of this alone. I'm here."

I let out a shaky breath. "It's stupid." I look down at my knees for something to focus on. "There's been a couple comments alluding to how the world would be better without me in it, and that's—"

"No." TJ's voice is sharp and my gaze snaps to him. He kneels down on the floor in front of the bed and grabs for my hands. He squeezes them as his eyes bore into mine. "There is *no* version of this world that's better without you in it. Do you believe that?"

I gulp down my emotions. "I know. I do," I whisper. I can't believe I'm talking about this with him or anyone, but the words start flowing before I can even consider keeping them cooped up inside. "I haven't considered hurting myself or anything like that. But sometimes when I read comments like that on those articles, I'd be lying if I said I don't think about how much easier it would be if I just wasn't ... here. If I'd died with my mom during childbirth, or if I'd gone to the store and stopped to get gas with my dad. None of this would have happened. I wouldn't have offended the entire entertainment industry and the general public. I wouldn't be struggling to string a sentence together when I used to be able to write pages and pages each day. I made everything so hard, and I hate it. I guess I could have kept my mouth shut and that would have solved the problem, too." I try to laugh it off, but a tear trickles down my cheek.

TJ reaches up to brush it away. "Can we be friends who hug?" he asks. "I'd like to hug you right now."

I nod, too overwhelmed to speak. He opens his arms. I crawl up on my knees and collapse into his embrace.

Chapter 24

TJ

I hold Lucy as she silently cries into my henley. I bring my hand up to cup the back of her head and gently stroke her hair. "I've got you," I murmur before pressing a quick kiss to the crown of her head. My heart pounds in my chest, protectiveness surging with each pulse. I wish I could take away all of Lucy's pain. I wish I could *do* something for her right now. I'm honored she felt safe enough with me to share this part of her story, and her raw honesty steals my breath. She's been through so much, and she's so brave, but I don't think she'd call herself that. In my eyes, the fact that she's still standing—or I guess, slumped into me right now—speaks to her inner strength. I want to make her see how strong she is … somehow. I want to make sure she knows she's not alone. That she matters.

Lucy leans back after a couple minutes and wipes at the mascara that's bleeding beneath her eyes.

"Thanks," she says, her voice hoarse from the tears. "I needed that."

I sit back on my heels, giving her a little space.

"I'm such a mess," she says and hits me with a look when I start to tell her she isn't. "I am. It's been a really hard year. I miss writing and writing well. That's always been how I've coped, so it's felt extra empty the past few months, not feeling like I can even do that." She pulls her knees up, hugging them to her chest.

"I get that. I can't imagine not having football as my outlet."

She nods and then lets out a small laugh. "I feel like I just laid myself bare. All my wounds right out in the open for you here."

Her cheeks flush, and I don't want her to regret her openness. I like knowing what she's going through. I'm humbled that she shared all that with me. I want her to know I see her, and in a small way, I get her.

"Would it make you feel better if I told you something about me?"

She looks at me with wide eyes, still glassy with emotion. "Only if you want to."

The thing is, I actually *do* want to. I don't overthink it. I summon my courage. I want to give Lucy a piece of me, something to go along with the shreds of her heart she placed in the space between us. I take a deep breath. "My girlfriend in college passed away the week before Christmas our sophomore year."

Lucy's lips part in surprise, and her hand flies up to cover her mouth. "TJ, I'm so sorry."

I swallow down the knot in the back of my throat. "She was alone in the house she and her roommates rented. It was a total dump. Classic college house. Their landlord was kinda the worst." I shake my head.

I've thought about how I should have made her move. I should have confronted the guy when, time after time, he didn't fix things when they asked him to. He was negligent, and no one called him out on it. If I had, maybe things would have been different. Maybe Tess would still be here today. I blink and find Lucy with her head tipped to the side, compassion in her gaze.

I plow ahead. "She had texted me that she was taking a nap. The rest of her roommates finished their finals and headed home earlier in the day. I waited to hear from her when she finished her exam, but she"—I swallow—"never texted me again."

Lucy reaches out and grabs my hand, squeezing it hard.

"When she didn't show up for her final exam that night, one of her friends from the class tried to reach her, and when she couldn't, she got in touch with her parents. They ended up finding her in her bed. She died from carbon monoxide poisoning."

"Oh, TJ." Lucy swallows and shakes her head. "She was so young."

"She was the best the world had to offer. Bright and funny and curious, but kind and always looking out for people." I cut myself off when my voice cracks. I haven't let myself dwell on Tess in several years, but it's not difficult to remember what a light she was, and how it felt so cruel that she was taken so soon. "I sometimes think if I had been there with her, I could have done something."

I don't admit that out loud very often. Probably haven't said it in years. I wish I could have done something—anything—to help her.

"Or you might have died too," Lucy says quietly after a moment. "It's hard not to hunker down in the place of regrets, trust me, I get it. But it doesn't change what happened. What happened sucks."

I huff out a breath. "It really does. I still feel like I should have taken care of her somehow."

Lucy presses her lips together and looks at me with a furrowed brow.

"What?"

She shakes her head slightly. "I think if Tess was here today, she'd say you *did* take care of her. She wouldn't blame you. It was an awful accident, and I'm so sorry for you and for Tess's family." She pulls in a breath. "Are you still in touch with them?"

My phone burns in my pocket where the email from Tess's mom is waiting for my response. I think about Tess's parents and how they took me in and treated me like their own son. I've kept in touch with them, but only over the phone and via email. I haven't seen them in person since the funeral. I gave all my focus to football. I didn't graduate, instead choosing to enter the NFL draft the spring of my junior year. I've been in Green Bay playing for the River Foxes ever since.

I know it's a lousy excuse. Tess's family lives in the suburbs of Chicago. It's a three-hour drive. Hardly insurmountable, even with my schedule.

"I've been cowardly." I glance at Lucy, my cheeks heating.

She releases her grip and brings her hands up to cup my face. "Not you. You're fearless, isn't that what you told me the night we met?"

"I lied," I whisper, relishing the feel of her soft skin on my coarse cheeks. "I'm afraid that people I love will always leave me. It's why I haven't dated seriously since Tess died." I gulp down my rising emotion. "I don't know if I can handle losing someone again, so I haven't gotten close to another woman since Tess." I blink and meet her gaze. It's open and kind, and I suddenly feel brave. "Not until getting to know you, actually. Thanks for being my friend, Lu. Thanks for being here." My voice cracks.

She presses her lips together as fresh tears spring to her eyes. "I'm really glad to be your friend." She swallows. "You're the first person I've let in in a long time, too."

"I know you said you haven't thought of hurting yourself, but I'm going to check in on you, because I don't want you to leave."

Her fingers press into my skin. "I don't mind. But you can trust me when I say that I'm not going anywhere."

I nod, and our gazes stay locked in. Lucy's eyes are bright with unshed tears, gold flecks sparking against dewy blades of grass.

"Thank you for telling me about Tess," Lucy says after a second. "I'm guessing she's the woman in the photo on your shelves at your house."

"That's her," I say.

Lucy nods.

"You also probably noticed my pathetic Christmas tree when you were at my place."

"Not gonna lie, I wondered about that. And about your comment when you walked in downstairs." Lucy scoots back and sits crisscross on the edge of the bed. "Guessing the timing of the holidays is tough for you."

I stretch my arms over my head. "Getting the news of Tess's death five days before Christmas put a damper on everything. My parents' car accident was also in December, so it's never been my family's favorite time of the year. Gram and Pa tried to make happy memories for me growing up, and I didn't always hate Christmas. I still don't hate Christmas," I amend. "It feels like a heavy time, and truthfully, I haven't really had anyone to share the weight of it with." I chuckle nervously. "That came out sounding way more vulnerable than I intended."

"Don't apologize. I think I understand." Lucy's eyes take on a faraway look. "My dad and I used to cut down our own Christmas tree every year. It was one of my favorite traditions, but I haven't done that in years. Ruby, my stepmom, prefers a fake tree. That's what we've had since my dad passed. I haven't cut down a tree in over a decade."

She's quiet for a moment, looking lost in memories of the past until she blinks, focusing her gaze on me and offering me a small smile.

My heart surges in my chest, beating more quickly with a desire to give something more to Lucy. "Want to go and cut down a tree with me?"

Her eyes go wide. "I don't want to do anything that's painful for you."

The thought of getting a Christmas tree and putting it up in my house has always felt like a betrayal of Tess, but sitting here, staring at Lucy, there's a voice in my head that sounds a lot like Tess saying, *Go, take the girl to the tree farm, you big oaf. Live, laugh, love.*

"Live, laugh, love," I say slowly.

Lucy's forehead creases, and a huff of a laugh escapes her lips. "What's that?"

A sense of peace comes over me, and I smile for real. "It's this dumb sign I have in my house."

"No, I know. I saw it when I was there. I just didn't know why you were saying it now."

I smirk. "First of all, I'm starting to think you might have gone through my drawers when I wasn't around, Lu." I wag my brows to let her know I'm teasing, but it doesn't stop her cheeks from turning pink. "Second, I'm quoting it because Tess and I used to joke about that. She had that sign in her house, mostly to make fun of it, but we used to say 'Live, laugh, love,' whenever we were trying to decide what to do next, or what our next move would be. It was a tongue-in-cheek thing."

A soft smile spreads across Lucy's face. "Tess sounds awesome."

"She was."

So are you.

The words are on the tip of my tongue, but I rein them in. I'll make sure Lucy knows she's incredible, too, but if I say so right now, it's going to sound like I'm saying it because I have to, or because I feel guilty for bringing up my former girlfriend.

Do I feel guilty? I always expected talking about Tess, reliving some of our time together, especially with another woman, would be upsetting and awkward. There is some of that, but not like I anticipated. It feels more like I'm taking a bandage off a burn wound. The adhesive sticks and pulls from being in place for so long, and it's not super comfortable, but underneath, the scar is smoothed over and not painful to the touch.

"She would be telling me to stop being a baby and take you to the tree farm. She'd be saying, 'Live, laugh, and love, TJ. Quit sitting on your butt like an oversized toad.'"

Lucy smiles. "Did she call you an oversized toad often?"

"Nah, I added that myself." I grin at Lucy. "So what do you say? Should we go for it?"

Lucy's eyes take on a glint of hope—anticipation. "Let's do it."

Chapter 25
Lucy

There must be something in the water in Wisconsin. These small towns are so charming. I didn't think anywhere would be as lovely as Cashmere Cove, but as we drive slowly down Mapleton Avenue, I can't help but think that Mapleton gives Cashmere Cove some competition. We passed an adorable park with a gazebo all twined with twinkling lights. Kids were skating on an ice rink, and there was a line in front of a mobile coffee pop-up nearby.

"This is the entrance. Turn right." I look up from my phone after navigating us to McGregor Tree Farm. A gorgeous farmhouse comes into view. We bypass the circle drive and follow the signs for the tree lot around back. TJ pulls his truck into an open spot.

I walk in front of the truck, meeting him on his side. He's assessing the grounds, and I fiddle with the tassel on my scarf. "You sure you're good with this?"

When he suggested cutting down a Christmas tree together, I could have cried ... tears of joy. It's been so long, and my heart pinched at the memories of my dad putting me up on his shoulders and hiking through the fields to find the perfect tree.

After hearing about everything with Tess, I'm not surprised by TJ's aversion to the holiday season, and I know he's doing this for me—for my benefit. That thought could make me cry again. I've blubbered enough for one day, so I firm my resolve and keep my gaze on the side of his face where his jaw is currently clenched to within an inch of its life.

"If it gets to be too much, say so, and we can leave," I tell him. "You don't have to pretend to be okay with me."

He relaxes his mouth and offers me a small smile. "And I can't tell you what a relief that is, but I'm good. I was thinking about Tess's mom."

I cock my head to the side to show him I'm listening, and he goes on.

"She invited me to a benefit dinner. They have one every year around New Year's in Tess's honor. It's this whole fancy thing, and they try to bring in a big-name speaker to get some media coverage to raise even more money for the scholarship they fund in Tess's name." His eyes take on a faraway look before he blinks and stares down at me. "I never go," he says quietly. "I've always thought it'd be too hard to be there alone, you know?"

I nod, my throat closing. A part of me wants to offer to go with him. Another part of me doesn't feel like that's my place. Add to that his mention of media presence, and I know I wouldn't be able to hide my identity.

"Maybe it's time," he says quietly.

I reach for his hand and squeeze it. "I'm sure it would be hard to be there, but it might also be healing."

He brushes his mittened thumb over my knuckles, blowing out a deep breath. "I know. Tess's parents are great. I owe it to them to show up. I've been letting them down for years," he says on a sigh.

I shake my head quickly. "You're allowed to grieve at your own pace and hold the boundaries you need to hold."

He nods once. "Thanks for saying that, Lu."

"It's true." I swallow. "I'll support you whatever you decide to do about the benefit dinner."

He offers me a small smile. "I wish you could come with me."

I suck in a breath. "I ... I don't know if that would be the best idea."

He shakes his head quickly. "No, I know. I'd never want to put you on the spot like that. It's—" He chuckles. "I don't know. Everything's better when you're around."

I roll my lips into my mouth, because now I'm really going to cry again.

TJ squares his shoulders and faces the tree farm. "Let's do this."

I nod and take a moment to collect myself. I wrap my scarf around my neck, letting it come up and cover my mouth.

He watches me closely as I straighten my beanie, making sure it's pulled down over my forehead.

"There," I say. "Ready."

We wander toward the fence marking the entrance of the tree farm. The grounds are gorgeous. Snow glistens over the trees. There's a big red barn straight ahead with a wooden sign on the door announcing free, homemade hot chocolate inside. My mouth instantly waters.

"Have you ever thought about ditching your disguises and coming clean?" TJ asks.

I glance up to find him studying me.

TJ motions to the scarf around my mouth. "Not that the bandit-on-the-run look isn't a good one, but..." He shrugs, cracking a grin.

I chuckle, but then shrug back. "I don't want to deal with people asking me questions."

"What if people think that what you said was valid? Like me."

"I don't think too many people are willing to see the good in me like you are." I still can't quite believe he does. Not complaining. Just being honest.

"Do those people really matter then?" he asks. His tone is kind, not condemning. TJ isn't asking about this to make me uncomfortable. He genuinely wants to know. He's not pushing me, just probing, making sure I'm considering my position from all sides.

"I'd like to say no, but I don't know if I'm strong enough to deal with the fallout," I admit. TJ looks like he wants to say something else, but I keep talking. "I'm not ready to come out of hiding. I don't know if I'll ever be ready."

I adjust the scarf, unease warming my chilled skin more than the knit fabric. Why do I feel ashamed of my answer?

TJ nods and doesn't press the point, but he's planted a seed in the back of my mind of a what-if question that I've been avoiding. I let it be for now, but I'm conscious that it's there, germinating right beneath the surface.

We make it to the barn entrance and are greeted by a pretty woman with a pregnant belly. She introduces herself as Laney and gives us the rundown on where we can find the different species of trees. TJ does most of the talking, and to Laney's credit, she isn't drooling at the sight of him in his winter attire. That makes one of us. Speaking from experience, it's difficult not to drool. The man is like a well-built lumberjack. His barn jacket, jeans, and work boots are really doing it for me.

I check my thoughts. I can focus on TJ's looks as the inspiration for Theo, but I shouldn't be ogling him for my own sake. I wish I could ask Laney how she manages not to be affected by the sight of him. I need some pointers.

"Saws and sleds are against the fence, and you can pay in the barn whenever you're done." She smiles and flicks her gaze to me.

"Thanks." I crinkle my eyes to let her know I'm smiling behind my scarf. It does make me feel a little sad to be constantly avoiding people—avoiding their gazes, avoiding conversations, staying solitary. I'm an introvert, so I do well alone, but that doesn't mean I don't like interacting with people. I open my mouth to say something—anything—to Laney, but she walks off toward the barn before I get a chance.

TJ grabs some gear for us and leads the way down the line of trees.

"It's gorgeous out here," he says over his shoulder. His hat is slightly askew, making him look youthful and delightful. "So here's what I'm thinking. If I'm going to do this, I may as well go all out, right?" He looks to me for approval.

"Live, laugh, love," I quote, and then immediately question if it was the right thing to say. That was TJ and Tess's phrase. Am I overstepping? "Sorry." I wince. "I didn't mean to—"

"No. You're right." He takes a deep breath. "I'm glad we're here together. Living and laughing and loving nature!"

I swallow around the wad of emotion in my throat. Will I ever have the type of relationship with someone—anyone—like TJ had with Tess?

Not if you stay holed away.

Ugh. There go my thoughts again.

Not the time or place, Lu. Not the time or place.

I force myself to focus on the wave of relief that rushes over me, and not on everything I'm missing out on. "I'm glad I didn't overstep," I tell him.

"Not at all." He hits me with a devastating smile. "You're good for me, Lu."

My heart stutters. "I—"

TJ talks over me, not giving me a chance to acknowledge the compliment. I wonder if that's intentional on his part, because he knows I don't process praise very well. I still don't know if I deserve it.

"I think we should go with a Balsam," he says. "I like the smelly kind of trees."

"A man who knows what he wants," I murmur with a small grin of my own. I'm bolstered by his commitment to this outing and his revived Christmas spirit. He makes me feel more free to just be—to not have to have myself all figured out.

"Absolutely," he says with a wink.

I roll my eyes at him, even as my cheeks flush with heat. "Quit being flirty. I don't know how to handle you."

"Oh, I think you do. Or you could." His eyes twinkle.

"TJ!" Without thinking, I slap him on the butt.

It happens in slow motion. Like an out-of-body experience. I freeze, stunned by my behavior as TJ starts chortling.

"That's one way to handle me."

I bury my face in my gloved hands. "I can't even believe I did that."

He's still laughing as he slings his arm around my shoulder. I chance a glance at him, and he looks down at me with a roguish grin.

"Don't even try to act like you haven't been thinking about doing that since you were staring down my perfect peach the night we met."

I shove him in the side and he pretends to stumble. He laughs some more, and I can't help but join in.

"You're not denying it, Cinderella." He wags his brows. "Who knew you were hiding this feisty side?"

"Shut up!" I shake my head at him, my face boiling beneath my scarf. "I can't be blamed for my behavior out here. The tree farm is enchanted and making me act completely out of character."

"Whatever you need to tell yourself to sleep at night, but if you want to know what I think"—he arches his brow—"I think you've got all sorts of bold behavior stored up inside, waiting for the time to come out and play."

I twist my lips to the side as if I'm pondering this. I want to deny it, but I also kind of like the thought that I'm not the wallflower I've always pegged myself to be. I hum. "No comment."

He looks triumphant.

"Now can we focus?" I attempt to sound serious, but my butt-slapping behavior doesn't really give me a leg to stand on. "Laney said the Balsams were up ahead, right?"

"That's where I was heading before you distracted me by smacking my tush." He smirks.

I groan. "You're never going to let me live this down."

"Definitely not. I'm already scheming up how I can get you to do it again."

"TJ! Walk," I say, laughing.

"Demanding." He clicks his tongue. "You're proving my point, Lu. Proving. My. Point." He spins and treks further into the trees, and I fall into step behind him.

I will neither confirm nor deny how often my gaze falls to his tush. In my defense, it's *right* there.

TJ's humming something that sounds like the music they play during football games on the sports channels. I don't know for sure, since I've been a football fan for all of three weeks, but I think that's where I recognize it from. It makes me smile. He's such a suave, confident man, but he's also not afraid to square dance with his grandparents and sing a little tune out here in the wild.

I wasn't kidding when I said this setting is enchanting. McGregor Tree Farm is straight out of a romance novel, and I make a mental note of my surroundings so I can record them and use them in a book somewhere down the line. The crisp blue sky. The feathered tree branches, coated with white snow. The well-trodden paths between the trees, filled with footprints of those out enjoying the tradition of cutting down their Christmas trees. It's this sort of place that I love bringing to life on the page because there's something so accessible about it for me, and I want to share it with readers. I want to make them feel like they're here when they read my tree farm scene.

The snow crunches under my boots, and without thinking, I bend and ball up a handful of it. "Hey, TJ?"

He turns, and I launch my snowball at him. It hits him in the stomach. He yelps. "What was that for?"

I grin. "Dad and I used to have epic snowball fights when we'd go tree shopping."

"In that case." He drops the saw and bends to collect some snow of his own. He launches a snowball at me, and I squeal, darting behind the trees to my right.

"You can run, but you can't hide, Lu," TJ taunts.

"Watch me!" I call out before ducking to get some more ammunition. When I stand and peek around the tree, my breath coming in quick bursts, I don't see TJ anywhere. I scan the tree line, and it's ridiculous that I can't find the giant football player somewhere around here. "Who's hiding now?" I call out.

"Not me!" TJ jumps out from behind the tree nearest to me and pancakes a snowball right on top of my head. The ice crystals cascade down my neck, getting inside my jacket.

I scream, my breath stolen by the cold. "You did *not*!"

"Sorry." He smirks, not looking sorry at all. He slings his gloved hands into the pockets of his jacket and rocks back on his heels. "This is something you should know about me: I'm fiercely competitive, and I play football in Green Bay, Wisconsin. Half our season is like one giant snowball fight, and"—he leans forward—"I always, *always* come out on top in snow games."

I pout, shaking the bottom of my coat out so the snow can escape. "Pretty confident in yourself, aren't you?"

"When it comes to taking you in a snowball fight? Yeah, yeah, I am." He grins.

"Well, then, you leave me no choice." I charge at him, letting out the cry of a snow-warrior. I open my arms out wide, going in for the tackle. I collide with his chest, and instead of taking him down into the snow, he barely budges.

I ram my shoulder into his abdomen and grunt, but rather than moving, his arms come up and wrap around me. He lifts me off the ground, hoisting me up so my face is level with his.

"TJ!" I squeal, kicking my feet but hitting only air. "Put me down. I was supposed to take *you* out."

He chuckles, and his breath is warm on my cheek. "You really thought you could, huh? Did you forget that I dodge grown men who are trying to tackle me for a living?"

I lean back so I can look into his eyes. "I was hoping to use the element of surprise in my favor."

His blue eyes dance, and I try to frown, but I can't help but smile.

I bury my face in the crook of his neck. "Don't make fun of me! I tackled my dad into snowbanks all the time, but I'm realizing now that's because he let me take him down."

I lean back, and TJ looks at me with warmth in his gaze. "We can go again, and I'll let you tackle me this time."

"Are you kidding? I'm better than a pity tackle, thank you very much." I stick my nose up in the air like I'm offended. "You can put me down, though. I'll plan a different form of attack. You better watch your back. I'm coming for you."

TJ loosens his grip, and I slide down his body. What a trip *that* is. I swear, I feel the ridges of his abs through our winter jackets, and his arms flex around me, making sure I land softly. Our eyes lock, and even after my feet are firmly on the snow again, TJ doesn't release his grip around my waist.

"I'll be looking forward to it." His voice is a low rumble, and his gaze flicks down to my lips. I lick them without thinking, and his eyes darken before bouncing back up and meeting mine. His arms tense around me, and I could so easily lean toward him right now. If he dipped his chin and I went up on my tiptoes, our lips would brush. There would be an explosion of color, like paint splattering the crisp white snow around us with bold, bright strokes. I've written this moment so many times, but the words on the page are like a drop of water in comparison to the ocean of feelings being this close to TJ is stirring up inside me. I'm hot and cold all at once, and it has nothing to do with the sun beating on my face or the melting snow making my back damp. I want to lean in, and I want to run away. I want him to kiss me.

His words from the night we met pop into my head: *I want to kiss you.*

He wanted me at the gala, when I was brave and outgoing and flirty and fun. Is it possible he could still want me now? Now that he knows I babble when I'm uncomfortable in conversations. That I made myself a public fool. That I'm awkward and not smooth at all.

A man who knows you. A man who'll savor you. Don't settle.

Those were his words, and all I can think now is that TJ *knows* me. He knows my secret life. He knows my past. I've shared more with him in the past few weeks than I have with anyone in years. Every time he looks at me, I feel like he's savoring me and desiring more of me. It's addicting, and I don't want to go back to anything less.

This was *not* supposed to happen. I'm not supposed to want him like this. We're friends, and that's enough for me. It has to be, and it *will* be.

I need to put the focus back where it belongs, and since I told TJ about my writing career earlier, it's only fair that I come completely clean. As my friend, he deserves to know the truth.

"I have another secret," I tell him, gazing up into his eyes.

His eyebrows hitch up, and his irises turn more navy. "You should definitely tell me. I love your secrets."

That shouldn't make me flush, but it does. As much as I don't want to step out of his embrace, I need to, because I need to get a grip on my discombobulated emotions.

I ease back and walk to where TJ dropped the sled and saw. He follows me and retrieves them. I head in the direction of the balsam firs, and he falls into step next to me.

He bumps his shoulder into mine. "I'm waiting."

I blow out a breath between my teeth. "Alright. Here goes." I wince. "I am *maybe* basing the main character in the book I'm drafting off of you." I press my lips together and cut a glance at him. "Please don't be mad."

His face goes from shocked to delighted to smug. "Are you kidding me? I'm honored!"

"Really? You don't care that I've been using you as inspiration without your consent?"

His eyes widen and then narrow. "Wait. *That's* why you said you needed inspiration the night we met?"

I nod and dip my chin, my cheeks flaming as those words he said to me play on a loop in my mind. *I want to kiss you. I want that very much.*

"Everything makes so much sense now." TJ's voice brings me back to the present. "So back there, with the butt slap and the snowball fight and the attempted tackle and the smoldering looks, were you acting out a scene or something?"

I swallow.

No.

I want to tell him that was all personal, but he's giving me an out, an easy explanation for the weird, blurred lines. I'd be stupid not to take it.

Also, he thinks I was smoldering? *Was* I smoldering? I can't explain why that makes my stomach tingle.

I shrug. "Kind of. I don't want you to feel like I've been using you. That's not my intention at all." I hear the desperation in my own voice.

"I don't feel used. But"—he wags his brows—"now that I know about this, I'm really going to have to turn up the charm. Give you a lot of material."

I cover my face again, and TJ laughs.

"Come on, there's nothing to be embarrassed about. I think I'll make for a great character."

"It won't be *you.* Though the guy's name is Theo," I say as an afterthought. At his shocked expression, I add, "I picked it before I knew that your name was Theodore."

"Freaky," he mumbles.

"Right?" I chuckle awkwardly. "Anyway." I hope he takes my cue that I'd like to change the subject.

He does not.

"So what's your pen name?"

"I'm not telling you that!" The thought of TJ reading my romance novels makes me want to crawl out of my skin. Why, oh why, did I have to blab to him about how I've never been kissed? If he reads my stuff, he's going to know I've never done any of the romance business myself, and it's going to color his entire perception of the story.

"Come on! You're basing a character off of me and not going to let me read it? What if you're slandering me?"

My eyes widen. "I would never."

He laughs. "Still. I want to read it!"

I squish up my nose. I've backed myself into a corner here, because TJ's right. He deserves to read the story that he inspired, whether it makes me supremely uncomfortable or not. The only person I have to blame for all of this is me. And maybe Cassie, for forcing me into going to the gala. Then again, if I hadn't gone, I wouldn't have met TJ, and I can't say I'm sorry about that.

I don't vocalize any of this right now. I'm not so fond of the idea of laying my muddled heart out for him to see in the middle of this Christmas tree farm, charming as the setting is.

I plaster on a mask of faux confidence and say, "Fine. I'll share a copy of the book with you after it's published, but that won't be till late next year."

"You're going to make me wait that long." TJ pouts.

"It'll be worth the wait. I promise."

The warmth in his gaze thaws the remaining bits of ice shrapnel coating my heart. "I don't doubt that."

Chapter 26
TJ

That escalated quickly. That's all I can think as Lucy holds the back door to my house open for me.

Five hours ago, I was on a date with another woman. Four hours ago, Anton texted me that Lucy was at Mood Reader. Three and a half hours ago, Lucy told me she's an author. I told her about Tess, and somehow, I felt lighter and more willing to get to living than I have in years.

So here I am, with a giant Christmas tree.

We stopped to get a tree stand on our way from Mapleton to Green Bay because I own no such thing. Lucy bustles inside with it now as I remain in the entryway of the living room.

"Can I take down your fake tree?"

"Please do." Gram scoots in the back door with Pa hot on her heels. "That thing is a bigger eyesore than Susie's carbuncle."

I wanted Lucy to have a full Christmas tree farm day experience, which is why I let my grandparents know I needed their help. They were all too willing to drive across town and meet us here for an impromptu tree decorating party.

Gram appraises the tree, giving it a nod of approval. "This will be quite an improvement." She hurries into the living room to help Lucy.

They move the table I had the old tree propped up on and get the stand situated. A minute later, I have the fresh tree in place. The spicy scent from the boughs and the crisp cold we brought in with us fill my small home.

"Looks good, son." Pa claps me on the shoulder. He doesn't say anything else. He doesn't have to. He knows this is hard for me. He's proud of me for taking this step. He and Gram—let's be real, mostly Gram—have been on my case about my lack of enthusiasm for the holiday season for several years.

I catch his eye, and questions furrow the lines on his brow, likely wondering what changed. Why did I suddenly let Christmas back into my life now?

The answer lies in the woman standing across the room, gently running her fingers over the needles on one of the tree's branches while Gram chatters away about her neighbor's hairless cat.

"The thing is mean, I tell ya. No one wants to visit over there. Pity the unsuspecting visitor who gets caught in that beast's crosshairs ... or lack of hair, I should say."

Lucy is being a good sport, making consolatory sounds in response. She reaches over to the bookshelf and moves the photo of Tess in the frame toward the front. She catches me staring at her, and she raises her brows, seeking permission. My entire body relaxes. It means a lot to me that she understands the line I'm straddling, trying to honor Tess while not overlooking her loss. It's something I'll navigate my whole life. Lucy seems to have a keen sense of how to help me walk this road.

"Who wants hot cocoa?" I ask.

Both Lucy and Gram's hands shoot up, and they dissolve into giggles like two peas in a pod. Something that was tightly wound in my chest loosens ever so slightly at the sight of them together.

"I'll take a mug, too, TJ."

I wrench my attention away from the women in the room and face my grandpa.

"I'm going to go grab that box of ornaments from the car." He starts for the door.

"Want me to get it, Pa?"

He shakes his head. "It's not that heavy."

Before I can argue, he disappears.

I begin assembling everything I need for hot cocoa. My store-bought mix is going to pale in comparison to the rich, chocolatey goodness we were treated to at McGregor's tree farm, but it's more about the thought, right? As the kettle is boiling on the stove, I check my phone.

Anton texted the group with Del, Poe, and me ... because of course he's going to make a big deal about me leaving Mood Reader with Lu in front of my closest friends.

Anton

How's your date, TJ?

I guess I should clarify ... the one with Lucy Dupree??

Del

Dude! Since when?!

Anton

Since he ditched his lunch date to come and see Lucy in Cashmere Cove. The two of them left together hours ago. <wide eye emoji>

Del

I can't believe you're holding out on us, Teej.

Poe

I'm all for this if it means you'll stop hanging around with jersey chasers.

Anton

Ditto.

Del

I third that. Don't leave us hanging. What's going on?

Anton

They're probably too busy making out for TJ to respond.

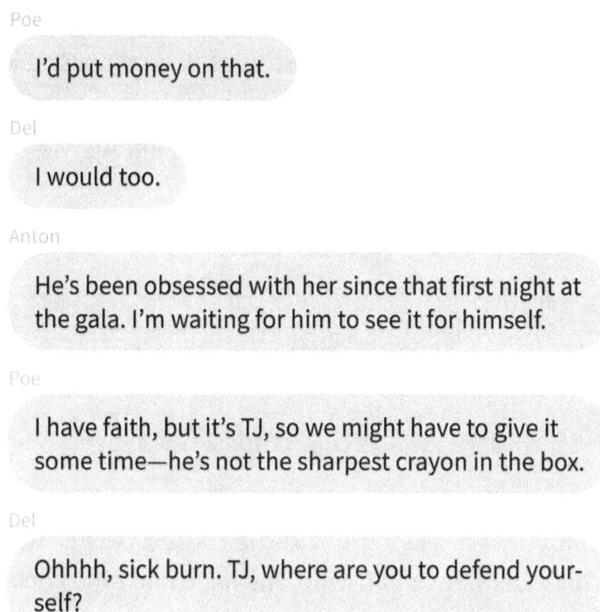

I roll my eyes at these hooligans, though I have to admit that their hypothesis about Lucy and me making out is reminding me yet again about how she told me she's never been kissed.

Today, out in the trees, I felt like we had a moment. A couple moments. The air was heated and taut between us, and a not-so-small part of me wanted to keep her in my arms and press my lips to hers.

Then she said I was her story inspiration, and now I'm not sure if any of what I was feeling can be considered real. If she was simply method acting—method writing, method brainstorming?—then she likely doesn't actually see me as someone she wants to kiss.

Then again, opening up to her and having her do the same made me feel like it was the two of us against the world. She promised she wouldn't leave. That has to mean something, right? But she could have meant she wouldn't let our friendship drop. We've established we're friends. That's all we've discussed. Aside from some flushed cheeks and longing glances at each other's mouths—not to mention the sensation of having her in my arms, which I won't forget anytime soon—things have remained completely platonic. It's all I wanted. Except with Lucy, and my new attitude regarding my past, I can't keep denying my change of heart.

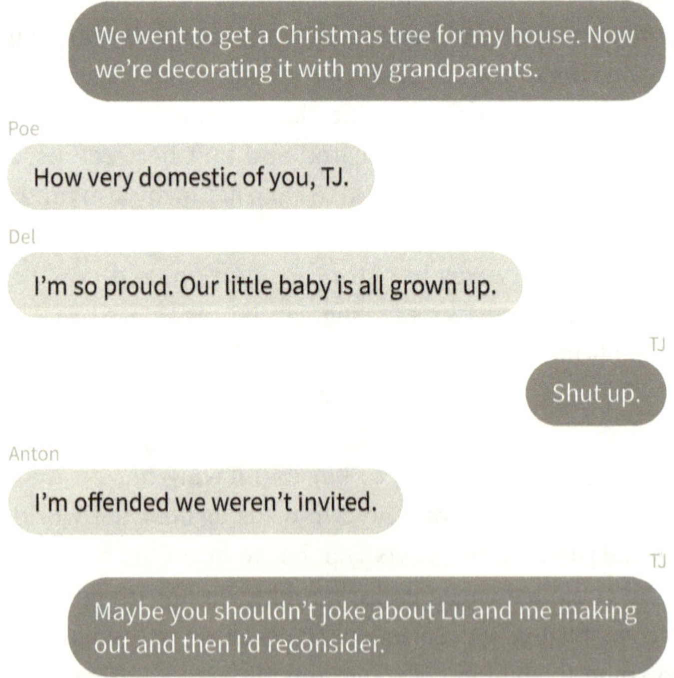

I snort out a laugh, pulling the kettle off the burner when it starts to whistle. I fill the mugs with one hand and type back with my other.

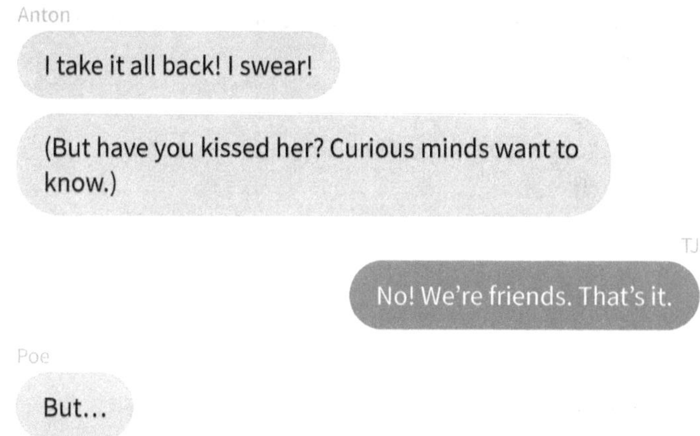

Darn it. Poe is the deep thinker of the group. Of course he's not going to let this slide. I don't understand how these men know what I'm thinking and through text message, of all things.

I scrape a hand down my face. I wish I knew what to tell them.

"TJ, everything good in there?" Gram's voice rings out from the living room.

"Yep," I call. "Be right there!"

I tap a final message out on my phone screen, because what else can I do?

I put my phone on the counter, but it buzzes right away in quick succession.

Anton

> We've got your back. Don't be afraid to take a chance with her.

Del

> I'm rooting for you two.

Poe

> Bring her to the game this weekend and my place after!

I sigh. I would love nothing more than that, but I don't know that *she* wants to come. She's hiding away. Granted, you can blend in in a football stadium, but she's Lucy Dupree. Gorgeous. Famous. Mysterious, thanks to her disappearance from the public eye. She's going to stick out.

TJ

> I don't know, guys. But thanks for being here.

Poe

> Just ask her!

Poe's last message rings in my ears as I load up the tray with four hot cocoa mugs and head back to face the explosion of Christmas that's happening in my living room.

"Oh good, TJ, there you are." Gram holds up a popsicle-stick angel with one of my grade-school pictures glued in place of the angel's head. "Look at this one. You made it in kindergarten!"

There's so much joy on her face that I feel guilty for the years I've spent not allowing her to celebrate this holiday because it was too hard for me.

I smile at her now. "Might have missed my calling as an artist."

Gram chuckles. "Stick to your day job, honey. You glued these sticks upside down. No one else's looked like this."

"It's called artistic expression, Gram. I was a savant even back then."

Lucy laughs lightly. Her cheeks are dusty rose and her eyes are bright. She thanks me for the hot cocoa when I hold out the mug. Her fingers brush over mine when she takes it from me, and a zip of pleasure flies up my arm. She sucks in a breath with enough force that I can hear it, which leads me to believe she also feels the crazy, electric connection coursing between us.

What does she want with it, though? Lucy told me in this very house the night of the Cinderella experiment that she didn't want anything more from me. Has that changed?

I take in the entire scene—Pa, stringing lights around the tree; Lucy, leaning toward my grandmother while Gram prattles on about another homemade ornament's origin story. Lucy's face is set in a soft smile, and she brings the mug of cocoa to her lips, nodding at something Gram said. I trace her movements, all velvety and sweet, and it's like a fire that had turned to ashes inside me ignites with the tiniest flicker of light. I want to pursue her, even though that means opening myself up to the possibility of loss. What I see now is how I'd also have the chance of gaining something truly great.

Chapter 27
Lucy

S itting in TJ's living room with his grandparents is the most comfortable I've felt in a long time. In the past nine months, certainly, but even before that. It's not that my stepmom and stepsisters aren't kind and welcoming. But this—sitting around, talking about old times, laughing and reminiscing, sipping cocoa and listening to Christmas music—is cozy in a way my life in California hasn't been since my dad passed.

It's simple and sweet, and I'm so grateful.

I look across the room at TJ, where he's dancing with his grandma to the low strains of Nat King Cole's "The Christmas Song." Loretta is about half his height, but she looks like she feels ten feet tall being in his arms. She pulled me aside before and thanked me for bringing their boy back. It made a wad of emotion clog the back of my throat, because I don't think I did anything. But this—TJ letting me into his home, letting me cut down a tree and decorate it—well, it's everything to me. He's letting me play my Christmas playlist, and every song brings me back to a memory I shared with my dad. It's bittersweet, but more sweet than anything to be given permission to enjoy it all here, surrounded by this family that so obviously loves each other.

I glance at the photo of Tess at the front of the shelf and say a quick prayer of thanks for whatever divine nudge TJ felt today to take a step back into the holiday spirit. I hope it's been a good step for him. His grandparents seem over the moon. I make a silent vow to continue to honor Tess's memory in any way I can, and to help TJ do so, too. From everything he's told me, she seemed like the type of person we could use more of.

My playlist switches to an Alvin and the Chipmunks song, and TJ wrinkles his nose. "Can this song even be considered music?"

I can't help but laugh, shaking my head in wonder. "You know what? My dad used to say the same thing."

It might seem crazy to say, but it feels like my dad had a hand in my meeting TJ. Like maybe he's up there in heaven, and he knew I needed a push. It was his chili recipe that kept the connection between me and the Wilsons going after the Cinderella stunt ran its course. I hope my dad would be proud of me trying to live and find joy despite some less-than-ideal circumstances this year.

TJ's gaze locks in on mine, and it's like he can see right through me. He crosses the room and reaches the pad of his thumb toward my face. "You've got some glitter here." The press of his finger is soft as he drags it across my cheek and then holds out the evidence for me to see.

"Thanks," I say with a shaky breath.

"You okay?" he asks, keeping his voice low.

Tears sting the backs of my eyes at his concern and his awareness. I don't know how he's so keyed in to how I'm feeling, but TJ continues to prove himself ridiculously good at reading me.

"Yeah." I nod. "I'm good. Thinking about my dad and feeling a bit overwhelmed, but in a good way. This has been the perfect afternoon. Thank you."

TJ shakes his head. His eyes never leave mine as he grabs for my hand. "I should be thanking you." He squeezes my fingers. "Thank you for holding space for Tess."

"You should always honor her however you can."

He flicks his gaze to the photo of her and then back to me. "I know. I will. My grief will always be with me in some way. But I don't want to stay there, stuck. Today, you helped me see that I owe it to her to live and laugh, which I guess I've been doing a decent job of," he says with a half grin before sobering. "But also, I think I owe it to her to try to love again."

My stomach does a swan dive to the floor before rocketing back up and settling at the base of my throat. "I—that's really good for you, TJ," I squeak out.

Really good for you? Come on, Lu. For someone who considers herself a wordsmith, what sort of pathetic response is that?

In my defense, I have no idea what to say to him. Is he implying that he wants to try to love again ... with me?

"It is good, I think," TJ says slowly, a small smile lifting the corners of his lips.

My pulse pounds in every corner of my body as he leans toward me. My senses are all on high alert. Is TJ going to kiss me, right here in the glow of the Christmas tree light? Would that be sort of perfect? Yes.

Wait.

No.

It would never work. Not with me hiding away and him in the public eye all the time.

Then again ... what if it *could* work?

If TJ can be brave enough to put himself out there to love again, couldn't I at least see if we could make a go of a relationship?

I hold my breath, cheeks warm with a flush of desire, heart hammering, and palms clammy. My eyelids flutter as he gets nearer to me, but I blink them wide open when I feel him bend to the side.

He reaches into the box of ornaments at our feet, and I press my eyes closed, hoping he didn't notice how I was leaning in. I take a second to collect my wits, but I don't have nearly long enough before he stands back up with the angel for the top of the tree.

"This was the tree topper my parents got as a gift for their wedding. Gram always told me it was a good reminder of the way they were looking out for me from heaven. I haven't gotten it out since Tess passed." He swallows, and my heart lurches toward him. I reach for his free hand, giving it a squeeze.

"It's beautiful," I tell him.

He stares at it for a second before blinking up at me. "You should do the honors, Lu." His low voice bowls me over, and even though he didn't kiss me, the way he's looking at me right now makes me weak in the knees.

All of that romantic stuff can wait. Right now, it feels like I'm watching healing in tangible, personified form.

I hesitate. "Are you sure?"

He nods and squeezes my hand.

"He absolutely is," his grandmother says as she joins us, tugging his grandfather in tow across the room. "He'll even lift you up to give you a fighting chance at reaching that top branch. Go on, TJ."

TJ shoots his grandmother a look I can't decipher before clearing his throat and turning to me, indicating my hips. "May I?" he asks, an adorable blush creeping up his cheeks.

I nod, not trusting my voice. He wraps his arms around my upper legs and lifts me up into the air. I try my best to focus on the task of placing the angel, but I'm acutely aware of the closeness of TJ's body to mine. This isn't the first time he's held me. I think back to the gala when he tossed me over his shoulder and brought me down from the scaffolding. Then my mind flits to earlier today at the tree farm. But this is the first time he's holding me since admitting that he's allowing himself to be open to loving again.

I get the angel in place, and TJ slowly lowers me to the ground, letting his arms linger around my waist, making sure I have my balance.

"Thanks," I whisper.

TJ's grandpa dims the overhead lights, and all four of us stare at the glow of the tree.

"It's perfect," Loretta whispers, like she doesn't want to raise her voice and risk disrupting the magical scene.

We stand in silence for a couple moments, each of us lost in our own thoughts as "Merry Christmas, Darling" plays over the speakers. The lyrics are all about wishing to be with someone on Christmas Eve. The song always makes me think of my dad, and then my mom, who I only know through the stories he told me. Tonight, after the rollercoaster day it's been, I can't help but be grateful for the people I *do* have with me. Cassie and Philly and Bex. My stepmom and stepsisters. And here, TJ and his grandparents. My heart swells because I know what TJ means when he says he doesn't want to stay stuck in his grief. Looking around, it's plain to see I have much to be thankful for.

When the song ends, TJ's grandpa flips the lights back on, and it's like I'm waking from a dream. I feel rested and at peace, like somehow everything's going to be okay.

TJ is watching me closely, and I offer him a small smile.

Loretta bustles about, cleaning up the mugs and the tissue paper remnants used to keep the ornaments safe in their box and ordering Martin around.

"Lu, dear. What are your plans for Christmas?" She pauses to look at me. "Are you headed home?"

I shake my head. "Not on Christmas. My family is filming an episode of their show, and we decided it would be better if I wasn't there."

Loretta frowns. "I don't understand."

I flick my gaze to TJ, and he shrugs. "Gram, Lu's family is sort of famous, but she's trying to stay out of the spotlight right now."

He looks to me for my approval, and I send him a grateful nod.

Right now. That implies that I won't be hidden away forever. How I want that to be true. The thought of putting myself back in the public eye makes me stomach flip uncomfortably, but I can't stay hidden forever.

Maybe someday I'll take back some ownership of my life ... but not yet.

Loretta arches her brows in TJ's direction, and Martin clears his throat. I look between the three of them, trying to decipher what I missed. "Everything okay?"

Loretta nods. "TJ has something to ask you about, so we'll leave you to it. Thank you for tonight and for letting us share in this. It's been lovely, but it's getting late, and we should go." She stops and hugs me.

Martin follows, kissing me on the cheek. "See you soon, I hope," he says with a wink.

Oh no. I'm going to get a pity invite to Christmas dinner, or something, aren't I?

They hustle out of the room before I can ask a clarifying question. I wait next to the Christmas tree while TJ walks them to their car, looking around to see if I can make myself useful, but there's nothing left to tidy up.

TJ returns, bringing with him the scent of awkwardness.

"You sure you're okay?" I ask, suddenly worried that all this Christmas was too much for him.

"Yeah, um. Yeah. I'm good." TJ finally meets my eye. He straightens his shoulders, as if making up his mind about something. "I was wondering if you wanted to come to my game this weekend."

Does he sound nervous? *I'm* nervous, so maybe I'm projecting.

"We play on Christmas morning," he adds, which is helpful for me because I didn't know they did football on Christmas Day.

"Oh, I—"

"No pressure. I know football isn't really your thing, and it's a huge crowd, and it's a home game, so it'll be freezing because it's December in Wisconsin. But"—he shrugs—"it'd be great to play for you. I mean"—he looks like a deer in the headlights as he course-corrects—"to play while having you watch, in person."

I chuckle softly.

TJ shakes his head. "I've been reduced to a babbling buffoon. This sort of behavior would be perfect for your book, wouldn't it?" He shoots me a wry grin.

"Well, now that you mention it." I tap my chin playfully. "Yes, it would be."

"Glad to be of continued service." He bows in an overdone way, and I laugh.

"Seriously, though." He pins me with his gaze again. "You're more than welcome to come to the game and the afterparty, if you want. My grandparents will be there."

"At the game or the afterparty." I raise a brow.

"Both. Gram and Pa can throw down."

"I never doubted them."

He smirks. "Honestly, the afterparty is a bunch of food ordered in at my friend Poe's condo. He has a huge gathering room he can rent, so we're all meeting there. Just my closest friends and their families—anyone in town for the game."

I nibble on my bottom lip as I turn this over in my mind. I want to be there for TJ. I'd love to spend more time with his grandparents, because I find them the perfect blend of hilarious and homey. It would be nice to meet his friends, too. But the thought of being surrounded by a bunch of other people I don't know and having them look at me makes me want to crawl out of my skin.

"I'll come to the game for sure," I say slowly, already thinking of my cold-weather gear. I can disguise myself well enough with something like what I wore today. "Can I let you know about the afterparty?"

TJ nods. "I don't want to make you uncomfortable. If it helps, know that my teammates would be cool. Rose Kasper will be there, so you'd know at least one other person. Plus me and Gram and Pa, of course."

"Of course," I say with a smile. "Thank you." I turn serious. "I was planning to spend a quiet day at the Inn, working on my story. I've got a lot of words to catch up on."

TJ assesses me. "Maybe you could get some inspiration from the game and the party."

I shrug. "Maybe."

Truth be told, I haven't thought much about my character, Theo, while spending the day with TJ, the real deal. The only time my book has been top of mind is when TJ has brought it up. Otherwise, I've been too busy savoring good times with good people. This must be what it feels like when reality is better than fiction.

Staring at TJ here in the glow of the Christmas tree lights, I'm half terrified, half thrilled to realize I want more of this real-life living. Interestingly enough, I'm also suddenly hit with ten plot ideas for my book.

"You alright?" TJ steps closer to me.

I blink. "Yeah, I'm good. I want to get to my computer. I have a story thread I need to tug on."

"Oh dang. This is it. This is how the magic happens, isn't it?" He crosses the room and retrieves my coat from the closet. "I feel like I'm witnessing the artistic process unfold before my very eyes."

I bundle up. "I don't think it's anything too crazy. Unless you think it's crazy that I'm going to type in my notes app while you drive me home so I don't forget this idea."

His eyes are wide and bright. "This is the coolest thing I've ever seen." He holds open the back door, shaking his head at me like I'm something that deserves marvel.

I blush. "Stop. It's really no big deal. I'm no big deal." I take a step out into the cold, but then get yanked back. TJ has a hold of my arm, and his gaze bores into mine.

"You're a big deal to me, and I won't have you saying otherwise about yourself." He leans forward, his face mere inches from mine, his eyes flashing with the fire of determination. My knees wobble as my gaze locks with his. "You've been filling your head with the words of people who are all too happy to tear you down. I'm about to change the narrative. Be prepared to hear me compliment you. Be prepared to accept my compliments. You'd better start believing them. Because you, Lucy Dupree, are a gem. Don't you dare let anyone, least of all yourself, dull your shine."

Dang.

"Can I use that speech in a book?" I squeak out, because my mind is short-circuiting as my heart does backflips inside my chest.

"Only if you promise me you'll try to believe every word of it."

I firm my lips and nod.

"Good." He smirks at me. "Come on, now. I hear creativity waits for no one."

Chapter 28
Lucy

I blink my eyes open and stare up at the ceiling of my room at Daisy's Inn.

"It's Christmas morning," I say aloud.

I went to church last night here in Cashmere Cove. I sat in the back, and everyone was so caught up with their families that no one paid me much attention. Mass was beautiful, with poinsettias surrounding the sanctuary and candles flickering in every window.

It was a tradition between my dad and me to go to Christmas Eve mass, and then have a slow Christmas morning, culminating with a big lunch and a birthday cake for Jesus for dessert. I allow myself a couple minutes to lie still. My mind conjures up the smiling faces of both my parents. My dad's favorite picture of him and my mom used to sit on our mantle. After he married Ruby, he gave it to me to keep in my bedroom.

I palm my phone on the nightstand next to me and click on my photos. I took a picture of a picture so I'd always have it with me. The two of them smile back at me from the screen. I zoom in on their youthful faces, their grins as wide as their cheekbones. Behind them is a sprawling tree farm with snow-dotted pines and a bright blue sky. I touch the screen, as if I may be able to actually feel them. Seeing them standing there, with their arms wrapped around each other, I realize the traditions my dad kept going for me were ones he and my mom started. I wonder if it was painful for him, doing what the two of them used to do together, alone. I never really considered it until now, and maybe it's because of everything that happened earlier this week with TJ and honoring Tess's memory, but there's something really beautiful about moving forward but carrying with you what got you this far.

The People's Picks are a part of my history now. I'm going to have to come out of the shadows eventually. At the thought, it feels like my mattress has turned into a pile of sticks. It's not a comfortable idea.

I blow out a breath. One thing at a time. Today, it's TJ's game. I promised him I'd be there, and this is the most public outing I'm attending since the award show, so it has to count for something.

"I wish I had the courage you had, Dad." I give the still shot of my parents' smiling faces one last look. "I miss you," I whisper, then click out of the photo.

I swing my legs over the edge of my bed and glance around my room. It's a disaster. That's how my living spaces end up when I enter what I call my writing cave. It's truly cave-like. There are take-out containers and used coffee mugs strewn about. A pile of laundry is thrown over the chair near the window. I've got Post-it notes stuck to the wall over my desk. Today, I'll enjoy Christmas. Tomorrow, I'll clean up.

My phone buzzes in my hand, and I look at the screen. I'm expecting to chat with my family in California, but it's not even seven o'clock, so there's no way they're awake right now.

TJ

Merry Christmas, Lu. You up?

My heart lunges in my chest.

Lucy

I am! Merry Christmas to you, too.

TJ

I'm outside. Want to let me in? I have a present for you.

I bolt upright. *Shoot. Shoot. Shoot.* I catch a glimpse of myself in the mirror over my dresser. I'm not in shape to entertain right now. My room is a disaster, so we'll have to stay downstairs. My face is also a disaster, and unfortunately, that has to come with me. I cross to the en suite bathroom while I type out a message.

Lucy

Give me five minutes.

TJ

<thumbs-up emoji>

I hurry to splash some water on my face and rid myself of the line of crusty drool that's running from the corner of my mouth to my chin when my phone buzzes again.

TJ

That thumbs-up emoji means I'm excited to see you.

I can't stop the goofy smile that spreads across my face. I stare at myself in the mirror over the pedestal sink, watching the blush rising into my cheeks. I tell myself not to overthink it, but the thoughts are being thought over and over again.

I let my fingers hover over the keyboard icons for half a second before deciding to be brave.

Lucy

Thanks for clarifying. I missed you this week. Be down soon!

I scramble back to my bedroom area and tug on an old sweatshirt over my pajama top. The flannel bottoms aren't the best fashion choice I could make, but they aren't the worst, either. I'm out of time, and mostly, I want to see TJ.

I pad down the stairs into the foyer of the Inn. It's quiet down here. I don't think Daisy has too many other visitors, though I'm pretty sure a couple families who are in town for the game are staying here. They're all still behind closed doors.

I exhale.

Anytime she gets new guests, I feel like I have to shrink away. It feels good to walk around without dodging glances.

TJ's silhouette darkens the glass sidelight window, and I flick the lock on the front door, giving myself a full view of him.

He's in head-to-toe River Foxes gear, from his branded gray sweatpants to his navy sweatshirt with the orange-and-periwinkle fox logo in the center. He's got a beanie on that's striped with all the team's colors.

"Morning, Lu." He grins down at me and holds out a box. "Merry Christmas."

"Thanks." I take it from him, shaking my head. "I didn't get you anything. Can you come inside for a second?"

"I don't have long," he says, even as he steps into the foyer. "I have to get back to the stadium."

He follows me into the hearth room. I set the box on the arm of the couch and sink onto the nearest cushion. He takes the upright chair to my right.

"Should I open it now?" My fingers toy with a rip in the corner of the wrapping paper. There's a slight gap in the paper on the side, showing a brown box underneath, and I can see the jagged edge made by the scissors line beneath the excess of tape being used to hold it all together. It's charming in its imperfection, and it makes my insides feel some kind of way to know, or at least to guess, that TJ wrapped whatever is in here all by himself. He didn't have some River Foxes staffer pull a gift together for me. This is all him.

I can't help but beam up at him when he nods and says, "Go for it."

I slip my finger under the frayed edge and rip the paper off the top of the box. The cover comes next, and I pull out a silky soft River Foxes jersey. "Number twenty-five." I hold it up and peek my head out from around the side of it, so I can see TJ's face. "I've heard he's pretty good." I wiggle my brows, flipping the jersey so I can see the back.

"Only the best for you, Lu."

I hug the jersey to my chest. "You didn't have to do that."

He shrugs. "I didn't want you to feel out of place at the game. I figured you didn't have a jersey, since you aren't much of a football fan."

"I'm a fan of yours."

A sly smile spreads across his face. "That's what I like to hear."

I make myself busy, running my hands over the fabric, tracing the letters of TJ's last name, and trying not to overthink how that last name will be on my back this afternoon.

Daisy bustles into the room, but stops short at the sight of us. "Oh, my dears. So sorry to interrupt! I didn't realize anyone else was up. Merry Christmas!"

"Merry Christmas, Daisy." I smile at my landlord and motion to TJ. "This is TJ Wilson. You may recognize him from the River Foxes."

Daisy beams. "I sure do. Welcome, TJ. It's a pleasure to have you here. Can I get either of you anything? I'm brewing some fresh coffee if you'd like a cup."

TJ shakes his head but smiles. "Thanks, but I can't stay long. Just wanted to get Lu her gift." He winks at me as he gets to his feet.

"I'll come and grab a cup after I see TJ out, Daisy. Thanks."

She nods. "Good luck today, TJ. Tell the team we're all rooting for ya."

"Will do."

TJ motions for me to go ahead of him, and I trail Daisy out of the room, pausing when I remember I want to retrieve the box and wrapping paper I left behind, but TJ has it in his hands. I smile at him as he joins me in the doorway. Such a simple thing, but the man is thoughtful like that.

"Hey, you two," Daisy trills from near the front desk. "Look up." She points above us and chortles before disappearing into the kitchen.

I look up and there, directly above where TJ and I are standing together, is a sprig of mistletoe. Immediate fire catches in my cheeks as I shift my gaze from the poison-kissing plant to TJ.

"Well, well, well," he murmurs. "What do we have here?"

I bury my face in my new jersey. "You do *not* have to kiss me."

"Okay." He chuckles.

I brave a glance at him, and he's looking at me with dancing eyes, like this is all hilarious to him. Little does he know I've been dreaming about kissing him since the snowball fight. If I'm being honest, it started before that, when he leaned in at the River Foxes gala.

I'm scared, and I'm self-conscious. I have zero experience, and he's TJ freaking Wilson.

"You look terrified," he says. "Don't worry, Lu. I'm not going to bite." He bends down. "I won't kiss you unless you ask me to."

Cue my heart doing some sort of record scratch. Because … what now? Is that an option? I need several more details and the permission to ask at least three clarifying questions, starting with TJ, *do you want to kiss me?*

He sets the box where he's stuffed the wrapping paper down at his feet and then holds up his empty hands. "You should see your face." He chuckles softly.

"This isn't funny!" I reach out and shove him, but he doesn't move. A wall of muscles wouldn't, after all. He catches my wrists, holding them in the center of his chest. My knuckles graze his sweatshirt, and my fingers itch to scamper over his chiseled chest.

"You've got to admit, it's a little funny." TJ holds my gaze, arching his eyebrows. "I mean, it's basically like a scene out of a book, right?"

I tip my head side to side, because he's not wrong. "I guess so," I admit. "I'd definitely write a killer mistletoe scene if given the chance."

He smirks, his gaze dropping to my lips. I lick them involuntarily, because my mouth is suddenly parched. When his eyes meet mine again, he's more serious. His Adam's apple bobs around a thick swallow, and his voice is low and restrained as he says, "I think I'd like to read that."

I slowly uncurl my fingers, letting my hands rest more fully on his chest. I can feel his heart beating through his sweatshirt, and it makes me feel bold.

"You seem pretty confident it would be a good scene." I slowly run my fingers in small circles around the upper part of his chest.

His breath hitches. "It feels like it would mostly write itself at this point, wouldn't it?"

I arch a single brow and hum. "I don't know about that. Why don't you tell me how you'd write it, TJ?"

His eyes darken, and then a flash of something that's like desire mixed with determination makes them glint. I can hear the blood thrumming through my ears. I keep my hands on his chest, bending my arms at the elbows as he steps closer to me.

"Let's see." TJ's voice is a low rumble as he speaks slowly, like he wants to get this exactly right. "First, I'd wrap you in my arms." He pulls me against him and folds me to his body, tucking my head under his chin. I sigh. He's so warm, and he smells so nice. "This way, you'd know that I was cherishing you, and that I want to be close to you."

"Mm-hmm." I don't trust myself to say anything else.

TJ dips his head and presses his nose into my neck, inhaling slowly, before tipping his mouth so he's speaking directly into my ear. My stomach bottoms out as he whispers, "It would also give me a chance to smell your sweet skin. There's something absolutely tantalizing about the smell of your skin, Lucy." His voice is sandpaper, smoothing out the coarse edges of my heart.

Is this man for real right now? I'm melting further into him, and I couldn't stop myself if I wanted to.

"I'd put my lips here." He moves his mouth to under my ear and speaks against the curve of my neck. "I'd kiss you on this smooth spot of skin, lingering a little while, because I couldn't get enough of you, and then—" He moves his mouth away, and I pull in a shuddering breath, because I *want* him to kiss me right there. Here, there, and everywhere.

He dips his chin and captures my gaze. His pupils are fully dilated and fully focused on me. His heart pounds wildly beneath my hands, and the only reason I'm still standing upright is that I'm grounded in him.

"—then I'd lean away like this and tell you I think you look beautiful in the morning."

A flicker of a smile twitches at the corner of his mouth, and I duck my head. I'm a mess, and I know it. In an instant, his fingers are under my chin, lifting it gently until I meet his gaze again.

"When you'd deny it, I'd tell you that, yes, you are beautiful, and I'd go on to tell you that I think your hair looks incredible up like that." He runs his finger from my chin, up my cheekbone, and over my nose. The callouses on his hands strike a match against my skin, and I'm bursting into fiery flames. "I like that I can see your full face, and these freckles, which drive me wild. I'd tell you that not only are you more beautiful than you think, but you're braver than you realize."

I bite my lip, and I didn't think it was possible, but his eyes darken further, and a low growl sounds from the back of his mouth. He brings his hands to my shoulders and massages them gently. "Even though I think you'd know it, I'd tell you that you're driving me out of my mind with want. All I can think about right now is kissing you, and I know once I do—" he clears his throat with a swallow "—once I *did*, one kiss would never be enough."

I pull in a deep breath, unable to speak.

TJ moves his hands from my shoulders to cradle my cheeks. "Then, I'd cup your face like this, and I'd lean in part of the way, taking it slowly and giving you a chance to stop me. Because this kiss has everything to do with you and what you want and how it's making you feel. You feeling cherished and beautiful and taken care of would be my entire goal. So ..." He stops, pausing with about an inch of space left between our mouths. My lips part in a gasp. "When I got to about here, I'd wait for you to close the rest of the gap, and—"

I am a millisecond away from doing just that when a squeal sounds from what feels like directly behind me.

"Dad! I'm starving! Hurry up!"

I jump away from TJ, and we spin to see a family of four come into view.

I quickly pull the hood up on my sweatshirt, and then I turn back to TJ.

He's got a dazed expression on his face, but then he blinks and smiles down at me. "How'd I do?"

"Um." I gulp. "Really well," I squeak out. "For an amateur, any-way."

His eyes flicker with heat and humor. "I'm happy to keep prac-ticing."

"Deal," I say on an exhale. TJ can explain-kiss me any day of the week, and it would probably be better than any real kiss I'd get from anyone else.

"Hey, is that TJ Wilson?"

My eyes bounce up and over to the family congregated by the coffee bar.

TJ holds up his hand in a wave. "Hey, guys, give me one second." He grabs the box and tosses my new jersey into it before taking me by the elbow and pulling me toward the staircase that leads up to my room. He uses his body as a partition between me and the family of fans. My heart swells.

"I'll see you at the game ... and maybe after?" he asks.

I nod, making up my mind then and there that I want to spend time with TJ. He'll take care of me and shield me from the public eye as much as possible. "I'll be there."

His shoulders relax, and he shoots me a grin. "I'll show off for you."

My cheeks flame. "I'll be watching closely."

He leans in. "Admit it. You really like how my perfect peach-shaped emoji butt looks in football pants, huh?"

I smack him in the chest. "TJ!" I hiss. "I can't believe I ever said that. I can't believe you *remember* that."

His eyes twinkle. "I remember everything, Lu."

Oh boy. Does that mean he remembers telling me he wants to kiss me? Does the sentiment still stand? Can I cash in on that ASAP?

He points to the box. "Wear that today."

"I will." I pull the box to my chest. "Good luck—and be safe."

He nods and stares at me for a moment longer, his gaze scanning my face and pausing on my lips for a second longer than the rest of my features. "See you later, Lu."

TJ turns and widens his arms to greet the anxious family. I use the opportunity to scamper back upstairs.

I close the door to my room behind me and rest my back against it before sinking to the ground and burying my cheesy grin into TJ's jersey.

Chapter 29
TJ

I'm usually pretty jacked on gameday, and this afternoon is next level. The residual effect of my time with Lucy this morning has seeped into my bloodstream, making me feel like I'm electrically charged. I'm even more energized than usual.

I bounce on my toes on the sidelines as I wait for my number to be called, signaling for me to head into the game. We're playing the team from Colorado. Our records are about the same so far this season, and we need this win to secure a first-round bye in the playoffs. We're mid-way through the second quarter, and the score right now is a tie. Seven to seven.

I pivot and look at the stands, up toward the box I'm sharing with Poe for our families. I can't see Lucy, but I know she's here, somewhere, with my name on her back. To be fair, there's a sea of people in the stadium with my name on their backs, but I don't care about them. I'm grateful for their support, sure, but they don't matter to me like Lucy does. I haven't paid attention to anyone wearing my jersey in years. Not since Tess would come to my college games.

I wait for the guilt to come, but it doesn't. Instead, as I close my eyes and blow out a breath to keep my adrenaline in check, I see a flash of Tess's smiling face in my mind. A wave of peace spreads over me, not unlike what I felt at the Christmas tree farm. Loving Tess was a gift, and it's as if now that I've owned that, spoken about her out loud and recognized how valuable the time I spent with her was to me, I can admit to myself that I don't want to live the rest of my life without striving for that type of connection again.

For a long time, I didn't think anyone would measure up to Tess, so I didn't even try. That, and I didn't want to open myself up to the hurt. But by closing off my heart to the pain, I've also closed myself off to the joy.

Lucy makes me want to love again.

Even though she told me when we met that she didn't want anything more from me, I can't help but hope that she's changing her mind. We've only talked about our feelings for each other in terms of a friendship, but if her reaction to me explaining how I'd write a kiss scene—which, let's be real, was me describing *exactly* how I want to kiss her—was any indication, our relationship is trending in the direction from friends to more.

I'm excited and scared to see where we end up. There's a very real possibility that Lucy could leave me. She's dealing with a lot in the aftermath of the People's Picks. Not to mention the fact that her family is in California, and my life is in Green Bay. We haven't talked about how long she's planning to stay in Wisconsin. We haven't talked about anything, but I'd like to think she'd give me—give us—a chance. I've maintained for years that I'm fearless, when in reality I've been living in the fear of losing another loved one. I'm ready to hope again. I want to be brave. In honor of Tess. And because Lucy is worth it to me.

I blink and look up at my box, hoping to catch a glimpse of Lucy. This time, I'm rewarded when I spot her next to my grandparents. She's wearing my jersey over her winter coat. She's got her scarf wrapped around her mouth, like when we were at McGregor's Tree Farm.

"Wilson, you're up!" My running back coach slaps my shoulder pad, and I tune into the game. A couple of my teammates jog off the field, and I get the play call from my coach and run to the circle of my teammates gathered around Anton.

"You good, Teej?" Anton asks, his eyes on the cheat sheet wrapped around his wrist.

I nod. "I'm great."

He calls out the play. The ball's at midfield, and it's third down and four to go. We're in the perfect position to run this draw play. The defense will be off balance, unsure whether we're passing or running the ball. Hopefully we can catch them on their heels. So far, I haven't been able to break off a long run, but I'm itching to get the ball in my hands again. I feel like I could fly, so if I get an opening, I'm going to soar through it, channeling the boost in energy that's in large part thanks to Lucy and making it count for the team.

If it impresses the girl I'm trying to impress, all the better.

Anton breaks the huddle, and I settle into my position, crouched about five yards behind where he's standing under center. Del hikes the ball and Anton drops back, selling the throw like it's his job. He's the best in the business. In my periphery, I see that the safeties are dropping back because they think he's about to pass the ball down field, but at the last minute, Anton drops out of his throwing stance and hands the ball to me.

I don't hesitate. The offensive line has created a hole you could drive a truck through, and Poe is blocking his man, allowing me the space to get into open field. I let my body take over, driving my knees and sprinting like I always do, holding nothing back and leaving it all on the field behind me.

Fifty yards later, I'm in the endzone. I slam the ball into the ground and it spikes back upward. Someone grabs under my arms and hoists me up from behind. The crowd is absolutely feral, and the noise is deafening.

"Heckuva run, Teej." Poe sets me down on the ground.

I spin and face him. "Will you pretend to be my Cinderella one more time?"

His eyes roll behind his face mask, but he obliges. We go through our little routine, which ends with me hoisting him off the ground and spinning him around.

"This is getting old," he mutters, but he's smiling.

"When are you going to make a move with your real Cinderella?" Anton joins us, and we tap each other's helmets.

"Yeah, man. I'm ready to hand over the reins to Lucy," Poe adds.

I grin and spin to face my box, where I see Rose has joined Lucy, my grandparents, and Poe's family. His sister is here with her daughter. The three of us point up at our people. Anton blows Rose a kiss. Poe makes a heart with his hands. My heart wants to explode out of my chest because of how badly I want to do *something* for Lucy. Something to show her how much she's coming to mean to me, but ... baby steps. For now, all I do is wave in her direction. I let my gaze linger on her as she waves down at me.

I jog off the field with Anton and Poe.

"Soon," I tell my teammates. "Hopefully very soon."

Chapter 30
Lucy

I don't think I'll ever be warm again, but it's worth the perpetual frostbite nipping at my fingers and toes to have witnessed TJ playing in person. The River Foxes Stadium is a venue unlike any other. Thousands upon thousands of fans *willingly* sitting on ice-cold, hard bleachers for a three-hour game? Are they crazy? Maybe. No one can argue with their commitment. Even when the River Foxes had the game under control early in the fourth quarter, no one left before the clock read zero.

I could have taken a break in the box and warmed up, but I didn't want to take my disguise off. It's difficult to explain why you're fully scarved with sunglasses on when indoors, and I didn't want to have to try.

I'm sitting in my car in the underground parking structure of Lawrence Poe's condo complex now. Freezing, but happy. It felt good to be there for TJ today, and if I'm being honest, I'm even more excited to see him tonight. Even if there are other people around. TJ has assured me that his friends are safe and that their families are good people. At some point, I'm going to have to trust him if I want to make this—whatever *this* is—between us work.

My nerves are on edge because the last time I spoke to him, the last time I saw him, he basically turned me into a puddle of love mush with his words. I would very much like to continue that moment immediately and then again and again, but I don't know how to do that. Or how to broach the subject with him. He's TJ Wilson—he could have his pick of any woman. I've told him on several occasions that I wasn't interested in a romantic relationship. We might have friend-zoned each other. Which was real stupid of both of us, if you ask me.

I square my shoulders. I'm going to walk into this party with confidence. I'm going to try my best to be how I was the night at the gala, even without the mask.

My phone buzzes on the console, and I pick it up to find a new text message in my group with Cassie, Philly, and Bex.

Bex

> Merry Christmas to my favorites! Lu, saw you on TV looking like a true fan!

> I mean, I only knew it was you because I know you, but still. There you were!

She sends a photo that she took of her TV screen. She's outlined my bundled-up body in yellow, as if I'd have any issues picking out the abominable snowman in the box.

Philly

> Aww, I missed this. Bex, since when do you watch football?

Bex

> Richie had it on. I was mostly watching for Anton and Rose content. Love those two.

I huff out a laugh and then tap out a message.

Lucy

> I'm about to see Rose and Anton. Should I ask for an autograph?

I'm being facetious, but Bex's response comes in too quickly for her to be kidding.

Bex

> Would you? Please!?

I shake my head.

Lucy

No! That would be weird. They're TJ's friends. I'm not going to fan girl.

Bex

<pouting face emoji> I thought *we* were friends, Lu!

Cassie

Glad you're getting out there, Lucy! Hope the game was fun. Where are you now?

Lucy

Afterparty at one of TJ's teammate's condos.

Philly

Does this mean you're more than friends with that hunk of burning love? <fire emoji> <hands covering face emoji>

I splutter out a laugh to my dashboard because it's hilarious that sweet little Philly would be talking about anything being a hunk of burning love. She's like an innocent lady from the 1800s, all steeped in propriety and morality.

Lucy

We're just friends …

Bex

I sense a but. Please tell me there's a but coming. Gimme the but.

Cassie

Quit saying but.

Bex

Not until Lucy confirms there's a but!

Why is TJ's very nice rear end the only thing I can think about right now? I shake my head. I will *not* be typing anything peach-related to my friends.

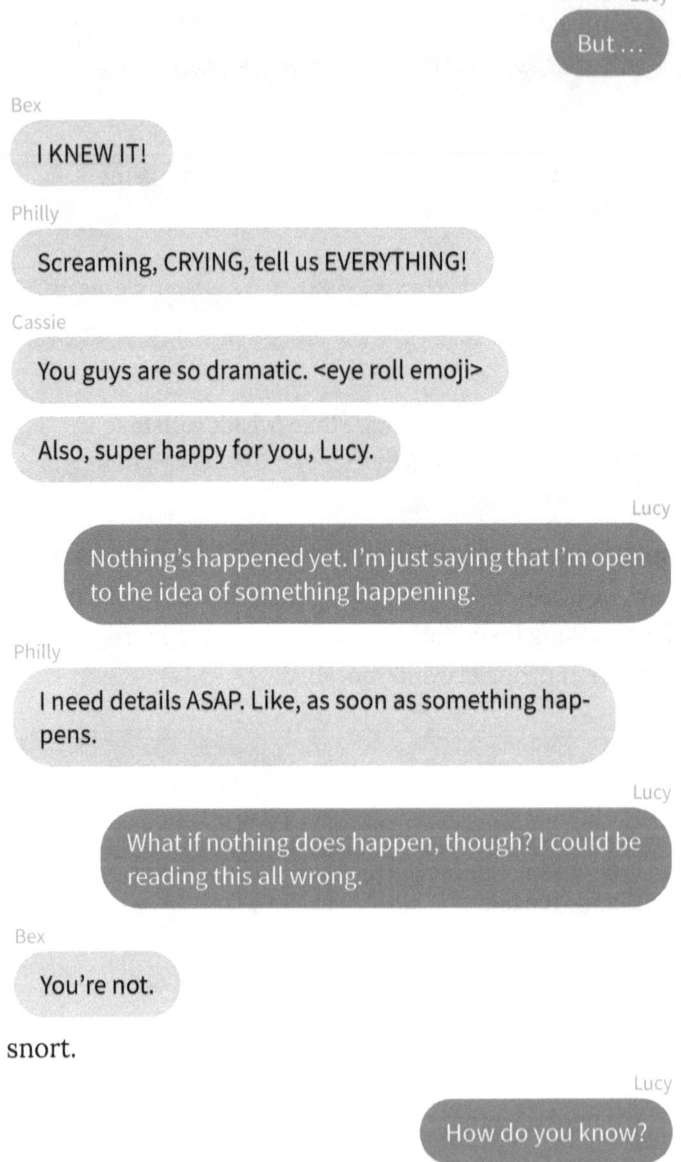

I snort.

Bex

Because any man would be a fool not to want some-thing with you. You're smart and fun and gorgeous, and you've got this big, big heart just waiting to love and be loved.

Philly

Bex, that's so beautiful!

Bex

<eye roll emoji> Tell me you're not crying, Phil.

Philly

I could tell you that, but it wouldn't be true.

Cassie

We're happy for you, Lu. Go get your man!

Lucy

Love you all!

I click out of our message and am about to stow my phone in my purse and finally leave my warm vehicle when my phone rings. It's Cassie.

"Hey, Cass. Everything okay?" I'm immediately on edge. We rarely talk on the phone. Plus, we were just texting, so this feels significant.

"Everything's fine," Cassie assures me. "Sorry, I don't want to keep you from your party, but I wanted you to know, as your agent, that there are articles circulating about you."

"Wait." I frown. "About Ava Reese? Or about Lucy Dupree?"

"About Lucy Dupree."

My skin prickles uncomfortably, and not from the cold. Dread pools in my stomach. "How do you know? What have you seen?"

"I have alerts set up for all my clients' names, so I get notified when any news is published about y'all." Cassie says it like it's no big deal, but it's another reminder that she's the best at her job, and I'm so dang grateful to have her as my agent. "For you, I get alerted for both your pen name and your real name. In this case, Lucy Dupree pinged. It's super minor—nothing to make a big deal of—but I know how much you value your privacy, and I want you to have all the information so you can decide how you want to go public with TJ ... *if* that's what you decide to do."

I blow out a long breath. "I'm overwhelmed," I admit.

"Hey, it's okay, Lu. As I said, this isn't a big deal; it's just a whiff of news. I'm going to send you the article so you can see for yourself, and then you can decide how you want to go forward, okay? I'm here for whatever you need."

I nod, and when I realize Cassie can't see me because we're on a stupid phone call, I say, "Thanks, Cass. You're the best."

"Everything's going to be okay, Lu. Better than okay. Don't let this change your feelings where TJ is concerned. I can tell you like him."

"Is it that obvious?"

"Only because he's gotten you out of your room more in the past three weeks than anyone's been able to do in the past nine months."

I consider this. TJ has made me feel both alive and taken care of. I've felt safe with him and his grandparents in a way I haven't felt in a long time. I've cherished the time I've gotten to spend with them. I love being in a bubble with TJ and his people. I only hope we can keep it that way for a while longer.

"Thanks for telling me about this, Cass. I'll talk to you soon, okay?"

"Okay. Love you, Lu. Have fun tonight."

"I will."

We hang up, and a second later, a link comes through. It's an article about the celebrity sightings at this afternoon's football games. There's an entire section on Rose and her relationship with Anton, along with a photo of her in the booth. It must have been taken around the time Bex took the photo of her TV screen, because I'm standing behind Rose. In the follow-up photo, Rose has pulled me forward, her arm draped around my shoulder. It was right after TJ scored his first touchdown of the day. We were celebrating together. The caption below the photo reads: *Mystery woman joins River Foxes families in the box. Does TJ Wilson have a new girlfriend?*

I let some air escape between my teeth. That's nothing too terrible or incriminating. I study the photos of me, and I don't think anyone would be able to pick out identifying characteristics linking me to TJ or to the River Foxes at all.

I frown when I realize that my name isn't mentioned, and yet Cassie still got an alert. I skim the rest of the article and scroll down to the comments, and that's when I see it. It's from a username called PopCultureFinatic007, and it reads: *Unhinged hypothesis, but does anyone else think the woman in the photo with Rose Kasper looks an awful lot like Lucy Dupree? We haven't seen her in months. Could she be cozying up with some pro footballers in Wisconsin? It sounds far-fetched, but honestly, I can kinda see it. Thoughts??!*

I reread the comment a couple times. It's been liked by a dozen other readers, and there are a couple replies. A few concur, and a few say PopCultureFinatic007 is reaching.

I give myself a second to digest this. It's like Cassie said. Nothing earthshattering. A good reminder nonetheless of how TJ's life is scrutinized down to the inch, and that's how my life was and would be again if I stepped back into the public eye.

I shove my phone into my bag. Rose told me to pack a swimsuit, but as I step out into the frigid outdoors, there's no way I'm going to want to put that on.

I make it to the side entrance of the condo complex, and the door opens. Loretta and Martin are standing in the entryway with matching grins on their faces. TJ is behind them, and he waves.

"Hello, dearie. You made it." Loretta opens her arms, and I step into a hug, feeling some of the stress and ick from the article melt away.

"I did." I lean out of the hug and smile at her, but then I frown when I realize she and Martin have their winter jackets on. "Are you leaving?"

Martin nods. "Gotta get this one home at a decent hour. Can't trust her after dark."

Loretta harumphs. "You like me most after dark, you big tease."

My cheeks flush.

TJ palms his face. "O-kay. That's enough of that, you two."

Loretta grins. "Anywho, we wanted to make sure we saw you. I hear you're going back to California for a bit."

"That's the plan. I'll see my family ahead of their New Year's Eve commitments. I should be back here by Thursday."

"TJ has an away game," Loretta says. "You can watch with us at our place if you're interested. No pressure, but you're always welcome."

"That's so nice." My heart pinches. I want to be part of that. I want to be around these people who are so kind and fun and caring. "I'll get in touch when I'm back in town, and we can sort out the details."

"Excellent." Loretta pats my arm as she walks by me, Martin trailing after her. "Bye, Lucy," he says, and then he leans in. "Take care of that boy's heart for us, will ya?" His voice is low, for my ears only.

Before I can respond, TJ steps forward. "I'm going to walk them out to the car. Wait here for me? I'll bring you into the party as soon as I see them on their way."

I nod and watch as the trio ventures out into the cold, wondering if it's possible that I could fit into their life in the way my heart longs to.

Chapter 31

TJ

I jog through the underground parking structure after making sure my grandparents find their way to the exit, returning to Lucy in under five minutes. She's right where I left her, and I exhale a relieved breath. I don't know where I thought she would have gone, but I'm still getting used to having someone be here for me.

Lucy looks up from her phone, her brows creased, but her expression clears and she smiles at me. "That was fast."

"Why do you sound surprised? I am one of the fastest men in the NFL, Lu. You saw me today."

"I did." Her eyes twinkle, and a warm pink hue colors her cheeks. "You're kinda hard to miss out there. You looked good."

"Past tense?" I grab for my heart, pretending she wounded me. "What about now?"

"Now you look like someone who's fishing for a compliment."

I laugh. "Pathetic?"

She considers me, fighting back a smile. "Endearing." She stares at me while twiddling with her phone case.

"You alright?" I ask. While I like this fun, playful side of Lu, I can tell she's got something on her mind.

She bites her lip, and I have to hold back a groan. This woman has no idea how tantalizing that sight is. It takes every ounce of self-control I have not to lean in and kiss her senseless.

When she meets my gaze again and I see the flecks of worry in her hazel eyes, all of my desires are replaced by one—to do whatever she needs me to do to take care of her and get rid of whatever is making her sad.

"It's no big deal." Lucy holds up her phone. "I … there's an article online, and one of the commenters is speculating that it was me at your game, in the box with Rose." She clicks the screen a couple times before angling her phone toward me.

I take it and scroll, guilt stacking up in my chest like cement bricks. "I'm so sorry. I shouldn't have invited you. I shouldn't have made such a show of pointing at you and waving. This is all my fault."

"TJ." She puts her hand on my forearm and squeezes. "No, it's not."

I shake her off. "I was being selfish. I wanted you there. I drew attention to you. I … I should have thought more about what you wanted. You've told me you don't want the attention, and I shone a light on you. I'm a fool."

"TJ." She takes her phone back and pockets it, returning her hands to my upper arms. I flex involuntarily. She smirks. "Are you showing off?"

"What?" I barely process her comment, but then I really look at her and she's smiling. Her eyes are twinkling. I take a deep breath.

"These muscles? You trying to make a girl swoon?"

"I … no." I sniff out a laugh. "But good to know that's what does it for you."

She grins before squeezing my arms again and turning serious. "Listen, you asked me what was wrong, and I wanted to tell you because I like that you care. I didn't tell you so you'd feel sorry. There's nothing to forgive. I chose to come to the game. I knew the risk of being out in public, and I opened myself up to being discovered. Because I wanted to be there. For you."

Her words coil around my heart like warm steam wafting from a mug of hot coffee on a cold morning.

She gives me a soft shake. "I promise I'm good."

"Okay." I nod. I want to trust her, and I need to take her at her word. But while she's talking a big game, I can see by the way she's chewing the inside of her cheek and the pallor of her skin that she's not unaffected by this. "What can I do? Do you want to leave?"

"No." She shakes her head. "I really don't." She stands up straighter. "I want to be here with you. To celebrate your win and to celebrate Christmas."

"If you're sure."

"I'm sure. Now ..." She pins me with a look, her eyes sparkling. "I believe we left off with you fishing for compliments."

"I would never."

She laughs, and it makes my heart beat faster. "Either way, I want to tell you that what you do out there on the field is wickedly impressive. And very attractive."

It's adorable how that last statement makes her face flush. What's even more enticing is the way she's holding my gaze. She's self-conscious, but still putting herself out there for me, and I am here for it.

"I was showing off for you. I wanted to make it into the end-zone in your honor," I admit, and then I lean in. "But football's just a game. Trust me, I'm even more determined when there's something important on the line."

She inhales. Her face is flaming, but she still holds my gaze. "What type of thing is important to you, TJ?"

"Right now? Time with you," I say without hesitation. "Poe has a great hot tub set up." I try to keep my tone casual, but I very much want to have her all to myself.

Lucy rolls her lips into her mouth again, considering this, and I can't stop the audible growl that escapes from the back of my throat. Lucy's eyes widen.

"Only if you're comfortable with that," I hurry to add. I'm not trying to force myself on this woman. "The hot tub would give us some privacy, and I'd really like to spend time with you."

Lucy searches my gaze, her eyes flitting across my face. "I'd like that too. But," she says, "we should mingle with your friends a little bit. I want to meet them, and I don't want anyone to think I'm ignoring them."

I smile down at her and grab her hand, placing a quick kiss on her knuckles. "Thank you for that. I'm really glad you're here."

"I am, too."

Anticipation flows through my veins as I lead her into the party room. We stop so I can introduce her to Poe. He's sitting on the floor, playing with his niece, but he stands when we approach, and his sister swoops in to watch over the young girl.

"Lu, this is the man who's been making the Cinderella bit happen on the field."

Poe rolls his eyes. "About that. Do you think we could do something else? Literally anything else?" He holds out his hand. "It's nice to meet you, Lucy."

"You too," Lucy says. "Sorry this one roped you into his tomfoolery."

I pretend to scowl. "That tomfoolery gets eaten up by our fans. I thought you liked it." I stare down at Lucy.

She shrugs. "It's not very original."

"See!" Poe points at me. "We can be done. I'm picking the next routine."

"Only if you score. That's the deal. If I score, we're doing Cinderella. It's a good luck charm at this point."

Poe scowls. Lucy surprises me when she pats him on the shoulder. "You're a good sport for putting up with this one."

Poe huffs. "Tell me something I don't know."

Lucy giggles, and a flash of jealousy pierces my core at the sight of her small hand on Poe's muscled arm. I know that's stupid, but it's like seeing this woman around another man has taken me back to caveman times. Poe smirks in my direction, like he can read my mind, but I don't even care.

I finally exhale when Lucy drops her hand and twines her fingers with mine again.

Someone calls for Poe from across the room. He looks past me. "I think my sister needs something. Make yourselves at home, and, Lucy, seriously, we all appreciate *you* putting up with this guy." Poe grabs my shoulders and gives me a good-natured shake as he takes his leave.

When he's out of earshot, Lucy rises up on her tiptoes, and I bend toward her. "For the record," she whispers, her warm breath against the shell of my ear sending lightning through my veins, "I love the Cinderella routine. Please don't stop."

Before I can respond, someone calls out her name, and her attention is drawn to where Rose is standing with Anton near the door to the deck. Since the hot tub is out there, I'm more than happy to move in that direction.

"You're never going to believe this," Rose says when we join the pair. "Oh." She glances at Anton and then motions to Lucy. "Anton, this is Lucy Dupree. Lucy, this is my boyfriend, Anton."

Lucy's face turns scarlet again, and I recall her saying that she settled in this part of the country because of Anton and Rose's love story. The green-eyed monster in my chest roars to life again, but I try to squash it.

"Hi." Lucy holds out her hand, and at the quiet sound of her voice, I'm immediately reminded of what she told me—about how she considers herself a lone wolf and prefers small groups of people whom she knows. She's here tonight, making the rounds with me and putting herself out of her comfort zone. My respect and appreciation for her increases tenfold.

"Between Rose and TJ, I feel like we're already best friends," Anton says. "They've had nothing but good things to say about you, Lucy."

"Oh." Lucy laughs a little, shooting me a wide-eyed look. "That's good, I guess."

I roll my eyes. "Way to make me sound like I'm obsessed with her, Bates."

"If the shoe fits," Anton says with his too-handsome grin. "She is your Cinderella, after all."

"Dude." I huff out a laugh. I look over at Lucy to see if he's freaking her out, but she smiles at me, looking bashful but happy. I squeeze her hand and she squeezes back, and my heart threatens to jackhammer itself out of my chest.

"Okay, as I was saying," Rose cuts in. "You're never going to guess the email I just got!"

Lucy tears her gaze from me and cocks her head to the side. "I'm listening."

"It's from Philomena Grace's agent." Rose is practically vibrating with excitement. She glances at me. "Philomena is one of *the* romance author icons of our time. I mean, her and Ava Reese, but Ava doesn't do interviews. No one knows who she is or where she lives or anything. Anyway, back to Philomena." Rose sucks in a breath, and I cut a look to Lucy, who bites her lip, and when she catches my eye, she looks away quickly. I fight a smile, committing the name Ava Reese to memory. "Her agent, Cassie, emailed me this morning. She apologized for the holiday email, but she wanted to reach out immediately, because Philomena had an opening in her schedule for April, and she was wondering if Mood Reader would want to host her. Can you even believe that?" Rose squeals. "It's like a Christmas miracle."

Anton pulls her to his side and kisses her temple. "I'm so happy for you, Sammy Rose." He starts to trail a line of kisses down her cheek, but Rose swats him away. He looks offended until she glances over at him and winks.

"That's incredible," Lucy says. "You'll have to let me know when she's here so I can put it on my calendar. I'd love to come."

"I absolutely will. It's going to be huge for Mood Reader. I can't wait to start planning a giant party."

"I like parties. Maybe I should tag along," I put in.

"The more the merrier, TJ. You a big romance reader?" Rose asks.

I side-eye Lucy. "I've been thinking about becoming one recently."

Rose glances between the two of us. "That tracks."

"You two want to hit up the hot tub?" Anton asks, hooking a thumb over his shoulder. "Looks like it's empty at the moment."

God bless him. Maybe he is more of a wingman than I give him credit for. Then again, he's a man in love, and he's been harping on me about how great it is to settle down with a good woman for months. Since meeting Lucy, I don't disagree.

"We were thinking about it," Lucy says, shooting me a shy glance.

Rose hooks her arm through Lucy's. "I'll show you where the bathrooms are so you can change."

"That would be great." Lucy looks over her shoulder at me as Rose leads her down the hallway. "See you out there?"

All I can do is nod.

"Dude," Anton says, laughing. He slaps me on the back, startling me from the trance Lucy put me under. "You've got it bad, and I am *here* for it. How soon is too soon to say I told you so?"

I shake my head. "It's too soon. I need to convince her to take a chance on me, Bates. I need to take this slow."

He nods solemnly. "Let me know if you want any tips."

"I'm not coming to you for romance tips."

Anton shrugs. "Your loss."

"Yeah, yeah." I make my way around him. "I'm going to change. I don't want to leave Lucy alone."

Anton snorts. "More like you miss her already, don't you?"

Guilty as charged.

I hurry away from the sound of Anton's knowing laughter.

When I climb into the hot tub a few minutes later, Lucy is already sitting on the far side. I can't help the groan that escapes as I sink into the bubbly water, closing my eyes. My muscles are knotted and sore from three hours on the field this afternoon. "This feels amazing," I breathe.

Lucy doesn't respond, and I blink to find her looking dazed. "You—your tattoos."

I look down. "Oh, yeah. I have a lot. Is, uh, that not something you like?" That could be a problem. I cock my head to the side. "Wait. Didn't you do your research on me after we met?"

She swallows and shakes her head. "No, I mean. Yes. I like them. And yes, I did." Lucy looks away, and my stomach bottoms out, but then she meets my gaze again. "I saw the tattoos in the photos, but I stopped short of studying them. It didn't feel right to ogle when I knew who you were but you didn't know who I was."

In a day and age where pro athletes are objectified for our bodies—and to be fair, I've leaned into that narrative in the past—it's nice to hear about someone holding something sacred or respecting me enough to at least want to get to know me before they examined me. I'm weirdly touched by that.

"Would you like to look at them now?"

She bobs her head, and I slide around to her side of the hot tub.

"I've been getting tattoos since I turned eighteen. Gram about had a heart attack when I came home with my first one." I tip my body to the side so Lucy can see my shoulder blade.

Lucy turns, her bare arm grazing mine. Goosebumps erupt on my skin, which is ridiculous given that we're in a hot tub, but there's no stopping it. Lucy is apparently too stunned to notice.

"Wow. It's ... wild."

I look over my shoulder at her to find she's trying to suppress a smile. "Was that supposed to be a pun?"

"Would you have preferred me to roar?" Lucy lets a smile break loose on her face, and I laugh.

"You can see why Gram lost her mind."

"The artwork is actually incredible." Lucy presses her hand to my arm and tilts me forward so she can study it again. The soft touch of her fingertips makes me lose my breath for a moment. "It looks like it's ready to pounce. Like it could leap off your skin." Her hand slides down my arm, leaving a trail of fire in its wake.

"I can't say I'd get the same tattoo if I were going in for one today, but I don't regret this one. It's big and daring, sure." I shrug, thinking back to the kid I was walking into the tattoo parlor at eighteen. "That's what I was going for. I graduated from high school and was off to college, walking on to the football team. My parents were gone, but my whole life felt like it stretched out before me. I had nothing figured out, but I wanted to live big and bold, with no fear. I thought if I did that, I could really be something, you know? The tiger is who I wanted to be."

There's something intimate about showing my tattoos to Lucy like this, here and now. Just the two of us. I glance over to find her staring back, and I'm suddenly insecure. The tiger tattoo is outlandish. In those online articles critiquing my body, it's often what commenters say downgrades me in my overall sex appeal. I don't really care what those people think, but I *do* care what Lucy thinks.

"You probably think that's juvenile," I add with a nervous chuckle.

"Not at all." She shakes her head. "I'm glad you told me about it. I like hearing the story behind it. I like when things have meaning." She scans my upper chest and then tentatively reaches out and places her finger on a set of Roman numerals, touching them so delicately. There's no legitimate reason I should feel her fingerprint like a stamp to my heart, but I do. "These numbers must be significant."

"The first two are my parents' birthdays." I watch her trace over the important dates of my lifetime. "Then the date they died. I added my grandparents' birthdays over here, along with the date

I got drafted by the River Foxes. My plan is to add to the lists when formative or impactful things happen to me. Things I want to remember and that are a part of me, in a way."

"That's really beautiful," Lucy whispers.

I swallow hard. Sitting here with Lucy—it's the first time in a long time I've let myself think about adding the date of my marriage. The thought of having children and including their birth dates makes my vision swim. I blink back my tears, lifting my hand and covering her fingers, pressing them to my chest.

We sit in silence, my heart hammering away under her palm. My head is spinning with thoughts of the past, and everything that got me to this point, while also churning ahead, sprinting toward an unknown future. I close my eyes and tell myself to be here now, in this moment with Lucy. I look at her and she smiles softly, holding my vulnerability like it's a treasure. I want to pull her closer, but I sit still. This is all new, and for Lucy, this is uncharted territory.

"What's this one?" she says after a few moments, dragging her hand across my pecs and to my opposite arm. She turns it so she can study the design on the inside of my bicep.

I grin as I recall the day I forced my teammates to get tattoos. "Funny story, but I got Poe and Anton to come with me, and we all got tattoos a few years back. They thought I was unhinged, forcing them into all sorts of shenanigans, but it worked out. Anton got a tattoo of a rose, which, after I learned about the real Rose, made a lot more sense. Poe got some poetry, which, honestly, is fitting. I got mine in honor of my grandpa. I knew my grandma would appreciate it, too, but it was mostly for Pa." I point to the design. "It's a reminder of what he always taught me about priorities. Faith, family, football." There are three symbols in the tattoo—a long cross in the center, the Triquetra, and an X and O pattern.

Lucy traces the cross. "So this is for faith. What's this one?" she asks, pointing to the three interlocking arcs of the Triquetra.

"That's a Celtic symbol for the trinity, which symbolizes the unity and connectivity of the family. These"—I take my hand and move her finger to the small drawing in the background—"are meant to show a football play call. The cross is the focal point, followed by the Triquetra, and then the football stuff sort of fades behind it all."

Lucy leans closer to study it, and the scent of her tropical shampoo makes my stomach pitch. "This one might be my favorite." She flits her gaze up to meet mine. "Do you think you'll get more?"

"Yes," I answer without hesitation. "Tattoos are a form of expression for me, and when I reach a milestone or have a breakthrough, I like to document it. Actually, I've been thinking about some new designs lately."

Lucy tucks a flyaway behind her ear. "Like what?"

"A pine tree, for starters."

She sucks in a breath. "That's beautiful, TJ."

"It's meaningful to me. That day at the farm was meaningful to me for a lot of reasons."

Chapter 32

Lucy

I press my lips together, watching as TJ shifts his position slightly so he's looking squarely at me. The intensity in his gaze—the desire and the care in his expression—is almost too much to bear. I look down and try to focus on the bubbling water swirling around me.

But then TJ's large, calloused fingers are under my chin, tipping it up ever so slowly.

"Please," he whispers. "Look at me when I tell you this."

I barely manage a nod. The reverence in his gaze makes me feel like he lit a snug, little fire inside me.

"You're meaningful to me, Lucy. I want to be clear when I say that. I've developed feelings for you." He chuckles at my wide eyes. "Don't look so surprised. You're extraordinary."

I squish up my nose. "I am not."

"You are, Lu." His voice is strong, firm. "You said at the gala when we first met, and then again several times after," he adds with a pained look, "that you aren't interested in anything more right now, but ... I am."

My heart, which was already racing in circles, starts levitating in my chest.

TJ reaches for my hands and holds them in his under the water, running his thumbs over my knuckles, and the temperature of the hot tub skyrockets.

"I'd like more with you, if you'd give me the chance," he says.

I close my eyes and squeeze his hands, trying to collect my thoughts. When I blink, he's looking at me with the open expression I've come to appreciate so much. He's all but handing me his heart on a platter.

"I ... I'm scared, TJ."

He inclines his head, moving it toward me so our foreheads are resting against each other. "I get it. I've closed myself off to this, or the idea of this, for years, Lu. But I don't want to let the fear of whatever may come prevent me from experiencing this with you. We can conquer this fear, like your fear of car washes and my fear of zebras ... together."

I smile at the memory of us hanging from the scaffolding, but before I let myself go down this path, I need to make sure he's sure. I lean back so I can get a good look at him and not be distracted by his nearness and his lips, which I very much would like to capture with my own right now.

"I'm afraid you're going to resent me because I'm not as social as you are." He opens his mouth to argue, but I shake my head and press on. "I was outgoing and fun the first night we met, but that's not really me. I'm introverted and boring. I'm ... still in hiding because most of the world hates me."

"First of all, I don't care about most of the world." The determined look he gives me arrives straight to my heart, like a steroid shot of tenderness. "Second of all, I won't resent you for being you. You say being bold and fun isn't really who you are, but I'm pretty sure the same person sitting here with me was the one behind the mask at the gala. That's the same you. I would know—I've been trying to drink in every detail since the moment I laid eyes on you."

This man and his sweet compliments. He's going to end me.

I stare at him, and I can tell he truly believes that. I have my doubts, but as if reading my mind, he cocks his head to the side and adds, "You don't get to tell me how I'm going to feel about you. I will be the one telling *you* how I *do* feel, starting by saying that you're exquisite."

"TJ," I breathe. "Stop it. You're being too ... too nice. It's too much."

"Not possible. Let me be nice. Let me tell you that I think you're fun and funny. I love how your mind works. I love that you truly listen to my grandparents when they talk to you. I want to hang out with you all the time. I like your bold side and your quiet side. I like all of you, Lu."

He's single-handedly taking a sledgehammer to every one of the arguments I had for not dating him. I'm very impressed.

"Okay." I say the word slowly.

He leans forward, closer to me. "Okay, like you're willing to give this a chance?"

"I am if you are." I nod, my heart ready to burst. The mile-wide smile that spreads across TJ's face is one of pure, unfiltered delight. It makes me brave. "I do have a question."

"Yeah? Anything."

"Do you remember when we were at the top of the steps at the gala, before they called you down to the stage?" I pause, waiting to see if the moment registers for him. He nods. "You said something to me then."

"I told you I wanted to kiss you." His eyes dip to my lips and then up again. "That I wanted to kiss you very much. But that you should wait until someone knows you and cherishes you to have your first kiss."

I hum. "I was wondering"—I glance down, biting my lip before meeting his gaze again; it's turned molten—"if maybe you could show me how that would go."

TJ's neck is taut with restraint, but he shifts his body, bringing one arm out of the hot tub and resting it on the side. He starts drawing languid shapes on my shoulder blade. The water droplets left behind by his finger cool in the frigid night air, only for my skin to be warmed again when he makes another pass. The sensation is addictive.

"That depends." His voice is low and careful.

"On what?"

"Are you asking for story inspiration?"

"I ... I was hoping this would just be for you and me."

He nods slowly. "Then I want you to know that I still very much want to kiss you. Not because you're beautiful. That's what I knew on night one. Now I know so much more, Lu, and I—" His voice breaks, and he swallows, trying again. "I am overwhelmed by you."

"Kiss me, TJ. Please," I beg.

"I want to go slow with you. I want to give you the control," he murmurs, drawing me in enough that he can press his lips to my forehead. He leans back so he's looking at me. "You take the lead."

Nothing has ever been more alluring to me in my entire life than this man, here, waiting on me and ensuring that I feel safe.

I gulp and nod. I have no idea what I'm doing, but he's managed to completely allay all my worries about whether I'm going to do this right. I feel at ease and cared for. I swing myself over so both of my legs are on the far side of TJ's body and I'm sitting on his lap.

"Is this where you want to be?" he asks, pressing his mouth to my collarbone.

"Yes." I wrap my arms around his neck, trailing my fingers through his short hair. "I want to be close to you."

He cradles my body against his, wrapping his strong arms around me and pressing his nose into my neck. He inhales a shuddering breath.

"I really like being held by you," I whisper.

"Good," he murmurs. "What else would you like?"

I shift, and he loosens his grip enough that I can look him in the eye. "I'd like to kiss you now."

I close the distance between us and press my lips to his. It's nothing and everything to me at the same time. It's like breathing—simple, necessary. Something I have to do. Something that's a *gift* to get to do.

TJ tightens his arms around my waist when I cup his face. He doesn't move. He's giving me time to explore his lips at my own pace. They're softer than I expected, and I like that. A big, tough football player with soft and sweet lips. I pause at the corner of his mouth and smile before I kiss the crease. I drag my lips across his and move to the other side, pressing another kiss in that corner. TJ's chest is heaving, and his eyes flutter open when I pull back. He blinks a couple times and gazes at me.

"Now," I tell him, "I'd like you to kiss me back. I don't want you to worry about going too fast or being too careful. I trust you, TJ. Please—"

He doesn't wait for me to say more. He drags his hands up my torso. Water splashes around us as he spears his fingers through my hair. He lets his thumbs rest along my cheekbones as he kisses me. Firm and strong and sure. The cold air swirling around us and the steamy haze off the water heightens everything about this experience. The liquid droplets on my cheeks cool and sting, but even that feels good right now.

TJ takes his mouth away from mine, and I immediately protest, but before I can complain too much, he's moved his lips to the column of my neck. I gasp and feel him smile against where my pulse flutters.

"I can't get enough of you, Lu," he says as he presses an open-mouth kiss to that spot.

I snap my eyes shut, letting my head roll back. "Kiss me there again. Please," I add.

This time, he scrapes his teeth against that spot, and my toes curl. I blink my eyes open to find him watching me, his gaze a blazing flame of desire. He smiles, keeping his eyes fixed on mine as he kisses me there again.

Having him hold my gaze with such care and adoration might be my undoing. His eyes shut as he sets to work trailing a line of sparks down my neck and back up again, and I feel like a firework about to explode.

I go up on my knees with my legs on either side of his waist and press my body into his, kissing him soundly on the mouth as he leans back, his fingers digging into the skin at my hips. He tastes like peppermint and fresh winter air, and he's delicious and wonderful and warm.

I expected my first kiss to feel awkward. In a lot of ways, I couldn't wait to get it over with so I could at least say I experienced it. It was like a looming box that I hadn't checked. Here, with TJ, I don't want to rush. I don't feel self-conscious. If this is on my to-do list, I'd like to do it forever.

I didn't realize how much kissing could be like a conversation without words. The back and forth, the humor mixed with moments of intensity that steal my breath. TJ keeps checking in, keeps making sure I'm happy and comfortable. He's respecting me while not treating me like I'm weak. He's showing me with his kisses what he's been showing me since the night of the gala—that he's dependable and strong and cares about my feelings.

For the record, right now, I am feeling some type of way.

Desired. Cherished. *On fire.*

"You're too good to me," I say between kisses.

"Not possible," he says against my lips. His breath is ragged. "You're so beautiful, Lucy. I could never deserve you, but I'm going to try."

Our kisses turn more languid and unhurried.

We take our time. I explore his mouth and manage to find a spot right at the hinge point of his jaw that makes him growl when I kiss it. It's a powerful feeling being close to TJ like this, seeing him be open with me in a vulnerable way. I vow to myself I'll cherish him the same way he's cherishing me.

I trace his tattoos again with my fingers, and we stay in the hot tub, tangled in each other. We talk and share secrets and dreams and goals and hopes and worries. As the cold wind whips around us, here, in TJ's arms, I feel like I'll be warm for the rest of my life.

Chapter 33
TJ

K issing Lucy brought me back to life.

All I can think about is seeing her and kissing her again. It's early on Monday morning, the day after Christmas. I have the day off, and Lucy agreed to let me take her out to breakfast. I assured her it was an out-of-the-way spot and we wouldn't be discovered.

I pull up outside of Daisy's Inn and take the steps two at a time. A family is walking out the front door, so I grab the handle and hold the door open for them, mindful to keep my head lowered. Flying under the radar is going to take some getting used to, but for Lucy, I gladly will.

I slip inside and shoot off a text to let Lucy know I'm downstairs. She appears at the top of the steps a few seconds later, and I can't stop smiling up at her like a happy puppy.

"Morning," she says shyly as she jogs down the stairs.

In response, I grab for her hands and pull her to the entryway to the hearth room.

"What are you doing?"

I glance up to where the mistletoe is still hanging overhead, and I grin down at her before lowering my mouth to hers and kissing her a proper good morning.

"Wow," she says, looking slightly dazed when I pull back. "That'll give a girl some energy."

I study her and frown. "You didn't sleep well?"

She shakes her head. "I slept great, just not for very long. I was wired when I got home, because"—her cheeks flush—"of the hot tub."

I am inordinately proud of that. I wag my brows at her, and she shoves me playfully. "Don't look so pleased with yourself."

"Can't help it. I've made it my mission to kiss you to the point where you're losing sleep."

Her eyes widen, and her blush deepens. "Well, you accomplished that yesterday," she says with a smirk. "I started tinkering with my manuscript and ended up writing almost ten thousand words last night." At my puzzled expression, she adds, "That's usually how many words I write in a week— a good week."

I let out a surprised expletive. "I mean dang, Lu. That's wild. All that writing and you must be hungry."

She raises her eyebrows at me. "Starving, actually."

The woman winks. She actually winks at me.

I cannot be held responsible for the growl that comes out of my mouth. I reach for her to pull her in for another kiss, but she side-steps me and laughs, taking off for the door. "Come on, TJ. I need sustenance." She glances at me over her shoulder and shoots me a wolfish grin. "For writing and more kissing."

The drive to the diner takes about twenty minutes. It's a hole-in-the-wall spot at the end of a strip mall on the outskirts of Green Bay. The parking lot is deserted when we arrive. It's early, and it's the day after Christmas, so I can't imagine we're going to have to fight too many people for a seat.

Lucy looks around at the vacant, poorly paved lot, and I have a moment of panic. Is this type of place not up to her standards? She's so normal and unassuming that I sometimes forget she's used to the finer things.

But then she takes one more look around, unlatches her seatbelt, and shocks me when she climbs over the console of my truck and sits in my lap.

"Hi." She smiles up at me and loops her arms around my neck. "Is this okay?"

"You don't even need to ask." I lower my mouth to hers and let myself get lost in her again. I love that she's comfortable enough with me to take initiative, to tell me what she likes and what she wants.

I'm quickly realizing Anton is right. There's nothing else I'd rather do than spend time with Lucy, doing what she wants to do, and making her feel like she's the most important thing in the world to me.

After a couple minutes and a few stops and starts, wherein Lucy was half out the door but I pulled her back to kiss her some more, we manage to leave the seclusion of my truck and get seated in a corner booth at the diner. I'm pleased to see the waitress standing behind the counter.

"That's Betsy," I tell Lucy, tipping my head toward her. She's a single mom in her early forties, and she looks tired this morning. I make a mental note to check in about her boys. "I've been coming here since I got drafted to the River Foxes, and she's never once blown my cover."

"I'm so hungry right now, I think I'd be okay being found out if it meant I got French toast."

I hand her a laminated menu. I don't need one, since I always get the same thing. "You're a French toast person, huh?"

"It's the superior breakfast."

"A whole platter of pancakes would beg to differ."

Lucy's brow puckers as she meets my gaze. "Pancakes don't hold a candle to French toast. Sourdough bread, built-in eggs, and fresh fruit toppings. Come on. No contest."

"I had no idea you were so passionate about this topic. Should I be concerned?"

"As long as you don't get in the way of me and my French toast, you'll be fine."

"Fair enough. Me and my measly pancakes will stay sequestered over here on this side of the booth. You can look down your nose at us."

Lucy snorts. "If you want to argue the pancake's case, be my guest. I mean, you'll lose the argument, but you can absolutely try." She bats her eyelashes.

I laugh outright. "You're feisty in the morning, Lu. I like that."

Betsy swings by the table. "Morning, Teej. Hiya, doll," she says in Lucy's direction.

Lucy offers her a tentative smile. "Hey."

"You know whatcha want?"

"The usual for me," I say.

Betsy nods and scribbles on her pad of paper. "Tall stack of pancakes, extra butter, extra syrup. Coffee and cream. And for you?" She flicks her gaze to Lucy, and then back down to her pad.

"Coffee for me as well, please. But with sugar. And I'll do the French toast."

Betsy scribbles some more. "Whipped cream on top for ya?"

"No thanks. Just the strawberries."

"Coming right up." Betsy pockets her notepad and is about to leave our table when she meets my eye. "A whole bunch of River Foxes merch showed up at our house on Christmas Eve. Know anything about that?"

I lift my shoulders in a noncommittal shrug. "Were the sizes okay?"

Betsy's mouth lifts into a smile. "Perfect. Thank you, TJ. If it was just me, I'd yell at you for your charity, but for the kids' sake, I'll allow it."

I nod at her, aware that she doesn't want to belabor the point. She nods back and bustles off.

Lucy watches her before turning back to me, raising her brows. "Sounds to me like you're a real-life prince charming. Or at least a knight in shining armor."

I shake my head. "It's not a big deal. It's the least I can do. They're good kids. Ten and twelve. Their dad got into some trouble and has been in jail since they were little."

Lucy's face falls and she flicks her gaze toward where Betsy disappeared into the kitchen. "That must be so hard. For all of them."

"Betsy is great. She's held it together, but I know it wears on her. I try to be her friend."

"You're a good friend."

I shrug. "So is she. Her discretion with me is worth more than twenty River Foxes jerseys." I reach across the table, holding out my hand, and she slips her fingers into it. "You good? Comfortable here?"

She stares at me with a soft smile on her lips before shaking her head slightly, allowing the change in conversation. "Yeah. This is great."

"No whipped cream?" I bring us back to our breakfast conversation as I flip her palm over and start tracing the lines on her skin.

"No way," she says staunchly. "You can't mess with perfection like that. French toast can stand on its own. It doesn't need any frills."

"You've obviously thought this through."

"Like I said, I take my breakfasts very seriously." She winks at me again, and I love it.

"You come here a lot, so the food must be good." It's a statement, not a question.

I nod. "Donald—the chef. He's awesome."

She tips her head to the side. "Not a name you hear often."

"I guess not."

"Sorry. My brain is in writer mode. I love that sort of thing. A unique name. A funny backstory. This whole place is screaming to be written into a story."

I look around and try to see the diner through Lucy's eyes. It doesn't look very special to me, but now that I'm looking for it, there are sweet details all around. Paper snowflakes dangle from the ceiling. Fresh holly and berries drape over the lip of a mason jar by the front register. The booths are lined with cracked leather, but the Formica table tops shine. It's worn, but well-loved.

"I don't mean to bore you," she adds, sounding embarrassed.

"You're not." I squeeze her hand. "I was marveling. You notice things that I would skim right over. Don't apologize for how your mind works, Lu. I happen to like it."

"Thanks." She smiles.

"How's the progress on your book coming?"

She blows out a long breath. "After the absurd number of words I wrote last night, I might just hit my deadline."

"How long do you have?"

"Till the end of January." Lucy cringes. "It's going to be close."

"You'll do it."

Betsy swings back and sets two mugs of coffee in front of us, along with cream and sugar. "Donny'll have your platters right out."

We thank her, and as soon as she's out of earshot, I lean toward Lucy. "By the way, I have a hunch that you know Philomena Grace."

Lucy focuses on her coffee, shaking a packet of sugar into the brown liquid and stirring it carefully. "What makes you say that?"

"Because I have a feeling that you coordinated getting her connected to Rose at Mood Reader. I'd even go out on a limb and say I could guess your pen name is"—I drop my voice—"Ava Reese."

Chapter 34
Lucy

I nearly spit out my coffee. If I had any hope of keeping this secret from TJ, it's gone with that reaction. Could I be more obvious?

I set down my mug, my hand shaking, before I hesitantly meet his gaze. "How'd you know?"

"I was watching you when Rose said that name. Don't worry, it wouldn't have been obvious to anyone else. But I see you." He looks suddenly bashful. "At least, I try to see you ... differently than most, I think. I hope you're not mad."

I shake my head. "Why would I be mad?"

"Because you didn't want to tell me."

"That's because I don't tell anyone, TJ. It's going to take some getting used to, knowing that you know this side of me, too. But I'm not mad. How could I possibly be when you know me well enough to read my cues and figure out a secret I've kept buried from everyone?"

He leans back on his side of the booth. "Then I should admit that I didn't get much sleep last night, either, because I stayed up until three o'clock, and I'm seventy-five percent of the way through A *Summit Lake Love Story*."

My pulse thunders in my ears. I open my mouth, but no words come out.

"Lucy, it's really good. Like, so good. And you're, like, really famous."

I glance around. Even though I know we're alone, and I know TJ trusts Betsy, I'm still self-conscious. "I'm not famous. Ava Reese is famous. No one knows she's me."

"Except for me. I'm so proud of you." His eyes are filled with sincerity, and I don't know what to do with it.

I press my hands to my cheeks because they're burning up. "You're doing it again—being too nice."

"Nuh-uh. You've earned it, Lu. It's incredible. You have a gift for storytelling. I can't wait to read everything. Especially the one you're working on now, to see how Theo fares."

"Theo'll get his happily ever after," I say with a small smile. I really like how invested TJ is. It's nice being able to share my writing with someone who isn't Philly, Bex, or Cassie.

"I should hope so. He's going to be your best hero yet." TJ puffs out his chest and then leans forward. "Did you add tattoos to his character?"

I tip my head to the side, imagining the ink on TJ's skin where it is beneath his shirt. "Actually, no."

His eyebrows fly up. "Why not? I thought you liked them."

"Oh, believe me. I do. I really do. But I meant what I said. Last night was for me and you. If I have anything to say about it, no one else will get to enjoy your tattoos from now on but me."

I cross my arms, and then it hits me—what I said. *Possessive much, Lu?* I open my mouth to walk it back, but Betsy appears with our breakfast, setting two piled-high plates between us. I thank her, and she glances at TJ, but he's staring at me with his jaw hanging slightly open, so she just shrugs.

"Enjoy, kids." She winks at me and heads back to the counter.

TJ blinks, shaking his head slowly.

"What?" I say, afraid it was too much and I pushed too far and I made this too serious between us too soon.

He keeps shaking his head as he wedges his giant body out of the booth. I panic for a second, thinking he's going to leave, but then he shoves his plate across the table and joins me on my side.

He takes a seat, his arm pressed up next to mine. "If you're going to say things as hot as that, then I'm going to need to be closer to you so I can kiss those pretty lips every time words like that come out of them."

I'm stunned for a second, and then I huff out a laugh. "You're ridiculous."

"Thanks to you," he murmurs, hitting me with a boyish grin.

TJ leads us in a quick prayer, and then we dig in. Our conversation shifts to things other than my writing. We discuss his chickens, his grandparents, and what he's planning for his teammates' next guys' night ahead of the game on Sunday. I tell him how I taught myself cross-stitch, and I share a little bit about my stepsisters. I tell him about Philly and Bex and Cassie, and how they're the best friends I could ever ask for.

"Cassie represents all of us. She's how I got to know Philly. That's how I made the connection happen for Rose."

"You realize Rose would lose her mind if she knew that she's been brushing shoulders with *the* Ava Reese and she has no idea?"

"Yeah, maybe. She can't know, though. No one can. Not at this point."

He nods. "I know. Your secret's safe with me."

I nod back. He's made me feel the most protected.

TJ leans in for a sweet kiss, but he cuts it off sooner than I'd like. "Sorry. My phone is blowing up. Let me make sure everything's okay, and then I'll silence it." He fishes it out of his pocket and stares at the screen. "I have a bunch of texts from Anton." He frowns as he scrolls.

"What is it?" I have the total body sensation that the happy bubble TJ and I have been enjoying this morning is about to burst.

"I think you've been found out." He flips the phone to me. Anton has attached a video of the front yard of Daisy's Inn. TJ clicks play. There are several media vans and a ton of reporters set up with tripod cameras. The video was taken from a distance, but it's obvious they're staked out there.

My stomach rolls, revolting against the French toast I love so much. This was always a possibility, but I'd gotten used to my anonymity here in Wisconsin. I let my guard down. I felt safe here. Now, though—

"Hey. Hey, Lu. Are you okay?" TJ's voice sounds far away.

I suck in a deep breath and will the oxygen to reach my brain so I can think. I blink and look over at him, shaking my head slightly. "What am I going to do?"

Chapter 35
TJ

I quickly handled our bill with Betsy and then got Lucy back into my truck. The mood was a complete one-eighty from the last time we were in here. I keep an eye on Lucy as I drive us to my house. I called Anton, and he's having one of Rose's sisters go into Daisy's and get some of Lucy's things. He's going to bring them to my place, and we'll figure out what to do from there.

Lucy has a vise-grip on my hand where it's holding hers on the center console. Anxiety and tension radiate from her. I'm tense because she's tense, and I don't know how to fix it.

I turn into my neighborhood, and my shoulders relax a fraction. It'll be good to be home. I wind through the neighborhood until I get to my street, and one look at my house makes any ounce of comfort I felt evaporate. There are all sorts of cars and media in my driveway.

Lucy slinks further down in her seat. She looks frantically at me as I casually drive past my house, never more grateful for the truck's tinted windows. "TJ, I'm so sorry. This is all my fault."

"Don't apologize. This isn't on you. The paparazzi have too much time on their hands."

She takes her hand from mine and uses it to cover her face. "I can't believe this. I brought all this media to your doorstep. Nobody has ever bothered you here before me, and now what are you going to do? Your home address will be splashed all over the internet."

"You're not the one leaking my home address."

"I know that," she grits out. "But you wouldn't be in this mess if you weren't tangled up with me."

"Tangled up with you is how I like to be." I grin at her, hoping my joke will lighten her mood, but all I get is a strained smile before her lips drop.

I switch gears, placing a call to Poe through my truck's Bluetooth feature.

He answers on the second ring. "What's up, Teej?"

"I'm with Lu. We need some privacy. Can we come to your place?"

"Can't you guys find someone else's hot tub to make out in?" Poe's usual deadpan voice is a balm to my frayed nerves.

"No can do, my man. Yours holds all my favorite memories now. We'll be frequent visitors."

"I just threw up in my mouth."

I chuckle. "Look, someone found out Lucy is in town. They're staked out at her place and mine. Can we swing over and figure out next steps?"

"That sucks." Poe's tone changes from dry to alert. "Yeah, of course, man. You didn't even have to ask."

"Thanks, Poe. Be there in ten." I disconnect the call, and Lucy lets out a deep breath.

"You have good friends," she says.

"The best. They always have my back. Yours, too, now." I cut her with a look, praying she believes me when I say, "You don't have to face any of this alone."

Chapter 36
Lucy

By the time TJ pulls into Poe's underground parking facility, I've formed a loose plan. I don't like it, but under the circumstances, I know it's necessary. I want to stomp my foot and throw a tantrum because things were going so well. I let myself believe in the fairy tale of TJ and me. I got comfortable and complacent, and it was so nice while it lasted. Now, the delicate life I've rebuilt for myself here feels like it's crumbling down around me. Once again, everything about my future feels uncertain, like it could get swept away in the wind at any given moment. It's a startling reminder that I'm not a princess, and happily ever afters don't just happen. TJ says I don't have to face this alone, but he's wrong. I do.

We take the elevator up to the condo, and Poe is waiting for us with a pitcher of ice water and glasses set on a tray on the ottoman inside his large sectional. TJ plops down on the nearest cushion, right at home, and he motions for me to sit.

"You need anything, Lucy?" Poe asks, following us into the living room.

"No. Thanks for—" I search for the right words. "Letting us in here."

Poe looks at me funny. "Of course." He swings his gaze to TJ. "I texted everyone else. Told them you were coming. Anton said he'll bring Lucy's things over."

"You guys are the best." My voice breaks.

TJ drops a kiss on the crown of my head. "Like I told you, Lu. You're not alone. It's all going to be okay."

"I know."

I want to believe that, and a part of me *does* believe it. This will blow over as all things do. The paparazzi are fickle. They'll move on to the next best thing as soon as fresh news drops. It's the way of the world, or at the very least, the way of the entertainment industry.

That doesn't change the fact that, right now, I'm in the eye of the storm. Worse, I've pulled TJ into the mess with me, debris flying all around us. If we could hunker down together, we'd be okay. I know he'd do everything possible to protect me, as would I for him. But we can't fool ourselves into believing that the bubble we were in didn't just pop.

If I stick around—if I stay close to him—I'm putting him directly in the path of the wreckage of my life, which has the very strong potential to mess up *his* life. He'll be caught in the crossfire, distracted from his work and his team because he's worried about me. He'll become the object of gossip and the public, all of whom will shout their opinions about him and our relationship. TJ deals with enough scrutiny on his own, even with his positive reputation. It's not fair of me to knowingly set him up for more, especially since I'm a disgrace in the eyes of the world. I care for him too much to let him go down with me.

I glance at Poe, and my guilt amplifies. TJ is part of a team—a major part of a team. If he gets dragged into this, so do they, and the whole team will suffer. He loves his teammates, and they've poured so much into making a run into the playoffs. I couldn't look myself in the mirror if I knew I could do something to spare all of them the interference that comes along with being made a public spectacle. That's the crux of it. It's in my power to *do* something, and as much as I hate it, I have to act—and I have to act alone. I want TJ and me to work through this, to get through it together, but ...

"What are you thinking?" TJ puts his arm around my shoulder, and I sink into his embrace, hating what I'm going to say next, but knowing that it's necessary.

I summon up my courage and take a deep breath. "I think the best thing for me to do is to disappear for a little while."

Chapter 37

TJ

Every muscle in my body tenses when Lucy says she wants to disappear.

She places a hand on my forearm. "I'm going to go back to California. I already planned on visiting my family between Christmas and New Year's. I was going to leave on Wednesday. I can move up my flight and get there late tonight."

My grip tightens around her shoulder. "How long would you stay?"

"Indefinitely. Long enough to give things a chance to quiet down around here. I don't want you to have to deal with extra media attention and the distraction of all this at the end of your season."

There's resolve in her gaze. She thinks this is for the best. I grit my teeth and attempt to keep the look on my face one of support, even though I hate the thought of her being half a country away from me. I don't want her to go. I want her to stay here and face this. I'll be by her side through everything, if she'll let me.

But I also don't want her to think I'm trying to tell her what to do. So much is out of her control right now, and the last thing I want to do is tell her what I think is best for her.

"You know what's best for you, Lu," I say. "I'm behind you the entire way. Whatever you need."

She sinks further into my side. "Thanks for understanding."

Poe clears his throat from across the room. "Will you come back to the Green Bay area when everything calms down, or … ?"

He flicks his gaze from me to Lu and back again. My pulse picks up. I'm at once anticipating and dreading Lucy's response.

"I honestly don't know." She looks up at me.

I squeeze her arm again. "We'll figure it out."

She nods, but she doesn't look convinced. She looks overwhelmed and fragile, and I want to go back to earlier this morning when everything was blissful and the future looked bright and full of sweet moments to be spent with Lucy by my side.

As much as I hate that Poe voiced it, he's not wrong in asking what's next for her. My life is in Green Bay. My contract with the River Foxes is for another four years, at least. Four years is a long time to live apart if she doesn't plan to be in this area.

I suck in a deep breath. I need to slow my roll. "One day at a time, that's all we can do."

The door to Poe's condo opens and Anton and Rose join us, followed by Del.

"Reinforcements have arrived." Anton sets a tray of smoothies on the island in Poe's kitchen. "With sustenance."

Del grabs one and takes a sip. "I'm here for moral support. Hope you don't mind, Lucy. We're real sorry about this."

Lucy manages a smile, and I make a mental note to thank my friends later. They're the best, and the fact that they're showing up for Lucy, making her feel cared for, means the world to me.

Rose opens her arms to Lucy, and Lucy accepts her hug. Even though my heart is still pinched at the continued stress lines on Lucy's face and the apprehensive flicker in her gaze, I can't help but feel a tickle of happiness that she gets along so well with Anton's girlfriend. It's a boost to my confidence—and my resolve. Lucy and I fit. She fits with my family and my friends and my friends' girlfriends ... or girlfriend, at least. I'm determined to make this work.

Rose rolls a suitcase in front of Lucy. "I had my sister grab as much as she could. I hope you don't mind that Poppy went through your room."

I hold my breath as my mind flies to Lucy's writing notes and her secret career. She's been so careful, and if her author life gets out before she's ready to go public with her work, I worry that it'll be devastating for her. I keep my gaze fixed on Rose. If Poppy saw anything that pertained to Lucy's books, she would have for sure told her. They're super close, and they all read romance novels, so it's not like Poppy wouldn't have known what she was seeing if any Ava Reese remnants were lying around Lucy's room.

"Good thing I cleaned my room this morning." Lucy shoots me a reassuring look, as if she knows I was panicking on her behalf. I breathe a sigh of relief, but then dread snakes through me as she takes the handle of the suitcase. "I can't thank you and your sister enough," she tells Rose.

"It's no problem at all. Daisy is keeping everyone out of the Inn. She told the reporters that, unless they had a reservation, they weren't allowed on her property. She's not confirming that you've stayed there, just telling everyone reservation records aren't publicly available. She also told a couple of paps who were trying to book a room that she was full."

Lucy frowns. "She's not full. I talked to her the day before Christmas, and she said she had at least three rooms opening up today."

Rose offers Lucy a knowing smile. "If Daisy says she's full, she's full."

Lucy's eyes well with tears. "You all are being so kind to me, I … I don't deserve any of this."

I pull her into my arms. She takes a shuddering breath and lets me hold her for a second—not nearly long enough—and then pulls back and swipes at the mascara leaking beneath her eyes.

"Sorry. I'm fine." She squares her shoulders and interlocks her fingers with mine. "Everything's going to be fine. I'm going to make some calls to figure out my flights and try to avoid attention while traveling, and I've got to let my family know I'm coming."

"You can use my office if you want some privacy." Poe motions for Lucy to follow him, and I watch her trail him down the hallway.

When Poe returns, the entire room turns and looks at me. They're quiet for a second, and then everyone starts talking at once.

"What are you going to do?"

"What do you need?"

"Can you go with her?"

"How's this going to work?"

I hold up my hands. "I don't know, guys. I can't go with her ... you know that. I have to be at practice tomorrow morning, and we have an away game this weekend."

I don't add that Tess's benefit is the following Monday night.

My chest tightens. Lucy was never going to be my plus one. An event like that is more public-facing and attention-garnering than she wants to be right now, not to mention that it's for my former girlfriend. Tess's family has said over and over again that they'd want to meet anyone I date in the future, but still. Lucy isn't ready, and I'm not going to push her. I *was* looking forward to her being here, in the Green Bay area, when I got back, but I will not feel sorry for myself. Lucy has bigger things to contend with than being the open arms I was hoping to come home to after an emotional night.

I blink, focusing on my friends. Anton and Poe's mouths are set in hard lines. Rose looks thoughtful. Del looks emotional.

"I'm going to fight for her and for us," I tell them. "I'm not sure what that looks like right now, but she's too important to me to let her go. This is a hiccup. A roadblock. It's temporary."

I don't know if I'm trying to convince them, or myself. The thought of Lucy not coming back to Green Bay makes me feel like my lungs are going through a paper shredder.

"How did they find her, anyway?" Del asks, his voice wobbly.

Rose raises her hand. "I can answer that." She pulls out her phone. "There was an article published after your game last night, and it had photos of me in the box. Lucy was in the background. One commenter suggested that the bundled-up woman reminded her of Lucy Dupree. The idea caught on like wildfire, and when I was mingling with the paps this morning—"

"You *what*?" Anton raises his voice.

"Don't worry." Rose rolls her eyes. "I was incognito." She turns to me. "One of them said a guest at the Inn confirmed a Lucy and TJ sighting yesterday morning."

"I didn't think the family whose autographs I signed yesterday noticed Lu." I scrub a hand over my face. "This is my fault."

"Stop, Teej. It is not." Poe's dry tone is sincere.

The door to Poe's office opens, and we all turn as Lucy rejoins us. She immediately comes to my side, tucking herself under my arm, and my heart squeezes.

"All set?" I ask her. "What do you need?"

"A ride to the airport would be good." She offers me a brief smile before turning to my friends. "I truly can't thank you enough. I hope I can repay you someday. None of you owe me anything, and I'm sure you've all seen my comments. I hope you'll believe me when I tell you what I told TJ. I shouldn't have told anyone they didn't matter, and I'm deeply sorry if any of you watched my outburst and took it personally."

"We didn't," Rose assures her. "Right, guys?"

"Absolutely."

"Right."

"I thought you were great. I like a woman who speaks her mind," Del says with a good-natured smile, and I could kiss his bearded face for making Lucy chuckle.

"Thank you all. I hope to see you again."

"You will," Rose says with a smile.

My phone starts ringing, and it's the special sound I have set for both my grandparents. "It's Gram. Gimme one sec."

I accept the call, stepping into the hallway beyond Poe's kitchen as my grandma starts rapid-fire questioning me about Lucy.

"Why is our Lu all over the internet news homepage, Teej? Went to check the weather and there she is! Is she alright? They keep showing this clip of her at some award show. She told us something about this, but I'd sort of forgotten." My grandma prattles on, and I'm half-listening while also trying to keep an eye and ear on the huddle in the living room. I can't hear what they're saying. Lucy is doing a lot of talking, and I just want to be close to her.

But I owe my grandma my time and focus, so I tune back in, explaining the situation and how Lucy is headed to California.

"You give her a hug for us, Teej. Tell her she's welcome back any time, and she's always got a place at our table."

"I'll tell her, Gram. Thanks."

Gram sniffs on the other end of the line. "Take care of our girl, TJ."

"I'm doing my best," I say, even though I feel helpless. She's about to walk out of my life ... at least for the foreseeable future.

No.

I'm not going to think negatively. I'll figure out how to be supportive and present ... even from a distance. I end the call with my grandma, promising to keep her posted, and walk into the living room as Lucy hugs all my friends.

"All good?" I ask as she joins me. I wrap my arm around her waist.

My friends nod, and Lucy smiles up at me. "I'm ready."

I force a smile. "Let's get you to the airport."

Chapter 38
Lucy

I stare at TJ's face on our video call, hating that I'm not in the same room as him. I want to trace my finger down his nose. I want to reposition the collar of his t-shirt so I can see his tiger tattoo. I want to be close to him.

He looks away from the camera. "I've gotta go, Lu. Coach assigned me some extra tape to watch ahead of our game." He glances at the camera again and attempts a smile. "Says I need to put in some more time after my terrible practice today."

I can tell he's trying to keep things light, so I do the same. "Tell him I think you're the opposite of terrible."

TJ laughs. "You tell him."

I smile. If only I could.

TJ hasn't come out and said it, but I think I'm the reason he's practicing poorly. He'd never blame me, but he told me he can't stop thinking about me.

Ditto.

I thought being apart from him would save him from worrying about me, but I guess I was wrong.

"I'll call you tonight."

I muster a smile. "Sounds good. Can't wait."

"Okay." He presses his lips together, looking just about as miserable as I feel. "Bye."

"Bye."

My list of recent calls replaces TJ's face on the screen. This has become the worst part of our video calls ... saying goodbye. Neither of us wants to. Neither of us knows how. It's been less than a week since I kissed him for the first time. Four days since the media descended on Daisy's Inn. Four measly days. That's how long I've been back in California, away from TJ, and already I feel like a stranger in my own skin.

I thought I was doing what was best—for him and for me—by leaving. But I don't know about that anymore. Something has to give. I'm circling around what that is and frustrated with myself for waffling, but I'm scared. Knowing I'm being cowardly is making me feel even worse. I toss my phone on my childhood bed and sigh.

"Knock knock." My stepmom's voice echoes from the hallway outside my room.

"Come on in, Ruby." I sit up straighter, trying to look less melancholy than I feel.

My stepmom swings the door open and walks into my room. She's dressed to perfection in jeans and a crisp white button-up. Ruby has a way of looking effortlessly chic every day, but you get her on overdrive when the camera crew is in the house. "We're about ready to film the dinner segment for the show, sweetie. I thought you might be hungry." She holds out a bowl for me, and I take it as my stomach rumbles. We share a small laugh.

My mind snags on the camera crew downstairs. *Is this my chance?*

"I haven't eaten since this morning," I tell her. I look down at the hearty bowl of chili and then flick my gaze to her. "Thanks."

"I was inspired to make it after you texted about the recipe," she says with a shrug. "Your dad had it perfected. I don't know that I've ever made a batch that matched up with his, but I tried." She bends over and kisses me on the forehead. "In any case, it's made with love."

I suck in a breath, keeping my eyes closed for a moment before blinking them open and staring back at Ruby's kind expression.

"You sure you're okay, Lu? You know you're welcome to join us. You're part of this family, and we're not ashamed of you or what you said."

I'm shaking my head before she's even finished talking. "I know, and thank you. I don't know if I'm ready to put myself out there."

It's my auto-response, but even as I say it, there's a tug inside me. *If not now, when?* Do I want to live in this weird limbo any longer?

"Whenever you are, we're here for you." Ruby takes a step toward the door and then looks over her shoulder at me. "For what it's worth, I hope it's sooner rather than later. You have a lot of life ahead of you, sweetie. Don't let one bad moment taint the whole picture."

She offers me a smile, and I nibble my lip as she closes the door quietly behind her. Her steps recede as she walks down the stairs.

I stir the soup. Steam rises as I instinctively try to separate the beans from the rest of the chili. Disgusting, fleshy little turd nuggets. But then I freeze, my spoon hovering over the bowl. My dad's voice rings loud and clear in my ear: "*If I leave out the beans, it'll change up the flavor of the entire soup. You don't have to like them—you can be disgusted by them—but that doesn't mean they don't have a purpose.*"

Slowly, I start mixing the beans back in. I curl my legs up beneath me on my bed and stare at the chili. Tears prick at my eyes. My dad feels so close to me right now. I can hear his laugh. I can see the smile lines around his eyes. My mind switches out the picture of him and replaces it with Loretta and Martin giving each other a hard time. I can see myself in the grocery store in Cashmere Cove, shopping for chili ingredients and meeting Rose. I flash forward to being on the square dance floor with TJ, and to every moment with him since then.

How many times have I wished I had kept my cool, kept my opinions to myself on the People's Picks stage, so I wouldn't be dealing with the fallout?

More than I can count. But what's done is done.

A bean in the chili of my life, to take the analogy and run with it.

It brought me to Cashmere Cove. It put me in the path of good people. People I never would have met if I hadn't left California in search of privacy and to try to figure myself out.

Have I figured myself out? I don't know about that. I'm getting there, maybe. I'll always be a work in progress. But I don't want to be stuck. I want to keep writing this story. I don't have to like how I acted on the People's Picks stage, but I can recognize that it was a catalyst for a lot of good.

My pulse accelerates when I think about TJ. I can't imagine not knowing him. Not having shared my heart with him and received his heart in return. This relationship between us is new, but it's got the roots of friendship and the promise of something true and good and beautiful.

I take a bite of chili, beans and all, and mull over my options.

It's time to stop running away, to own up to what I did and said, and allow the public to make of it what they will. I'd rather people didn't hate me, but if they do, I can't control that. What I can control is who I surround myself with and how I spend my time. My family is downstairs, with an offer on the table for me to join them. They are good, and they love me. If I'm going to face down my demons—those of my own making, and those made by the public's perception of me—there's no better way to do that than with them at my side.

Something settles deep in my chest—a feeling of peace I haven't known in a long time. I bask in it for a couple minutes, talking to God, talking to my parents, chronicling this moment, because it feels like it's a big one—one that'll be a turning point in my life.

I know what I have to do. I grab my laptop. I'm going to need more hours in the next day, but I'll do my best with what I have.

For now, I scramble to make myself TV-ready, throwing on a black turtleneck and exchanging my oversized sweatpants for a decent pair of black denim jeans. I take a minute to swipe on some fresh mascara and touch up the rest of my makeup before I pull out the necklace I ordered for myself in a fit of late-night online shopping when I first got to California. It's subtle, but when I clasp the chain behind my neck and straighten out the two discs that are etched with a T and a J, it feels like I may as well have rented out a billboard to broadcast my feelings for TJ. He's not here with me now, but he's here in spirit. I know he's my biggest champion as I own my mistakes and speak my mind.

I smile at myself in the mirror. I can do this, and I'm not doing it alone.

I'd rather not draw all the attention to myself, but since filming has already started, it's inevitable. The cameras are rolling, and they capture the surprised looks on the faces of Ruby and my stepsisters as well as the shocked expressions from their guests, who didn't know I was here, as I step into the dining room.

Ruby bustles around to set an extra place at the table for me, and after a couple beats of awkward silence where we all just stare at each other, I take a deep breath and begin.

"I have some things to say."

It's time to start living again.

Chapter 39
TJ

"I have so much I want to say to you. Both of you." I indicate Tess's parents, Sarah and Roy.

"We're so happy to see you, TJ. You look good." Sarah's eyes glisten. "Are you taking care of yourself?"

"I'm trying to. I'm sorry it's taken me so long to show my face around here. It was selfish of me to stay away, and I—"

Roy holds up his hands. "It's alright. We all grieve differently. We understand."

Sarah tucks her hand into the crook of her husband's elbow. "What matters is you're here now." She glances past me. "I was wondering if you brought anyone with you."

"That's what I wanted to talk to you about." I pull in a deep breath. "For a long time, I didn't think there would be anyone special after Tess, but I met someone recently who has made me feel ..." I pause, searching for the right words to describe Lucy while being cognizant of Tess's parents' feelings. "She's made me feel like loving might be worth it again ... even though the future is unknown and there's always the risk of pain ahead."

Sarah sniffs, and Roy pats her hand. "I know that's what Tess would have wanted. She loved life, and she would have wanted you to live yours to the fullest. That's what we're trying to do, too. Some days, it's easier than others—" Sarah's voice cracks. "But we owe it to her to try."

I nod, my throat thick with emotion. "I won't ever forget her. The woman I'm seeing helped me remember that I should honor Tess's memory by being willing to love again."

Roy glances at his wife and then smiles at me. "Sounds like she's good for you."

"She really is." A weight of longing presses down on my shoulders. I wish Lucy could be here. I know why she can't be, but man, it would be good to see her, to be near her, and soothe my aching heart with her presence.

"Oh my." Sarah stands up straighter. "You *did* bring someone."

My entire body freezes. It can't be. Can it?

"Or I should say someones." Sarah motions with her hand, waving forward whoever is behind me.

I turn to see Anton, Rose, Poe, and Del, along with a couple of my other teammates and their significant others.

Anton clasps me on the shoulder as Del wraps me in a bear hug, lifting me off the ground.

"What are you guys doing here?" I ask, once he sets me down.

"Lucy asked us to come before she left for California." Poe straightens the collar on his tux. "You're lucky I love you, man, because I still feel like an overdressed penguin in this thing."

I splutter out a laugh and make introductions between my teammates and Tess's parents. The whole time, my mind and my heart are filled to the brim with memories of Tess and longing for Lucy. I picture her standing in Poe's living room, huddled up with the guys, while I was on the phone with my grandma. She didn't mention anything to me about inviting my teammates, but she was looking out for me even then. She knew this would be a difficult day, and she did everything in her power to ease the burden of me having to bear it alone.

"Should we head inside?" Anton jars me from my thoughts.

Roy motions for us to lead the way. "We're waiting on a few people, but we'll see you all in there in a bit."

I stop to hug Sarah one more time as the guys and their dates enter the ballroom where the benefit dinner is set to begin any minute. She squeezes me tight. "I'm so happy you're here. I'm so happy for you. You found a good one."

She releases me, and someone else joins her and Roy. I make a quick retreat, and it's only when I'm halfway to my table that I start wondering how Sarah knows who I found. I didn't once mention Lucy's name.

I dismiss the question, assuming she was speaking generally. I take my seat at the table with Anton on my right and Poe on my left.

Rose leans across Anton's place and smiles at me. "It's really good you're here, TJ. We're proud of you."

I smile back. "Having you all around for this makes it easier."

"Tess sounds like she was quite the woman," Poe says from my other side. He's got the event program open to the bio they've included of Tess.

"She was." Before I can say more, Sarah and Roy are onstage, giving their opening remarks.

"It's humbling to have you all here with us tonight as we remember our Tess and join together to do some good in her honor." Roy puts his arm around his wife, and the entire room applauds. "This year, we have a special guest who reached out to us after hearing Tess's story."

Sarah turns and holds out a hand. "Ladies and gentlemen, Lucy Dupree."

My stomach bottoms out as Lucy joins Tess's parents on stage. She's in an understated and unassuming long black gown, but my heart still stops as she walks forward in a pair of sky-high heels. If I wasn't so stunned, I would be out of my seat and making sure she made it across the stage without tripping.

Poe slaps my back and Anton leans over. "Surprise," he whispers with a grin.

Without taking my eyes off Lucy, I say, "You knew about this?"

"Only since yesterday. Lucy texted Rose that she was coming."

I shake my head slowly as Lucy makes it to where Roy and Sarah are standing. Roy leans forward and speaks into the mic again as Sarah hugs Lucy. "We're bowled over to have Lucy

Dupree here with us tonight, and even more in awe of her generosity. Lucy, if you'd like to say a few words."

My eyes are locked on Lucy, and my heart is thundering in my chest as she steps forward. Her eyes scan the crowd, and I know the minute she spots me, because her shoulders sink ever so slightly and a small smile lifts the corners of her mouth.

"The honor of being here is all mine," Lucy begins. "I didn't want to make a big deal out of this, but apparently when I get on stage these days, people are on the edge of their seats, wondering what I'll say next." She gives a self-deprecating chuckle, and the entire audience titters. "But this isn't about me. It's about Tess Stewart and the life she lived. I was made aware of what an amazing person Tess was from a friend at the time, and he was inspired by Tess, and in return, I was inspired by him. There's something to be said for living each of our days to the fullest. Tess did that, and I want to be better about doing that, too. That's why I'm here.

"For the past year, I've lived my life in hiding, tucked away because of what happened at the last stage I stood on. I'm not proud of some of the things I said, but thinking about Tess and how none of us know when it'll be our time made me realize that I don't want to have regrets. My past and the mistakes I made have formed me into who I am, which is a work in progress. I don't want to miss out on life and love because I'm too afraid to embrace it. Even though I didn't know her personally, I know Tess's legacy is one of living life fully, freely, and for others. Her heart lives on in all those who love her and in all of you in this room. It is my honor to make a donation to the Tess Stewart Scholarship Fund."

Lucy steps back from the microphone as the audience claps. I'm halfway out of my chair, my body instinctively moving in her direction, when Sarah steps forward and lowers the mic so she can be heard.

"What Lucy is too humble to tell you is that she's donating one hundred thousand dollars to Tess's fund and matching the next fifty thousand dollars we raise tonight."

The room gasps, and I do, too.

Lucy shakes her head, holding up her hands like she doesn't want to make any of this about her. My heart is ready to explode as the room erupts in praise and applause.

I track Lucy as she hurries off the stage and down the stairs to the far side. I have to weave through the tables, and I lose sight of her for a minute. My entire body goes into panic mode. Where is she? I need to find her, to hold her, to thank her. Then I spot her, standing out of view of the rest of the audience. She turns and our eyes meet, and she holds up a hand in a shy wave, a tentative smile on her face.

I'm to her in three long strides, and I wrap her in my arms, lifting her off the ground and holding her to me in a crushing hug.

"Thank you for being here," I whisper into the soft skin of her neck.

"I'm sorry I didn't have the courage to be here for you sooner," she says quietly. "I shouldn't have left for California knowing you had to face this. I should have told you I'd come with you from the start."

I lean back so I can look at her. She brushes her hand over my forehead. She doesn't lean in to kiss me. I can tell she's doing it out of respect for Tess and her family, and it makes me love and respect her even more. I set her on her feet and press a kiss to her forehead.

"I didn't expect you to come out of hiding for me."

"I know you didn't. But I meant what I said up there. I don't want to live my life in the shadows. Not when doing so stops me from showing up for the people I care about." She reaches for my hands and squeezes them. "I care about you, TJ. A lot."

My eye catches on something silver and shiny hanging from her neck. I reach out to touch the discs with my initials on them. I flick my gaze to hers. Her cheeks turn pink.

"I ... I was missing you, and I wanted a way to keep you close. Is it ... too much?"

"Too much?" I say with disbelief. "Considering I was thinking of tattooing your name across my arm so everyone would know how gone for you I am, no, I don't think you having my initials hanging around your neck is too much."

Her blush deepens. "You're going to get a tattoo for me?"

"I told you. I get tattoos for the things that matter the most to me. That's you."

Her eyes well with tears, and I pull her to me in another hug, relishing that she's here and that I get to hold her. I don't know what life has in store for us—none of us really do—but here and now, Lucy is by my side, and there's no one else with whom I'd rather face whatever comes.

Chapter 40
Lucy

A knock sounds on the door of the duplex I'm sharing with Rose. I toss my cross-stitch hoop down and jump up.

It's been three months since TJ and I officially became a couple. Three months since my cover at Daisy's Inn was blown. Three months since I flew to California and then flew back to Chicago for Tess's benefit. Three months of stepping into the spotlight alongside TJ, facing down the critics with humility but also with my chin held high. TJ has been my constant support.

The producers of *Dinner with the Duprees* decided to air the unedited sequence of events, with me coming to dinner and having a heart-to-heart with my family and those in attendance, explaining myself and offering an apology. They felt like it was the most direct way to reach the most people, and it's been mostly well-received. Some people are still absolutely vicious with their words and opinions, and they often hide behind their computer screens, more than happy to tear me down. Other people—both online and in real life—have willingly forgiven and offered me validation and well-wishes. It's been a mixed bag, but I'm grateful to be on the other side of my stint in hiding. It's good to live in the light instead of hiding away in the shadows.

"Somebody's excited for her date." Rose grins at me from her end of the couch. I moved in with her in January, and it's been such a good fit. She's got her laptop out, and we've been working alongside each other in amiable silence for the past hour. She's writing a story of her own, and it's been killing me not to tell her about my author career. Soon. The two of us have become close as roommates and as we shared the ups and downs of watching the River Foxes win their second straight Super Bowl together earlier this year.

I stretch my arms over my head. "It's a tough job, dating a sexy and sweet football star, but someone's got to do it."

She laughs. "Co-sign!"

I cross the room and open the door to find TJ looking devastating in jeans and a worn, brown barn coat with a tan, corduroy collar.

"Hey, you." He steps forward and sweeps me into his arms, kissing me soundly. "Missed you," he says as he buries his nose in the crook of my neck and inhales.

I sigh in contentment. These are the moments I live for. "Missed you too."

He leans back and his eyes bounce up and over my shoulder. "Oh, hey, Rose."

"Hello, you sweet, little obsessed man," she coos back.

"Guilty." TJ grins.

I laugh at the look of puppy love on his face. I could say something about how he's being silly, but I know he's not. He constantly shows me how much he adores me—how much he values me. He dropped off an afternoon coffee at Daisy's Inn every day while I was pushing to meet my manuscript deadline back in January. He planned the coziest winter date nights where we watched romcoms and adventure flicks and laughed and talked and kissed until well into the early morning hours. We've cooked family dinners together with Martin and Loretta, and we play cribbage at their senior living complex whenever we have a Thursday night free. I'm helping TJ with a new crop of chicks, which are currently living in his basement until they get big enough to join the rest of the ladies in the coop. Last month, after his Super Bowl win, he flew home with me to California and proceeded to charm Ruby, Hilary, and Kait to within an inch of their lives.

TJ is considerate and warm, and we talk about everything and nothing. He's my biggest champion and my soft place to land.

"You ready for this?" he asks, tucking a strand of hair behind my ears.

I pout. "Ready to get it over with."

He grins. "You're gonna be great." He grabs my hand as we turn to go.

"See you tonight for dinner?" I say to Rose, playing it cool. Every month, we have a standing dinner date at Guadalupe's with her sisters and our other friend, Mallory.

Rose is looking at her screen, but she bobs her head in response. "I'll be there."

"Good. I'm in the mood for tacos."

"Same here. You two have fun. Show that car wash who's boss, Lu." Rose winks.

I nod with determination as TJ leads me to his truck. He opens the driver's side door for me. I take my seat behind the wheel and he joins me on the passenger side.

"Do you think she suspects anything?" he asks as he clicks his seatbelt in place.

"Not a chance." I grin, glad to have something to focus on as I back out of the duplex's driveway that is not my upcoming standoff with an automated car wash. "How's Anton holding up?"

"He's a wreck. In a good way," TJ adds with a grin. "The guy has been ready to propose to Rose for over six years now. He just wants to do the dang thing."

Little does Rose know that when she shows up to girls' night later, it won't be us waiting for her, but Anton.

I do a little shimmy in my seat. "Second chance romances are the best."

TJ's hand finds my thigh and he gives it a squeeze, which makes me shiver for a whole other reason. "I think our romance is the best," he says.

I flick my gaze over to him and smile. "That goes without saying."

He leaves his palm resting on my thigh, and I glance down at it and over to him again. "Maybe the car wash can wait. I can think of some other things we could do in this truck."

I stop at one of the only red lights in Cashmere Cove and glance over to find him staring at me, eyes smoldering. He leans across the console and kisses the tender spot behind my ear, making me gasp and grin, because I think I got him, but then he whispers, "Good try."

He leans back in his seat and I groan, focusing on the road as the light turns green.

He chuckles. "Be a good sport, Lu. You promised you'd conquer the car wash today."

"Why are there so many car washes in Wisconsin?" I grumble. "It's like they're popping up on every corner for the sole purpose of taunting me. I could wash my own car. Or your truck. I could wash your truck!"

When TJ doesn't respond right away, I cut him with a look. He's got his lips pressed together and his eyes closed. He cracks one eye open and glances at me with a wolfish grin. "Don't mind me, I've got a great mental picture going. There's bubbles, and you in a bikini, and me laying you down on the hood of my truck, and—"

I reach over and swat at him, laughing. "TJ! You're the worst."

He catches my hand and kisses my palm. "You put the thought in my head, sweetheart."

I try to pout, but I can't help but smile.

TJ kisses my hand again. "To be fair, you're always in my head." He pulls my hand over and places it on his chest. "But more importantly, you're always here, in my heart."

I feel like I'm floating on a happy little cloud of love dust. The best part of my relationship with TJ is that we can be both fun and playful and serious and thoughtful with each other. I have never once worried that he's only into me for my looks.

I turn into the car wash parking lot, and my heart starts beating faster. "Alright, what do I do?"

"I promise this is not going to be as bad as you think. I'm right here to walk you through it." TJ directs me where to drive, and I get through the touch screen prompts without issue. There's a car in front of us, so we have to wait.

"Of course," I grumble. "We have to draw this out. As soon as it's warmer, we're going to the zoo. It's only fair."

TJ grabs my hand and runs his thumb over my knuckles. He doesn't tell me to chill. He doesn't make fun of me for my temper. He just sits with me. He's exactly what I need.

I sigh and rest my head back against the headrest, turning so I'm facing him. "You really are the best, you know that?"

"I do," he says easily, grinning.

I huff out a laugh. "And always so modest."

"Nah." He turns serious. "I'd better be the best when it comes to you. You deserve nothing less."

I shake my head. "How is it possible that you are smoother than any main character in any book I've ever written? Or read, for that matter?"

He shrugs. "Because I was made for you."

I smirk. "There you go again, basically writing romance novel lines for me." I lean across the console and kiss him as the car in front of us pulls out and the garage doors open. The lights are blinking and the arrows are flashing, telling me to move forward.

"It's my turn."

"You've got this. Ease forward, lining up your tire with the track," TJ coaches.

I do what he says, and I feel my tires lock in place.

"Now put it into neutral," he instructs. "And take your foot off the brake."

"Okay. That's done. Now what?" I'm gripping the wheel for dear life, but TJ reaches over and gently pries my hands off it.

"You don't want to accidentally get us off track. That's all." He keeps my hands in his as the water starts spraying all around us. The truck moves forward on its own, and I look around.

"Really? That's it?"

"That's it. You did it." He brings my hands to his mouth and kisses every finger. "I'm proud of you, Lu."

I beam. "So now we wait for it to be done?"

He nods.

"Dang." I free one of my hands from his and tap my chin, arching my brows with feigned innocence. "I should have brought my cross-stitch hoop. Got any ideas about how we can pass the time?"

As the water and soap foam around us, TJ deftly unhooks my seat belt and lifts me into his lap. "I'm sure we can figure something out."

He covers my mouth with his, and it's official. Car washes are my new favorite thing.

Epilogue
Lucy

The following month, Mood Reader is packed for Philly's event, and Rose and her co-owner Mia are flittering around, making sure everyone has what they need and is all settled before the Q&A begins.

TJ places a kiss on the sensitive spot on my neck that I love so much. "You ready for this?" he whispers into my ear.

"Yeah." I stand up straighter. "Yeah, I think I really am."

He wraps his arms around me as Rose takes her seat in one of the armchairs at the front of Mood Reader. "It is an absolute delight to welcome one of my favorite authors to Cashmere Cove tonight. Philomena Grace is the bestselling author of five small-town contemporary romances set in the American South. She lives in Texas with her emotional support houseplants. She loves her writing group and nineties romcoms, and has recently embarked upon a personal journey—a quest, if you will—to bake the perfect chocolate chip cookie." The crowd titters. "So put your hands together and give Philomena Grace your warmest Mood Reader welcome."

TJ and I clap along with the rest of the crowd as Philly walks out from behind the nearest bookshelf and takes a seat next to Rose. Mia hands her a microphone.

Cassie joins TJ and me from where she was with Philly behind the bookshelf. "You good?" she asks out of the corner of her mouth.

I can't help but chuckle. "You guys must think I'm going to faint or try to bolt or something." I flick my gaze between TJ and Cassie, dropping my voice to a whisper. "I promise. I'm good. I'm excited."

I tune back in to Rose and Philly's conversation. "Talk to us a little about your process," Rose says. "What do you do when you get the seedling idea for a new story?"

"That's one of my favorite parts of the process, actually. Those early days when the world is my story oyster. Anything is possible, and I'm brainstorming to my heart's content. There's something so freeing in that. And—" Philly gazes out over the crowd. Her eyes connect with mine, and her smile grows. "I'm blessed to have the best writing partners in crime. Two other well-known authors and I share the same agent, and we bounce ideas back and forth all the time."

My pulse picks up.

"Can I ask who your writing pals are?" Rose leans forward.

"Of course." Philly smiles. "Ava Reese and Beatrix Bell."

Rose lets out a low whistle. "Does this mean you know the elusive Ava Reese?"

"I absolutely do." Philly grins. "She's the best. She's actually here tonight."

"What?" Rose squeaks into the microphone as the entire audience starts buzzing.

"That's your cue, sweetheart." TJ places another kiss behind my ear. "Go get 'em. I'm so proud of you."

"Lucy Dupree, ladies and gentlemen." Philly stands and holds out her arm, motioning me forward.

I keep my eyes on the stage, and I walk down the center aisle of chairs that Mia and Rose set up.

Rose's jaw is on the floor. The audience is cheering as I join them. I catch some shocked expressions, but the overall mood is positive. It's a relief.

"Are you kidding me, Lu?" Rose shakes her head. "All this time I was fangirling over Ava Reese, and *you* were—are—Ava Reese?"

She shakes her head again. "Let's all sit so we can discuss this. I have lots of questions for both of you."

Mia appears with another chair and hands me a microphone, her eyes wide and sparkling.

I take my seat and, at the back of the room, spot TJ grinning widely. Cassie has her phone out. She's recording this for my official Ava Reese social media pages.

Philly grabs my hands and squeezes, looking at me with question marks in her eyes. I love her for wanting to make sure I'm alright. I squeeze her hand back and smile. I knew this would be scary, but I'm actually more excited right now than anything.

"Lucy—er, Ava—welcome." Rose laughs breathlessly. "Sorry, I'm floored. I'm afraid I'm going to totally butcher this."

"You could never," I tell her with a smile. Rose is one of the most capable people I know.

"First of all, I have to say thank you to Philly for letting me piggyback on her event. The real news of the day is how absolutely incredible her latest release is, am I right?" I look out at the crowd, and those in attendance cheer in agreement.

"Lucy definitely helped shape it into what it is," Philly puts in. "It's so nice to finally be able to give her some of the credit she deserves."

Rose glances between us. "Why now, Ava? What makes this the right time to share your identity?"

I sit up straighter, wanting to get this right. "It's been quite a year. After a very public incident, which has been rehashed to death at this point," I add with a chuckle, "I thought I'd never be able to admit that I'm a romance author. I was afraid readers would blackball my books. But I couldn't live in that fear anymore. I started dating an incredible man, and together we realized that we don't want to do life halfway. We owe it to ourselves to hold nothing back. So this is another step in coming out of the shadows and living my life to the fullest. I'm proud of my stories, and I feel safe enough in who I am to let others know I'm behind them. They're not going to be for everyone, just like I'm not for everyone, but I hope they continue to find the right readers. It's always an honor when someone gives my book some of their precious time. Now that my identity isn't hidden, I'll be able to interact with readers and thank them in person. That's my main impetus for stepping forward now."

The rest of the conversation passes in a blur, and it's two hours later by the time Philly and I finish chatting with those who came out.

TJ has been by my side through it all, and I lean back into him as Rose closes the door to Mood Reader behind the last fan.

"Well," Cassie says, her heels click-clacking on the wooden floor as she joins us from the back storeroom. "I'd say that was a huge success."

"I still don't even believe this. You little stinker!" Rose points at me before she wraps me in a hug. "I'm so proud to know you."

I laugh as I ease out of her hug. "I'm still me."

"And you're exceptional." TJ kisses me on the cheek before turning to scan the room. "Would you ladies mind if I stole Lu? There's something I've been wanting to do for literal hours."

My friends nod, and TJ wastes no time spinning me around, scooping me into his arms, and cradling me like he's about to carry me over the threshold.

"TJ!" I wrap my arms around his neck. "What are you doing? Where are we going?"

"You'll see." He walks me out the back door and sets me in the passenger seat of his truck.

I ask a million questions, but he's tight-lipped as he drives us away from downtown Cashmere Cove. We're headed in the direction of Green Bay—I can tell that much. When I realize TJ isn't going to talk to me about what he has planned, I sit back in my seat and relish the feel of his hand holding mine.

He pulls up to the River Foxes stadium thirty minutes later and helps me out of the truck. The stadium is dark and quiet. He leads me through the player entrance, his hand in mine as he weaves us through a few hallways.

"TJ." My heart flutters, guessing what he's doing. "Where are you taking me?"

He looks over his shoulder as he stops in front of a nondescript door. "You're not afraid of heights these days, are you?" he asks with a small smile.

My breath catches. "Not with you, I'm not."

"Good." He opens the door and squeezes my fingers.

TJ

"TJ," Lucy says carefully, her usually airy voice sounding deeper and raspier. "What are we doing here?"

I settle down next to her on the scaffolding overlooking our stadium's atrium. I look over at her—this woman, this most beautiful woman. I smile. "Don't you know? You have to know, Lu. You've written this scene countless times before. Back where it all began. The story coming full circle."

Lucy shakes her head and opens her mouth, but then closes it again as her eyes fill with tears.

I squeeze her hands and lean forward to kiss the apples of both of her cheeks. "Don't cry, Cinderella."

She sniffs out a laugh. "They're happy tears."

I hum. "Why's that?"

She smiles up at me. "Because this is so much better than any of the stories I've ever written."

"I haven't even done what I brought you up here to do yet."

"Well." She smiles slyly at me. "Get on with it, then. I'm waiting."

I grin. "I've been waiting to ask you this for weeks, Lu. Months, even. When we were here in December, I had no idea the gorgeous woman in the vintage wedding gown would be the woman who cracked open my outer shell and showed me that I was living a half-life. I thought I was okay, but a life devoid of love isn't really a life at all." I keep my eyes fixed on hers, watching as they glisten with growing pools of tears. "Lucy, you have shown me so much about inner strength and facing the hard stuff with courage and integrity. I adore your shy side and your spitfire side. I love when you're bold and brave, and I want to be by your side when you need to tuck yourself away and restore your sense of peace."

Lucy lets out a small sniffle, but she's smiling, so I take that as a good sign.

I wedge the ring box out from under the lip of scaffolding near where I'm sitting and flip it open. Lucy gasps as her eyes fly down to the round center stone flanked by a smaller stone on each side. "It's an honor to stand by your side and watch you shine. Your mind amazes me. Your heart humbles me. You're my best friend, Lu, and it would be an honor to be your husband. Will you marry me?"

She throws her arms around my shoulders, and I gather her close, clinging to the ring so I don't drop it.

"Yes, TJ. Yes, of course I will." Lucy grips me tight, and I hold her, my own emotions wedging their way into the back of my throat.

I can't believe I'm here. I had given up on this—had given up trying for more because I was afraid. But come what may, it's all worth it for any moment I get to experience with Lucy.

She leans away and cups my face, drawing my mouth to hers in a kiss filled with so much promise, my lungs seize.

"I love you forever, Lu," I whisper, when she pulls back.

"I love you too, TJ." She exhales. "This ring is incredible. I've never seen anything like it."

I hold it up so she can examine it.

"It's pretty special to me," I tell her. I point to the stone on the left side of the center stone. "This was my mom's diamond."

Lu's hands fly up to her mouth. "Really?"

I nod and move my finger to the other side, keeping my eyes on her. "This was your mom's diamond."

"What?" Her watery eyes search mine. "How?" she whispers.

"Ruby helped me. Your dad had it in a safe for you, for some day. I hope it's okay," I add, watching her to make sure this is what she wants. "I thought it was a beautiful tribute to the past, with the center stone reminding us to live in the present. The whole ring itself is my promise to you of my heart and my life, whatever the future may bring."

Lucy lets out a sob as I slip the ring on her finger, and then she scoots into my lap, holding me close as I cradle her and whisper my love for her into her ear.

"You sure you're not a closet poet, TJ? That was so beautiful." Lucy holds out her hand to study the ring. "I cannot get over this. It's perfect for me." She kisses my temple. "You're perfect for me."

The sound of feedback coming from below makes us both jump.

"Sorry to interrupt!" Gram speaks into a megaphone. "I'd like to hug my granddaughter-to-be, so if you two could move your hineys down here, we can get this engagement party started."

Lu splutters out a laugh. "You invited your grandparents?"

"Yeah." I rub the back of my neck. "And my teammates, and your writer friends, and your family from California." I swivel her in my arms so she can look down as everyone trickles into the Atrium below. They're all cheering and clapping for us.

"Did she say yes?" Poe hollers up.

"Yes!" Lucy yells down with a laugh, shaking her head and waving as all our favorite people wave up at her, before turning to me. "This is the best day."

I kiss her, swift and deep. "As much as I'd like to keep you to myself, are you ready to head down to our party?"

We stand and make our way to the door that leads to the stairs. Lucy pauses. "We'll get there faster if you carry me." She bats her eyelashes, and I hoist her over my shoulders.

She giggles as I charge down the steps.

"Be honest," I say. "You only asked to be toted around because you like the view."

"Guilty," she says with a pat to my butt.

"Knew it, you little sneak."

"You're stuck with me, TJ, and this perfect peach is all mine."

I make it to the bottom of the stairs and set Lucy on her feet again. Her cheeks are pink from being turned upside-down, and her hair fans out around her face. Her eyes are sparkling with delight, and I can't believe she's mine.

I laugh because this is living, and then I lean down and kiss her.

Bonus Epilogue
Lawrence Poe

The engagement party for TJ and Lucy is in full swing when my phone rings. I reach into my pocket to silence the call, but my sister's name is on the screen, so I take the stairs up and out of the atrium, away from where Anton's in charge of the playlist that's currently blasting Taylor Swift's "Love Story."

I glance back at the scene, and I can't help but smile. TJ, certified player, both on the field and off, has turned into a one-woman man, and he couldn't look happier about it. He and Lucy are a great match. They balance each other out and function like a true team.

I'd love to find a partner like that, but I'm enough of a control freak to know that I don't do well having to share with anyone, so I'm not sure a long-term relationship is in the cards for me.

I turn away from the explosion of love and happiness and accept my sister's call. "Hey, Felicity."

"Hey. Am I interrupting?"

I glance over my shoulder. The true answer is yes, but I never want to make Felicity feel like a burden. She's a single mom with so many variables stacked against her. I do everything I can to help her out, even though she lives on the East Coast and I live here in Green Bay. "You're good. What's up?"

It's quiet on the line, and I check my phone to make sure the call didn't drop. "Felicity? Is everything okay?"

I hear her exhale. "Yes. No. It could be, but I need a favor."

"Name it."

She laughs nervously. "Remember you said that."

I lean against the wall. "Spit it out, Lis."

"Okay. I got orders, and I'm deploying, and I need help with Ana, so I was hoping she could come and stay with you."

The words come out in a rush, and it takes me a beat to process them. When I do, my mind immediately starts cataloging, organizing, and delegating.

"When?" I ask first.

Felicity sucks in a breath. "Middle of June."

Every muscle in my body tenses. "That's OTAs, minicamps, and then I've got training camp and the preseason, Lis."

"I know. I know. I thought of that, too. But I've figured out a workaround."

I can't help but smile at that. Felicity and I were raised in the same household. She's not quite as task-minded and systematic as I am, but it's close.

"I'm listening."

"Beni will come with Ana. She can stay with you and—"

"What? No."

My mind glitches at the mention of Anastasia's godmother and Felicity's best friend from high school, Beni Fitzgerald. She is my polar opposite. She hates me, which she's made abundantly clear over the years. In her defense, I said some things I'm not proud of, but I thought we were past that, until she raked me over the coals. She proved herself revengeful and spiteful, and quite frankly, I don't think she's a great influence on my niece.

"Lawrence." Felicity sounds tired. "I know you two don't get along, but I need your help. Neither of you can watch Ana full-time. If Beni stays with you, she can cover when you're at work, and vice versa."

"I could hire someone," I argue. "Easily. I'll get the best nanny I can find."

"If I wanted Ana to hang out with a stranger, I would leave her here on base," Felicity says, and I know she's right. "Look. This is a huge ask. I get it. But please, Lawrence. This deployment will go a long way in ensuring that I get to spend some more time shoreside in the future, which means more time with Ana. Can you set aside your beef with Beni for three months?"

Three months. It's a mini deployment. Felicity has been on a ship for as long as nine months at a time. Usually our mom watches Ana, but she'll be living in Europe for the summer with her best friend.

I rub the back of my neck, not seeing a way to get out of this.

"Lawrence?"

I grit my teeth. "Fine. We'll make it work."

"Thank you." The relief in Felicity's voice is palpable, even from hundreds of miles away. "You're the best big brother a girl could ask for."

I chuckle. "You're lucky I love my niece."

"And she loves you! She'll be so excited to come and stay. She and Beni will fly your way in June. I'll work out all the details. Don't worry about a thing."

I squeeze my eyes shut. Does my sister know me at all? I worry about all the things, all the time. I'm going to have the most precocious, precious three-year-old in the world underfoot. I'm a good uncle. I truly believe that. But caring full-time for a child is a huge deal. I need to bring my A-game.

Especially since my partner in this is Beni Fitzgerald. An unreliable slob. A careless free spirit. And the only woman who has ever made a complete fool of me.

Yeah, I'll have a lot to worry about with her living under my roof.

Don't miss Lawrence and Beni's story in *Second Down and Second Chances*! To see how Anton and Rose reconnected, check out *Exes Don't*.

Acknowledgements

All glory to God, now and forever!

Thank you to you, dear reader, for picking up this book and spending some time with TJ and Lucy. I hope you enjoyed their story. A special shout-out to all those who read *Exes Don't* and clamored for more River Foxes romances. Your enthusiasm and excitement for this fictional football team is a big reason this book exists. You continue to make my author dreams come true every time you pick up one of my books. Thank you!

I've been blessed to work with the best on the nuts and bolts of this one. Thank you to Melody Jeffries for taking my vision for this cover and executing it to perfection. I'm still not over how perfect the hashmarks are! You are, as always, a delight to work with. Thank you to Caitlin Miller for your editing expertise. I love getting your feedback because I know it's going to make my story better *and* because you are such a sweet cheerleader. I'm so grateful.

Thanks to my beta readers—you know who you are. I have you to thank for the car wash scene and for helping me to believe in this book. Thank you to my ARC team for being willing to read advanced copies and generate some early buzz. You're the best!

To my local writer friends, booksellers, librarians, and the bookish community in northeast Wisconsin—I love being in this business with you! Thanks for the support, commiseration, enthusiasm, and connection. While author life can feel like a solitary endeavor at times, I love getting the chance to join forces with you.

My immense gratitude goes to my friends who inspire me daily to be a better wife, mom, and all-around good and faithful human. I've heard it said that you become more like the people you spend your time with, and I really hope that's true, because you guys are truly wonderful. I love you all.

Similarly, to my family—near and far—your love and support mean the world. I couldn't do any of this without you. Thank you for showing up at every book event, for being thrilled about each new release, and for your encouragement through it all. Love you, guys!

My sweet kids, you're my favorites. Getting to watch you grow is the greatest privilege of my life. All my love.

To Nick, thanks for being my biggest champion. You make me better in every possible way. I love you madly.

About The Author

Leah Dobrinska is the author of the River Foxes Football Romances, the Songwriter Sleuth Mysteries, the Fall In Love series, the Larkspur Library Mysteries, and the Mapleton novels. She earned her degree in English Literature from UW-Madison where she was awarded the Dean's Prize and served as a Writing Fellow. She has since worked as a freelance writer, editor, and content marketer. Leah lives in Wisconsin with her husband and their gaggle of kids. When she's not writing, handing out snacks, or visiting the local library, Leah enjoys reading and running.

www.leahdobrinska.com
Instagram: @whatleahwrote

9 798988 597889